He is good. He is doing all the right things, and all the wrong things, all at the same time.

There is a click, as the hammer on the Winchester snaps home on a cartridge filled with sand.

At the same time there is a small, crisp explosion. And between and above the eyes God gave him, Lewis suddenly has a third eye. It is black and perfectly round, and even as it appears, it begins to weep blood . . .

THE HARD HIT
John Wainwright

Berkley Books by John Wainwright

DEATH OF A BIG MAN
THE HARD HIT

THE HARD HIT

JOHN WAINWRIGHT

A BERKLEY BOOK
published by
BERKLEY PUBLISHING CORPORATION

This one is for John and Nicky...
nice people,
by any yardstick

THE LOUDSPEAKERS ON the arrival platform are saying:

"... *Will Mr. Stanley Hemmingway come to the station-master's office, please. Calling Mr. Hemmingway. Will Mr. Stanley Hemmingway come to the station-master's office, please...*"

I ignore the yap; I do not even look up at the speakers but, without looking up, I come to the firm conclusion that somebody, somewhere, has granite boulders where his brains should be.

Let me tell you...

It is mid-evening, starting to snow a little, easing towards zero centigrade temperature and I have already had one sweet hell of a day. I left Amsterdam airport, in a British United Dakmaster, at about three-quarters after two, this afternoon. We touched down at Newcastle, just after five. Since then, I have made two train changes.

All this to make sure no smarter-than-average goon is bumping into the small of my back. All this zigging and zagging, to make damn sure.

And now this!

I do a quick, visual check of my fellow-arrivals. Five of them. A middle-aged biddy with thick legs, a fur coat, a ridiculous hat and four suitcases; she has nailed one of the porters—a guy as old as herself—and, any minute now, she is going to cross his palm with silver and foretell his future... that he is just about to rupture himself. A trio:

1

man, wife and kid; the guy has that paunchy, well-married look about the eyes, his wife looks like Rocky Marciano in drag and the kid has his ma's jaw, his pop's ski-run nose and eyes he filched from a jet mine . . . three people, each a walking argument in favor of birth control. And one soldier boy; a young, smooth-cheeked kid in khaki; typical top sergeant meat . . . one of the babies paid to keep the guns greased, pending World War III.

Five characters who are definitely *not* "Stanley Hemmingway."

I give thanks for the dog-collar, carry my brief-case in my right hand, hold my ticket, ready for collection, in my left and walk along the platform.

The guy in B.R. uniform takes my ticket. He nods and smiles, and I smile back, and it makes his day; he figures he has worked a quick in with one of St. Peter's drinking buddies.

I make for the steps. On the way, I pass a light which is working hard not to become part of the darkness. There is a sign alongside the light, and the sign reads THIRSK and, standing to one side of the sign, there is a wide-shouldered creep with "gorilla" stamped all the way across his puss.

The fink with boulders under his skull . . . that, for sure!

He does not notice me. He is too busy not watching a door marked "Station-master's Office."

The loudspeakers are still saying:

"... *Calling Mr. Hemmingway. Will Mr. Stanley Hemmingway come to the station-master's office, please . . .*"

I have been waiting here fifteen minutes, and I am cold. There is a coating of snow across the shoulders of my charcoal-gray mac, and the mac is not lined; it is no wind-cheater and the wind which is sneaking into this station approach would make a brass monkey invest in a welding kit. I must have been in colder places . . . but, offhand, I cannot remember.

I keep myself from freezing to death by mentally cursing the dumb bastard responsible.

The other five have left. The soldier boy marched past, with the collar of his greatcoat pulled high. He was followed by the family; the kid howling, the wife beefing and the husband not listening. Shortly after, a taxi arrived and the dame with the fur coat and the suitcases moved out in style.

Me?

I am sitting here, on this bench. I am being snowed upon and I am being refrigerated, and I am keeping my eye on a smart-looking 3-liter Ford Capri which is parked near the station entrance steps. It is the only car around, therefore I figure it to be *the* car.

I am right.

The dumb bastard strolls down the station steps. Even from this distance, I can see he looks worried; the lamp above the entrance throws shadow-lines across his forehead and, south of his smashed-in nose, his mouth is pulled down at the corners. He tightens the belt of his overcoat, shoves his fingers into some fancy driving gloves and climbs into the Capri. The exhaust gas clouds out from the rear and the car eases its way towards me.

I straighten up from the bench, and flag it.

The dumb bastard winds down the window, and says, "Yeah?"

I say, "Stanley Hemmingway?" and make it into a question.

"Uh?" His eyes widen.

"Or fuzz maybe?" I suggest.

He makes the "Uh?" noise again.

"Or maybe *I'm* fuzz," I say.

He blinks at the dog-collar a couple of times, then says, "I dunno you, reverend. I think you're making some sorta..."

"Mistake?" I ask.

"Yeah." He nods.

I give him the cold-eye treatment, and say, "Were you waiting for somebody, mac? There, on the platform...were you waiting for somebody?"

He hesitates, then scowls, then gives a nod and says, "Yeah. I was..." At which point, the clouds roll by, the scowl broadens into a stupid grin, and he says, "Hey! I seen you on the station. You just come in on the train from York...right?"

"Right," I agree.

"You're the man I was..."

"Am I?"

"Sure." I am puzzling him, again. "Look—the costume...okay. But you don't talk like a Holy Joe. Right?"

"Don't I?"

"Hey—buster—don't gimme that..."

"Don't call me buster," I snap. "You are here strictly to drive this thing. It is not the start of a beautiful friendship."

"Yeah...okay," he grumbles, and looks sulky. He leans across to unlatch the nearside front.

"The back," I say.

He shrugs, turns in his seat and opens the nearside rear.

I climb into the car, close the door and begin to thaw a little.

He says, "You dress like a preacher-man, how the hell am I to know you're Hemm—"

"Skip the names," I warn. "What you did at the station was too damn dumb to believe."

"How the hell do I know what you..."

"What I look like?"

"Yeah."

I say, "Thanks to you, everybody could have known."

"I was waiting. I was gonna head you off."

I give him a nasty laugh, and snarl, "Sure...then, maybe, somebody could have headed us *both* off."

"I ain't that stupid," he mutters.

"Work at it," I crack, "it'll come." Before he has time for an answer, I ask, "Okay... what about you?"

He does the "Uh?" sound again.

"I am sitting in a car," I say. "I would like to know who with... and why he is here."

"Bishop," he growls.

"Does that mean something?"

"Bishop—Reg Bishop... that's me."

"So? Am I supposed to ask for an autograph?"

"Tipp's man."

"Tipp's beef?" I sneer.

"Yeah... Tipp's beef." This one is too thick to insult.

"Tipp being?" I ask.

"Darley's rep, in these parts."

"Yeah?"

"North-east," he explains. "Tyneside, down to the Humber. We watch Darley's interests."

"We?"

"The Tipp outfit. We're organized good."

"Is that a fact?" I mock.

"Yeah." In the glow from the dash, I see his head nod. His is very proud of this organization of which he is a part. He says, "Darley sends word up to Tipp, for him to fix with one of his boys to meet a guy called Hemm—"

"Forget the name," I say, in a tired voice. "Like the collar, it is phoney."

"Oh!"

This dumb bastard—this whole Tipp crowd—needs teaching a lesson. So, I do some scaring.

I say, "Y'know what, fink? You do not know from hell itself who I am. You have asked for nothing... but *nothing*. I flag down this car, you ask me inside, then you spill your guts. The whole bag... from you, all the way up to Darley. So, tell me, dumb-bell, what happens if I now flash the tin?"

"Uh?"

"The badge? If I am a bull? A dick? Fuzz? The law? What if I am *that*, dumb-bell? Tell me—I am interested—how do you crawl from under?"

"Jesus!" he breathes.

"How do you draw diagrams, to give Darley a way out? How do you explain things to this Tipp creep?"

"I—I . . ." He twists in his seat, blinks at me, and says, "Hey—you *ain't* the law . . . right?" and he is not one-hundred-per-cent sure.

"Right," I say, heavily. "Quit wetting your pants, junior. I am not the law . . . but I *could* be. You, too. You could have been the law, back there on the platform."

"Me?" His eyebrows lift at the thought.

"I have," I say, "known some very ugly-looking cops."

"Oh!"

And (I swear) he even looks insulted. This Neanderthal goon thinks he is good-looking; he figures himself as a latter-day Valentino.

I sigh. There are some things you can never do; some horizons you can never reach . . . they are long gone, and well beyond the grasp of mere mortals.

I say, "Eyes front, buster. Get this thing under way. Let's do something different for a change . . . let's have a Bishop playing chauffeur to a make-believe priest."

At least, he can drive.

Five miles, and we swing left at a traffic roundabout, and we are on a dual-carriageway; the A.1, and travelling south.

It is a nice car, with plenty of stretching space in the rear. There is a wicker picnic-basket on the carpet, along-side the seat, and I figure that it contains food. It does; cold chicken slices, crisp-crusted bread rolls and best butter. There is also a bottle of wine *(Sancerre)* and a Thermos. I leave the wine, and check the Thermos. It is filled with hot noodle soup.

I sit back and enjoy noodle soup, chicken slices and buttered rolls, after which I feel much better.

I re-pack the picnic-basket, settle into a corner and smoke a pipe of tobacco . . . and gradually (very gradually) the world becomes okay again. Even the dumb-bell behind the steering wheel has a place in the scheme of things.

All this time, I keep checking through the rear window; that no vehicle is keeping steady station behind us. I also keep to one end of the seat; a position where I cannot see Bishop's face in the driving mirror. Because . . . if I can see *his* face, he can also see *mine*, and he has seen it for too long, already.

These are simple, basic precautions—like a good gardener checking that his tools, even when not required, are clean, oiled and rust-free . . . they make things that less difficult. They are one reason why I have lived free for more than half a century.

I have this great ambition.

To die in a warm and comfortable bed . . . and of old age.

North of Doncaster we move onto the motorway network, and the Capri settles down to a steady 65/70 mph run south. Not too fast, because the snow is now coming like dollar-sized confetti and almost beating the impatient sweep of the wipers; it is building up, like a white shroud, along the central reservation—drifting a little at the uprights of the crash-barriers—white-streaking past the side windows of the Capri.

The traffic is not heavy—only mugs are out at night, this weather—and we pass a couple of lumbering grit sprayers . . . warm-looking and homey in the wash of their amber-flashing lights.

Odd—but I like this country . . . and I cannot put my finger on the reason. I liked it, even in the war years; when everybody was a little crazy and the G.I. flood was something the English couldn't decide whether to love or hate; when London was the first stop from the battle front and a furlough started to mean something only when you reached Piccadilly Circus; when a few days in the capital, and a few days in the provinces, was a good enough reason for killing Germans . . . and a very *good* reason for killing Germans.

Happy days. We-ell—maybe not happy . . . but different. Very uncomplicated. Very basic. Very simple.

Which (maybe) is why I like this country a little more each time I visit it. It does not have the flash-Jack, clapboard frontage of much of the U.S.A. It does not have the brittle con of Paris, or the smiling double-talk of Rome, or the elephant-heavy hints of Berlin. It is a very honest country, and when it is crook it is crook . . . and makes no bones about it. It can, like most places, be a smiling killer but, even then, it does not resort to trickery; it leaves you in no doubt that it wants your life.

As I say, I like this country. It is not the country of my birth but, if it was, I would be satisfied . . . as things are, I look upon it as the country of my adoption.

It is therefore (and if a man like myself can ever lay claim to such a place) "home."

Bishop has switched on the car radio. He has tuned it low, and it makes for easy listening; a sound upon which to float passing thoughts . . . thoughts which do not amount to concentration. The music is not quite my style and the D.J.—as usual—is giving with too much empty gab, but this stuff is what the kids of today want and, as always, the kids of today set the pop scene . . . and, anyway, there is an occasional Sinatra, an occasional Nat King Cole, to stir the memories of those who have memories.

The bridges of the service area cafes look good, in the falling snow; their lighting give the flakes pastel shades and, if you ignore the slush on the parking lots, the buildings and roofed-over walkways are beginning to look like Christmas-tree villages.

Christmas is a nice time, in this country. Nicer than anywhere else on earth. Dickens might not agree but, compared with the rest of the world, England still stays a little Dickensian at, and around, this time of year.

Which is one reason why I like England...suppose England gives a damn!

I take off the clerical collar and its bib. I take off the shirt. From my brief-case I take the nylon drip-dry, with collar attached, and the fancy-patterned tie. I pack the clerical collar and bib away, and close the brief-case.

I re-dress.

I am no longer a priest. I am now an ordinary, somberly-dressed John Doe with a harmless weakness for flashy ties.

We pull off the road, and into the Newport Pagnell motorway services complex. It is now past ten o'clock, I have been travelling more than eight hours, and I am beginning to feel a little bushed.

Bishop steers the Capri to a parking space near the toilets, brakes, stops the engine and climbs out. He leaves the radio switched on.

I watch him as he strolls into the gentlemen's john, give him a couple of minutes, then I get out of the car, walk to the main building and climb the stairs to the cafeteria.

It is part of the routine agreed upon. The switch-over. Bishop will now drive the Capri south, to Junction Thirteen, swing left through Bedford, join the A.1 and scoot back up north to report "Mission Accomplished" to the Tipp guy.

I hope.

Meanwhile, I join a small queue at the cafeteria counter, pay for coffee and a doughnut and find a table.

I relax and enjoy sitting down...which, upon reflection, is crazy. I have been "sitting down" for hours. In the Dakmaster. In the trains. On the bench. In the Capri. My rump has done so much non-stop work, it is damn near dead. Yet, this is different—like the train was different, and the Capri was different—and more relaxing...like *they* were different until the newness wore off and was replaced by the same old numbness.

I sip lukewarm coffee, chew a soggy doughnut and philosophize to myself...about the mysteries of sitting down. Maybe the butt, too, has feelings? Maybe it, like the rest of you, likes a change? Maybe—even to *it*—a change is as good as a rest? Who knows?

Who the hell cares?

I have more than an hour to kill. The pick-up is not scheduled until eleven-thirty and, in this profession, eleven-thirty means just that...on the button. Could be the contact is here, already. Could be he is the thin guy, toying with pie and chips; glancing up, over his rimless spectacles, and giving everybody the once-over while pretending not to. Could be he is the contact—but I doubt it...and, if he is, I am going to say some hard words about mice hoofing around playing at "tigers."

Could be the contact is a woman. Maybe not just the one person—maybe two people...maybe two women.

Maybe the two floozies who have just walked past this table; the two with trays loaded high with cream-plastered goodies; the two who don't give a damn about their calorie-counts.

Or could be...

The hell with it!

I grab hold of myself. I am getting jumpy, and I do not like getting jumpy. Getting jumpy means just that—*jumping*...and it is very easy to jump in the wrong direction.

I swallow the last of the coffee, pick up my brief-case and walk out of the cafeteria. I cross the landing and stroll to the middle of the bridge. It is cooler out here; cooler and less stuffy than in the cafeteria. I fill my pipe—slowly, and with care—light it and stand watching the traffic through the glass.

Have you ever done this?...stood on a motorway bridge, and watched the traffic speed past under your feet?

It is a little like being a giant. Like being the Rhodes Colossus, with motor cars instead of ships passing beneath you. It makes you feel big—important...a sure way of beating the shakes.

I have less than five minutes to go...

I buy another coffee and doughnut at the cafeteria counter, walk to a table and sit down. I open the brief-case and take out a copy of the Irving Wallace novel *The Prize*. It is a paperback edition. I open it at page two hundred and make-believe I am reading it. I *am* reading it—the first four lines of the page...I have already read and re-read them enough times to know them by heart. I re-read them again.

The man carries his tray to the table, unloads tea and a cellophane-wrapped sandwich, leans the tray against the leg of the table and sits down, opposite me. He unwraps the sandwich and, as he does so, he glances at the clock on the wall of the cafeteria.

He checks with his wrist-watch then, still stripping the cellophane from the sandwich, he speaks.

He says, "I would put it this way, more precisely—I made a discovery, and then I made an invention."

Without looking up, I read the next line from the book.

I quote, "But it was the invention that won the prize, nevertheless."

He says, "It is possible," and bites into the sandwich.

I close the book, rest the palm of my hand on the cover and look at him for the first time.

I murmur, "You're word-perfect, friend."

He nods, smiles and chews.

He is a younger man than I expected, and this also surprises me...that I unconsciously "expected" any specific type of person. But the goons who play this particular game are usually just that...goons. They fit into a general mold. Middle-aged because, in our company, years beget a degree of reliability. Dead-eyed— or maybe I should say cold-eyed—because years also bring mistakes, and mistakes have to be paid for, and a stretch behind the wall leaves its mark...especially around the eyes.

These and other things.

There is a stamp about these men and, if you know what to look for—and if you have seen it enough times—it is as obvious and as immediate as a skin pigmentation.

This man does not have it.

He is twenty—if that...certainly no more than some spot in the early twenties. He wears his hair long and modern; not shoulder-length, but longer than usual and it has the healthy sheen of good condition and regular shampooing. He has a moustache of the modern drooping-corner style; trimmed and well-kept. He wears a zippered, soft-leather wind-cheater above a nylon roll-neck of royal blue and both garments look expensive and well cared for.

In other words, he looks clean, healthy, young and intelligent...qualities not too common in this walk of life. And the blatantly obvious combination of all those qualities makes him something of a collector's item.

I have been watching him for a few moments, in silence.

He, in turn, has been watching me.

He flicks his eyes to the paperback, and says, "Have you read it?"

"No."

"You've seen the film, perhaps?"

"No."

He says, "The book is better than the film. The film isn't as long-winded as the book. You take your choice."

"That," I remark, "must be very nice."

He bites into the sandwich and, as he chews, he says, "The American reading public like value for money. Long novels. Lots of characters . . . lots of verbiage. They buy a book . . . they want it to last."

I nod and express slightly sardonic interest.

He says, "Films don't work that way, of course."

"No?"

"Action . . . with as little dialogue as possible. No more than six main characters . . . otherwise the audience can't follow the plot."

"Is that a fact?"

He says, "It must be hell scripting a book like that for the screen."

I move my head—as if in agreement . . . as if I give a damn.

This young man fascinates me. Already. There is an air of smooth self-assurance about him. Not cockiness. Not bravado or brashness. Okay—these qualities I have seen many times . . . every would-be-young-turk has them, before they are smashed out of him. But, with this one, it is not cockiness, or bravado, or brashness. It is something else.

It is what makes a Toledo blade unbreakable.

It is what makes the Rolls Royce the best motor car in the world.

Class!

This young man has class . . . and he wears it as easily,

as naturally, as unconsciously as a skin.

I watch his face and, very quietly, say, "Darley."

He swallows, drinks some tea, then bends his lips into a half-smile.

"Darley," I repeat.

"I know a man called Darley," he says.

"Yeah?"

"Not an uncommon name . . . not too uncommon."

"Not common," I say.

"Darley," he muses. "George Darley . . . a Dublin man. An Irish poet . . . but all Irishmen are poets, aren't they?"

"Not George Darley," I murmur.

"Felix Octavius Carr Darley?" He grins. "No . . . it wouldn't be him. He was an American artist—a very good book-illustrator . . . but it wouldn't be him. Would it?"

"No." I shake my head, and can hardly prevent myself from returning the grin.

This boy is good; he is everything Bishop was not. He is pushing me into making the first real move. It is a game, and he knows it and I know it, and whoever wins this game can claim a small victory.

He fishes a pack from the pocket of the wind-cheater, and lights a cigarette.

As he is lighting it, he says, "Let's forget Darley. Let's try another name. Let's try Fleischer. David Fleischer . . ."

"Forget it!" I snap.

"He calls himself 'Fletcher' . . . so they tell me." He drops the spent match into a tin ashtray, takes a long pull on the cigarette, then murmurs, "German father—English mother . . . American citizen. So-o . . . Fleischer. Why not?"

"Okay," I growl. "Darley—the man we both know . . . Edward Darley."

"Well, thank you, Mr. Fletcher." He smiles and nods his head. There is good-natured mockery in the smile, and

the nod of the head is equally mocking...it is a little like
the friendly bow of a victor to the vanquished. He says,
"He sends his regards, and warned me to drive carefully."

Like I say...this boy is *good*.

London, in the small hours...

It never sleeps. It never even cat-naps. It may quieten,
and relax a little (like now) but it always has one eye open,
ready to bat the hell out of anybody foolish enough to
take too many liberties.

I have known this city in many of its moods. I make no
claim to have known it in all its moods—it has too
many—ask me, and I'd say the man who claims to know
London in *all* its moods is a fool and a liar. I only claim
that I have known it in many.

Take Sunday mornings...

On Sunday mornings, this city—this massive, pulsat-
ing London—takes on the mantle of an overgrown
village. A near-deserted village. A village which suddenly
has trees you have never before noticed; patches of
greenery—village greens, if you like—which you have
passed, without seeing, scores of times. And villagers...all of whom know each other. For a few hours, each
week, London stops being cosmopolitan, and becomes
very Olde Worlde English...and, of all the cities in the
world, only London can pull this particular trick.

Or take London, when I first knew it...

I first knew London more than a quarter of a century
ago, when it was having its guts blown out; when its
entrails were fire-hoses and its broken bones were what
was left of buildings after the bombers had returned to
base. And its mood, in those days, will never again be
matched. It was all England—more than that, it was all
the free world—concentrated in one blazing and bleeding
heart which refused to stop beating.

That was the London I first knew...and first loved.

But I learned that it has less magnificent—less graceful—moods.

It has a mood which rejects the old and the homeless; which convicts them of poverty, and sentences them to sleep under newspapers, in dark corners; which is merciless, and which exposes them to the weather, and freezes them, and starves them and, eventually, kills them—slowly...an inch at a time.

It also has a mood which embraces men (and women) like myself. A dark mood. A brooding and savage mood. A mood which suits the rogue animals of society; men (and women) who know what they are, but don't want to change, because they are satisfied to *be* what they are. Not necessarily bad. Not necessarily wicked—not by their standards—but, because of what they are, outlaws of society...and yet, and despite their outlawry, part of society.

And London is their Valhalla—their happy hunting ground—and the mood of *their* London is the mood of every jungle on earth.

I know London...I know it well.

We ran out of motorway at Hendon and, since then, the boy has eased the route of the van towards the west; through Brent and through Ealing. We have passed cops and we have passed patrol cars, but none of them noticed our passing—and who can blame them?...what is there suspicious about an Austin van being driven carefully and at only moderate speed, even at this hour?

And the boy can drive. As well as—maybe even better than—Bishop. He handles that gear-stick like it was Saladin's sword stroking its way through silk. Nor can his pedal-work or steering be faulted. He is good; like all good drivers, he is an extension of what is under the bonnet and what is moving us along the road surface... he is part of the vehicle.

There is no radio but, instead, there is conversation. And I mean that. Conversation... not just talk. This boy knows how to communicate; how to say something... and when to stop saying, and start listening.

His name is Lewis. Timothy Lewis... Tim Lewis, to his friends. He has had a good education; up to, and including, a first year at university. His subject was English Literature... which means he has read more than most people, and has understood what he has read. His education stopped suddenly, when his father kicked it.

Since then...

I say, "Why this?"

"Darley?"

"Yeah."

He smiles, and says, "Why not? It's a living... a good living, given luck."

"Yeah," I agree, sarcastically. "A block of prison cells makes for real high life."

"The good ones don't," he remarks.

"All of them," I assure him. "The good, the bad—the Krays, the Messinas, the Richardsons... all of them."

"Darley?"

"One day." I nod, and am sure I am right. "There is a gray suit, somewhere. It fits badly... but it is *his*."

He chuckles, quietly, glances at me, switches his eyes back to the road, then says, "And you?"

"Maybe," I growl. "Maybe an electric chair—maybe a gas chamber—maybe a guillotine... who knows?"

He lets another quiet chuckle escape from his lips, but does not argue.

I watch the road ahead for a while; the mottled brown slush which is the carriageway, flanked by the snow-covered sidewalks. Come a few more hours and the

sidewalks, too, will be covered in chocolate-colored slush.
The white—the unspoiled beauty—will be trampled upon
and will become sullied and filthy. Then, given time, the
rain will wash the sidewalks clean . . . and the beauty and
the filth will be one more memory.

Lewis says, "You'll be here over Christmas."

"Could be," I agree.

"I like Christmas," he muses.

"Yeah . . . me too."

"Kids. Kids *make* Christmas . . . don't you think?"

"No."

"No?" He sounds surprised. Almost hurt.

"I dislike kids," I say, impatiently. "They have one
thing going for them . . . just that one thing."

"What's that?"

"If they live long enough, they'll grow out of it."

In the gloom of the cab I feel, rather than see, him grin.
He says, "And dogs?"

"What about dogs?"

"Do you hate them, too?"

"Why the hell should I hate dogs?" I ask.

"W. C. Fields. He once said . . ."

"People say a lot of things." I cut in, and my voice has a
harsh edge. "People like Fields—people working to build
up an image . . . they say things. Most of it is carefully
thought out crap."

"Like the killer with the candy-covered heart?" he asks,
quietly.

I make my voice hard . . . real hard. I put ice in it. I like
this boy. I want he should recognize the truth when he
hears it.

I say, "The animal does not exist, kid. Don't let 'em
fool you. A killer is a killer . . . period. Anything extra is
pure crow-shit."

● ● ●

Valda...

Who the hell ever christened a kid "Valda?" Who the hell ever lumbered some squawking infant with a handle like that? It is a whore's name. It belongs to the bawdy houses and the bordelloes.

Valda... for Christ's sake!

Without even looking at her, I know what she is. The name tells me; it tells me her whole history. What she is, and what she has been.

A hooker... before the "Valda" label was thought up. Some kid who figured she had something to hawk; something different; something unique; something the boys were going to queue up to pay for.

Sweet Jesus!

Then some pimp got hold of her. Some slimy bastard who offered to "organize" her; some two-timing, sweet-talking turd who held out an ersatz edition of the one thing the customers *never* gave... affection. He said things she wanted to hear and, even though she didn't believe them, they sounded nice—even when he was saying them... so she paid him to say them.

And, maybe at some time in this period of her life, the name "Valda" arrived. She was given a new name—she was re-christened—she was re-born, if you like... and the world she was re-born into was one hell of a high-smelling place!

The rackets... what else? She became one of a crowd, in a cat-house. She was clothed, she was fed, she was housed, she was given pocket-money and, for these things she worked. She functioned when she was told to function; she took men like a fruit-machine takes dollars... and with the same unemotional, mechanical expertise.

She learned the tricks—learned her trade—and became good. She moved up the cat-house scale until she was Number One Girl. Then—when the lines began to show around the neck—when the legs became a little skinny and the breasts a little less proud—she was promoted to madame. She ruled over dames who were what she herself had once been. She watched for the short-changers. She sweetened the vice cops . . . and those she couldn't sweeten she set up for a fix.

Then, eventually, she became too old; too old, even, to be a madame. She lost the sparkle—the bite—necessary to control a team of hot-spirited grafters. So-o . . . the boys had to step in and mark a few, to keep the rest in line. Maybe they had to step in, more than once. Maybe some real roughing had to be resorted to. Whatever . . . a marked grafter is so much dead weight until the marks wear off, and the boys who run the rackets work strictly for cash.

So, out goes Valda, and in comes some other madame who can muscle the girls into line.

Which is why Valda is here; tenant of this not-too-crummy maisonette, above a betting shop, in a Hammersmith dead-end.

I can write the words, and set the words to music. Valda has been one of Darley's racket-girls for years. The betting shop is also one of Darley's concerns. Great . . . so the maisonette is a safe "dropping spot" for anybody Darley wants to keep off the streets, and little old Valda is Darley's eyes and ears.

All this I know. By the whore's name she answers to . . . by the general set-up. I do not have to be told; I have already heard it too many times not to be bored.

She watches me from across the coffee table; watches me as I straighten, from untying my shoes and relax back into the comfort of the armchair; watches me as I unknot my tie.

She watches me, and sips whisky and lime.

"No drink?" she checks.

"No drink," I confirm.

She looks at me with interest; like a bug-catcher might examine some new crawler he has found. I do not fit into any of the neat slots which, together, add up to her life; I am supposed to be "tough," and "tough" men soak up booze—but I don't ... and it throws her a little.

"Anything?" she asks.

I smile, and say, "Nothing at all. Just to unwind a little, before the sheets take over."

She takes another slug of whisky and lime.

I rest my neck against the back of the armchair, half close my eyes and, for a few moments, we watch each other.

I see a woman ... a woman who, once upon a time, was an attractive woman. It is still there; the stamp of near-beauty. The facial lines mask it slightly, but the mask is transparent and, under the mask that which drove men dippy is still around. I figure her to be about sixty—maybe a few years younger ... her chose profession plays hell with prolonged youth! She had dress-sense, in that she dresses her age; there is no little-girl-grandmother about the clothes she is wearing; they are smart, but subdued. Her hair is tinted, but that is no crime; it has a raven-black sheen ... but, without the dye, my guess is that it would be a frowsy gray. Her make-up is too thick; that is my only criticism ... that she has the belief held by every other ex-hooker, that youth can be plastered back into position if the pot it comes in costs enough dough.

Other than that, she would make some middle-aged guy a very nice mother.

She says, "Darley sent word. Anything you fancy."

"Nothing," I grunt.

"A woman?" she suggests.

She makes the offer like anybody else might offer a cigarette... and, to her, the two offers would be on a par.

"No woman," I say.

"A man?" This time the question is shot with a hint of contempt.

"Do me a favor," I growl.

She moves her shoulders, and says, "Some people... y'know."

"I need sleep," I say. "I do not need sex... of any sort."

"Sure. Just that Darley said..."

"I will," I sigh, "be seeing Darley, sometime tomorrow... later, today. I will make a point of telling him you offered. And that I refused."

She moves her head in a single nod; as if she is satisfied; as if a small, but nagging, weight has been lifted from her shoulders.

I let myself settle deeper into the upholstery. I try the old yoga trick of concentrating my thoughts on each muscle, in turn; of consciously making my body relax, inch at a time. Let the toes hang loose inside my socks... then the feet, one foot at a time... then the ankles... then the calves...

The theory goes that, before you reach the face, you are asleep.

Maybe it works... for some people.

Maybe I am doing it all wrong. Maybe I am concentrating too much... or, maybe, not enough. The trick has never yet worked for me.

Maybe I am concentrating on the wrong thing... on Valda.

There is a look which she is trying to push away from her face; an expression she is trying to keep from her eyes, but cannot. It is a little like the old bobby-sockser look... a little like that, but not much like that. Hero-worship?... we-ell—not quite that, either. Respect?... yeah—some brand of respect is there.

Curiosity?...could be—but it is the curiosity of the mouse for the trap; it is mixed with apprehension and not a little timidity.

She begins, "Darley..." then stops.

"Yeah?" I encourage.

"He—er—he thinks you're big," she says, awkwardly.

I move my mouth into a non-committal twist.

"You've met him?" she asks.

"Darley?"

She nods.

"Yeah...I've met him. Twice."

"When you've been..." She stops, again.

I know what it is she can't say. I answer the unasked question.

I say, "No."

"Oh!" She sounds vaguely disappointed, then cheers up a little and roots for her boss. She says, "He's important. Y'know...important."

"Darley?"

"What he says goes."

"So they tell me," I grunt.

"He can fix things. Anything...he can fix it."

"Yeah. They all can," I say, in a bored voice.

"Eh?"

"They can all fix things. All the master-minds. All the big-fixers. Until it comes to the king-sized fix...then they send for me."

"You?" There is a breathless quality about the one-word question.

"Guys like me," I correct myself.

Then comes the atmosphere. The same old atmosphere...the same old feeling.

I figure the guy who pulls the switch in the death house—the guy who drops the capsule in the gas chamber—the guy who pulls the lever which operates the drop...all these people will know what I mean. They, too, will have been subjected to this kinky fascination; this frightened probing, by people who have some sort of dark passage in their minds.

Nor are these people a minority. Nor are they all bent.

Twice—twice, already—I have been offered heavy bread by big circulation magazines for my "memoirs;" to be knocked out by some hack writer and published under some crappy *nom de guerre* which every cop in Christendom would recognize as a cover-up for "Dave Fletcher."

My profession interests people. Lots of people—more good than bad, more honest than dishonest...and why the hell it should I do not know. I deal in a commodity. The doctor and the midwife deal in the same commodity...but from the other end. But who asks a quack for his "memoirs?"—who asks a midwife?...so, why ask *me*?

But it happens...every time.

People are crazy.

The Valda dame is as crazy as the rest.

She moistens her lips then, in a near-whisper, asks, "What's it like, Fleischer?"

"The name," I snap, "is *Fletcher*."

"Eh?"

"Fletcher...David Fletcher. And, lady—as far as you are concerned—not even that."

"I'm—I'm sorry." She is suddenly scared. Why?—God only knows...but she is suddenly scared. She tries a quick slug of liquid courage, then says, "It's the name Darley..."

"Darley is a very mouthy punk," I growl. "This I suspected. This I now know. This I will tell him."

"You—you ain't scared?"

"Of Darley?"

"No. No...you wouldn't be." She says it like she has suddenly realized something which is very obvious.

"Fleisch...Fletcher wouldn't be scared. Not even of Darley."

"Lady," I say, wearily, "I have had a long, hard day. It is now climbing up to two, and I am tired. Let's skip the rest...eh? Let you just show me the bed. Then forget who I am, and I will forget who you are, and we will both hit the sack and sleep...okay?"

"T-together?" She asks this damn fool question in a timid, little-girl-doesn't-know voice.

"Come again?" I stare. I think I know what she means...but I need to be sure, before I blast her.

She says, "Darley said I was to..."

"Darley," I snarl, "has lost his goddam marbles! He is shag-crazy, and must figure every other guy the same. No, lady...I do not require a dame with which to warm my bed. Nor do I require some ass-happy fairy. And, sure as hell, I do not want Methuselah's grandmother."

Okay...so, I should not have said it. I should not have made that particular remark. I should have eased the message across to her more gently.

I know...she has offered me the only thing she possesses—the only thing she *has* to offer—herself. I also know that nobody can offer more than that...more than themselves.

And this is a great argument, of course...the sort of argument cheapskate intellectuals toss around. But what she has offered me—what she had *actually* offered me—is the body of a has-been-harlot. Something ten thousand other men have already used and worn out.

So-o...what does that make me?

Okay...I should not have thrown the offer back into her teeth that way. I could have been more polite.

But, who wants to waste time being polite?

I am a bastard...ask anybody.

Which is why I am sleeping alone, and is why I do not

give one lonely damn about whether or not I have insulted a stupid dame called Valda... which by my reckoning is not even her real handle.

So, goodnight nurse... and screw everybody!

Lewis eases the cab out of the cul-de-sac and into the traffic.

I lean forward from the rear seat, and say, "Where?"

"Reve Street. You won't know the place. It's off..."

"It's off Soho Square," I chip in. "Between Soho Square and Dean Street."

"Okay... you know." He strokes the gear-stick and we pick up knots. "Sit back. I'll get you there."

I say, "Just drive towards, kid. I'll tell you what, when we reach."

"You're the fare, friend."

I growl, "Yeah," and lean back.

It is just after ten, and I have lived two hours of the day already.

The Valda dame shook me at eight. She brought tea and the morning newspaper; she even brought them with a smile... which, after last night, proves that she has good powers of recuperation.

I drank tea and filled my eyes with the latest slice of the world's troubles. Then I did press-ups—the usual twenty—before wandering into the bathroom for a toothbrushing, a shave and a shower.

Back to the bedroom, where I dressed in the clothes which had been stored in the wardrobe for me. The nice, quiet gray suit. The cream shirt. The tan tie. The new socks. The pair of soft-leather shoes.

Everything fitted. Everything was fine.

After that, breakfast.

Breakfast was a not-too-inspired meal; it was not the sort of meal to live on in my memory. Scrambled eggs (unseasoned)—toast and marmalade and... (but of course, in the U.K.) more tea. And, as always, the vital part of the breakfast—the vital part of *my* breakfast—the first pipe of the day; charged carefully with well-rubbed tobacco; lighted expertly and with the exactitude which only comes with experience; drawn deep, slowly and pleasurably into the lungs...after which, I was more or less alive and kicking, and capable of staying that way for the rest of the day.

I'd allowed myself to check that other members of the human race were still around. I'd eyed the world through the window of the maisonette and, for a change, what I'd seen had not brought on the usual urge to dive, head first, from the top of the Empire State.

With holly, a couple of reindeer and the three wise men it could have been a Christmas card.

The cul-de-sac was white-covered. The ploughs and the gritters had given it the go-by and no traffic had, so far, used it. The footprints of the milk-delivery man, the postman and the newsboy were the only indentations in the whiteness. Later, when the betting shop opened for business, there'd be more. The virginal beauty would be dirtied by men tramping all over it—okay...like Valda.

Meanwhile...

Meanwhile it was nice to look at and, although it had stopped snowing, the sky was lead-heavy with a lot more of the stuff not yet delivered.

A cab had called for me, just before ten.

The driver of the cab is the boy...Tim Lewis.

We hit the places everybody knows; the parts of London people mean when they say "London," Kensington Gardens and Hyde Park. Marble Arch, and then Bayswater Road becomes Oxford Street.

This is no Christmas-card-land. It is the wrong color. This is sewage-colored mush, and the only snow is the cotton-wool snow piled high behind the plate-glass frontage of flashy stores.

I say, "What does he call this place?"

"Eh?" Lewis cocks an ear for a repeat.

"Darley... the clip-joint he uses as base. What's its name?"

"The Striponium Club."

I breathe, "Christ!"

Lewis chuckles.

I say, "Reve Street... right?"

"Yeah."

"Okay." I lean forward and give instructions. "Regent Street, Shaftesbury Avenue, Charing Cross Road. Then into Soho Square, via Sutton Row. Carlisle Street, Reve Street—drive not too fast—then left, left again down Dean Street... down to Leicester Square tube, and drop me."

"What the hell..." he begins.

"Do it, sonny," I snap. "Then give me thirty minutes. Same place—Leicester Square tube... I'll be waiting."

"I hope you know what you're doing," he says.

"All the time," I assure him.

"Darley won't like it."

"So?"

"He's a busy man."

I say, "Great. He should congratulate himself. The time to worry is when you are in the bread line."

We do it my way; Regent Street, Shaftesbury Avenue, Charing Cross Road, Sutton Row, Soho Square, Carlisle Street, Reve Street.

He drives smoothly and slowly along Reve Street, and I see the dead neon above the door of the dump. *The Striponium Club.* It is the usual—one of a million—a hole in a wall, and the hole is surrounded by glass-fronted cases in which are touched-up photographs showing round-assed dames who have tits... big deal! The door—the entrance to *The Striponium Club*—is having some difficulty finding space between a crummy-looking massage parlor and a sex-magazine mart.

And this, for Christ's sake, is known as "the under-world"... this pukey-looking trio of pornographic con-shops. I have this feeling—as always... show it soap and water, and it will move so fast it will leave a trail of dust.

There is a pale blue Merc parked not far from the club entrance. It has no covering of snow; it has arrived this morning. It is empty.

A colored guy is shifting some of the slush from the sidewalk. He moves in bottom gear; he keeps his eyes down and his shoulders bent.

A couple of teenage jerks are feasting their eyes, and working up their imagination, on the goods displayed in the sex-magazine emporium's window; they are just looking; they are not going to buy anything; if they could afford that junk, they would not be wearing the shoes they are wearing... not in this weather.

Along the street, the refuse cart is collecting the empties from last-night's shoot-up. Three guys—two of them colored—are muscling the bins around.

There are other things—other vehicles—other people—and I check them all as we pass.

Then we are out, and into Oxford Street, then left and left again, into Dean Street, and the cab is picking up speed towards Leicester Square.

Lewis drops me at the tube station.

I use the next thirty minutes to make sure...

I watch Lewis's cab lose itself in the traffic heading towards Long Acre, then flag another cab. The instructions are the same; Charing Cross Road, Soho Square and up Reve Street... a re-check to see what has, and what has not, happened.

Not much.

The refuse collection is almost through. The colored guy is still moving slush from point A to point B. The two jerks are still feeding their eyes on cover-girl nudes. The pale blue Merc is still parked.

I stop the cab in Dean Street, pay the driver and start using Shanks's carriage... along Carlisle Street and back up Reve Street.

The two jerks have moved from the porn-mag shop and are now admiring the scenery in the glass cases which front the entrance to *The Striponium Club*. The slush-pusher figures he has pushed enough slush for one day; he is wandering through the door of a two-bit cafe, a few yards along the street from Darley's joint. The refuse cart has disappeared. There are pedestrians and there is traffic... different pedestrians and different traffic.

There is also the blue Merc.

Alongside the Merc, I stop to load my pipe. I load it without looking... I use my eyes for other things.

The doors of the Merc are unlocked, and the keys are still in the ignition switch; which means the owner is either a lunatic or some guy with enough local weight to *know* he is safe... and lunatics do not own thoroughbred cars like this.

So-o...

I make a guess, and make a wager with myself that my guess is right.

I continue up the street, to Oxford Street, flag another cab and return to Leicester Square.

I wait and, as I wait, I smoke my pipe.

I have already mentioned... the boy has class.

I am watching for a cab, and he shows up in a V.W.; a battered "beetle," with an engine in its rump which does not sound at all battered.

He pulls in at the curb, opens the nearside door, and

calls, "When you're ready, Dave!"

I climb in, alongside him, close the door and we move off.

"What's with the Dave?" I say.

"What else? I had to call you something. Would you rather I call you..."

"Forget it," I growl. "You have made your point ...don't over-state your case." I jerk my head at the ceiling of the V.W., and add, "Why the change?"

He smiles, and says, "What you've been doing...a logical extension."

I watch his face out of the corner of my eyes, and wait.

He says, "You've been back—to Reve Street—I don't know, for sure...but that's what I guess. To check that nobody is watching. To check that everything is safe. In your position, it's what I'd do...I think it's what *you've* just done."

"And?"

"A logical extension." He smiles, again. "Just in case somebody *is* watching—*did* see the cab, first time round...a different jalopy."

Like I say...the boy has class.

And now, Darley is doing his beef routine; he is flapping his mouth and making rude remarks.

Edward Darley...Ed "Safron" Darley.

"Safron" because of the color of his skin; it fascinates me...I cannot decide whether the tint is yellow or orange. It shines, like it has just been polished; like it is silk-textured and without pores; like facial hair is something is has never known.

The face is high-cheekboned, thin-lipped and dark-eyed, and the eyes slant upwards, ever so slightly, at the outer corners. The overall effect is vaguely oriental...but not *quite* oriental. Some place in the dubious pedigree of Darley there is a full-blooded yellow man (or, maybe, a yellow woman) and, some place else, colored blood has been introduced, and Darley carries a splash of both. It is what makes his skin and his eyes . . . but no other part of him.

The rest is all hoodlum; flashy, over-dressed and loud-talking.

His mouth belongs some place up, or around, Liverpool. He talks like his tongue is in cramp, and lets go of the words before they have travelled beyond the back of his throat. "Adenoidal" is the way to describe Darley's conversation; he talks like he has adenoids as big as footballs . . . and muscles to match!

I turn to go back up the stairs; to return to the comparatively clean air of Reve Street.

"What the hell y'think you're doin'?" bawls Darley.

I keep walking.

"Hey! Fleischer!"

I stop. I turn. I eye Darley very coldly.

"What the hell . . ." he begins.

"Call me that again," I rasp, "and I will break your purple-pissing back."

"You will *wha-at*?"

I do not repeat it. The fink heard it the first time round, and I do not do encores for germs like Darley.

We are in the main room of *The Striponium Club*—which means we are in a room slightly bigger than the average call box—and we have an audience of two.

Tim Lewis watches with an interested half-smile hooked onto his mouth. The other guy—broad-shouldered, heavy-bodied and with features which look like they have been bombarded with rocks—watches, scowls and moves forward.

Darley's personal bouncer is about to thread me through the mangle . . . that's what *he* thinks!

I ease myself onto the balls of my feet, flex my knees a little and wait for him to arrive. He gets to within

punching distance, and swings; he does not telephone its
time of arrival... he damn near sends a postcard. I duck
under it, straighten when it has passed, and smash a basic
Karate chop at his throat. It stops him and he takes time
off to find some air.

From then on, it is easy. I give him the toe of my
shoe—hard—under each knee-cap and he drops, yelps as
his knees touch the carpet, then sprawls forward on
stiffened arms. I give the elbows the shoe-toe treatment
and he flattens out on his face.

I drop onto him. Full-weight. Knees landing at each
side of his spine in the small of his back. As I go down I
grab one of the bottles from a table—one of the fancy
bottles which Darley uses as candle-sticks in this
dump—and smash the bottle on the edge of the table.

I grab a handful of the bouncer's hair, yank his head
back and drive an edge of the broken glass into the side of
his neck. The blood runs and spills onto the carpet.

I ask the fink a question. I ask it in a voice which makes
it a very serious question, and a question which demands
an answer.

I say, "How do you want him delivered, Darley?... dead, or alive?"

Darley gets the message.

He looks like he would enjoy grilling me over a slow
fire, wets his lips, makes with what he hopes is a smile, and
says, "We—er—we started wrong... *Fletcher.*"

"We did?"

I lean forward a fraction and the broken glass bites a
little deeper.

The goon with part of a bottle in his neck makes
gurgling noises.

Darley says, "I did," and it almost strangles him. "I
have this thing—y'know... about being kept waiting."

"Yeah. I, too, have a few 'things.'"

"Sure. Sure. But..."

"I do not like being treated like a dog, Darley. I do not like being made to lose my temper . . . it upsets me. Okay?"

"Okay." He nods, and hates me at the same time. "Let's—let's forget it. I'm sorry. Let's start at the beginning again—eh?"

For a few moments I make-believe I am giving it careful thought. Then I push myself up from the goon, toss what is left of the bottle into a corner and dust off the knees of my pants.

The goon hauls himself upright. He is bleeding down the front of his shirt. He is also looking very scared.

Darley looks at him, despises him for a second or two, then snaps, "Out!"

The goon makes as if he would like to argue.

Lewis murmurs, "The man said blow. Be advised . . . blow. You're only bleeding. It could be worse."

The goon puts thunder-clouds in his expression, but he holds his neck and shambles out of the room.

Darley goes to the fancy bar, at the rear of the room. He fingers the colored bottles, like they are jazzed-up organ-stops, then says, "Okay . . . what's it gonna be?"

"Tomato juice," I say.

He stares at me, and there is suspicion in the look. He figures this might be some new crack he does not follow.

He says, "Anything, mac. You name it . . . we've got it."

"Tomato juice?" I make it a question, this time.

"Yeah. But . . ."

"Tomato juice," I repeat.

"Okay." He shrugs. He concludes he is dealing with a nut. He switches his offer to Lewis, and asks, "And you?"

Lewis grins, and says, "Tomato juice. If it puts that breed of tiger in a man's tank, that's what I want . . . tomato juice."

Darley turns sarcastic.

He says, "Nobody minds if I drink something a little heavier . . . eh?"

"If you can lift it, drink it," I remark. "Who cares?"

I heave a chair away from one of the tables and sit down. I use the time it takes for Darley to fix the drinks to give *The Striponium Club* a quick once-over.

It is sucker-bait... every inch of it. It is a wallpapered sewer, with subdued lighting. It is carpeted with a carpet which, even in this myopic gloom, can be seen to be well-stained and with plenty of burn marks where cigarettes have dropped. Most of the carpet is covered with tables; too small for sense and too close for comfort. There are chairs at some of the tables, and other chairs are stacked, in a nest, along one wall.

There is a stage, and the drapes are drawn back. The stage is maybe twenty foot wide and ten foot deep; an overgrown rostrum with a black, sequin-studded back-cloth. It is a typical stripper's platform, and it puts the G-string damn near within groping distance of the first tables.

There is also, of course, the bar. The bar balances the stage, at the other end of the room, and is just about size-for-size with the stage. It is well stocked, and it goes in for colored booze; the bottles have tiny lights behind them, and shine green and pink, golden and red, orange and even blue; they look nice... and the chances are they all taste lousy!

It is a clip-joint-cum-strip-cellar-cum-porn-parlor, and the only good thing about it is that it does not pretend to be what it is not.

Lewis and I wait at the table, and Darley joins us. He dumps tomato juice in front of Lewis and myself. His own booze is whisky and ice.

He notices my interest in the place.

As he grabs a chair, he says, "Nice... innit?"

"I have," I say, sourly, "seen nothing I have not seen before."

"You ain't seen the show, yet."

"True," I growl.

"That's a gas."

"Yeah?"

"They come for miles."

"From," murmurs Lewis, and sips at his drink.

"Eh?" Darley stares at the box.

"From," repeats Lewis, gently. "They come *for* the show...and they come *from* miles."

Darley frowns, then grins—a not very happy grin—and says, "Ain't he a gem? Educated. Y'know... educated."

"Upstairs," I jerk my head. "The bookshop—the masturbation joint...all the same complex?"

"I aim to please." Darley swallows some booze, smacks his lips, and says, "They wanna watch it. They wanna read about it. They wanna pull-off. Okay...I oblige."

"For bread, of course?"

"Is there anything else in this world?" He grins.

Lewis looks at me and droops a slow eyelid...the one Darley cannot see.

I taste the tomato juice, and even the tomato juice is crummy. Lewis lights a cigarette; he takes his time and makes it look like it was an act thought up by Marcel Marceau. Darley swirls the whisky around in his glass, and the ice-cubes make soft knocking noises.

We each wait for the other.

Me?...I am prepared to wait until hell grows icicles. I am here for a purpose; I was sent for. I am selling—Darley wishes to buy...therefore, Darley makes the first move.

"You—er—y'know why?" he says, at last.

"What?" I play it stupid.

"Why you're here?"

I move my shoulders.

He says, "I wanna make a contract...right?"

I smile.

"I—er—I want you to do a job...right?"

I taste the tomato juice.

"There's . . . Y'know . . . there's this guy."

"Yeah?" I show mild—*very* mild—interest.

Lewis does the eyelid-droop trick, again.

Darley is sweating. Not much—not yet . . . there is a shine of moisture across his upper lip. Nevertheless, he is sweating.

He says, "I want him—y'know . . ." He hesitates, then clears his throat, and ends the sentence, ". . . handled."

"Handled?" I polish the tomato-juice glass with a forefinger.

"Y'know . . . seen to."

"Not altogether," I murmur.

"Uh?" Darley blinks.

I say, "You keep telling me 'I know.' You use the expression a lot. You are mistaken, friend, I do not 'know' . . . not until you tell me."

"Christ . . . you *know*." The impression is that, if his arms were not otherwise engaged, Darley would flap them.

I shake my head and keep a deadpan expression.

"You're a—you're a . . . Christ, you *know* what you are."

"Yeah. I am an American citizen."

"Jesus!" He speaks the word low enough for it to be called a whisper. He is worried—scared of what he is doing—scared of what he wants to ask me to do.

They always are. *Always.* If they were not scared, they would do it themselves; they would save dough, and I should live a little harder. My job—to do that which scares the hell out of them . . . but, first they must spell it out. They must at least do that. I have made it a rule . . . and I do not break rules.

I wait.

Lewis also waits. I have this feeling . . . that Lewis is more than merely interested. That he is watching every move. Listening. And remembering. There is a relaxed concentration there; relaxed, because that is the nature of the kid—it is what makes him better than average... but the concentration is, nevertheless, one-hundred-per-cent.

Darley takes a long, hard swig of the booze, gasps as the stuff hits his throat, then speaks in a rush.

He gabbles, "I want you to hit him for me."

"Hit him?" I cock an eyebrow.

"Shoot him. Kill him. Kill the bastard."

Having said it, he is breathless, and the sweat is now on his forehead, and under his eyes.

"Shoot him," I say. "Specifically... shoot him?"

"Any way." Darley's voice is a snarl. "Just kill the bastard... that's all."

I nod. I sip the tomato juice.

Very quietly, I say, "Ten G."

"Look! He's..."

"Who he is—what he is—where he is—is not important," I chip in, gently. "Just that he is not immortal. Just that you want him out. And, to get him out, will cost you ten G."

"I—er... Jesus! I didn't expect it to cost..."

"You expected it, Darley."

"Naw. I thought, maybe..."

"Darley—you are a liar." I speak in a tired voice, because I am tired of this same old spiel. It happens— every time... the punks act like they are bargaining with some Arab street-trader. They act like they are buying lemons. They know what they want—they know they are going to have to pay—they know they will *have* to pay... and, every time, there is this red-hot poverty routine. As if I am stupid... as if I do not know that poverty is something they are not on speaking terms with. I say, "You are wasting air, friend."

"Ten thousand dollars is heavy bread, man. I dunno whether..."

"Ten thousand *pounds*," I say. "I use the currency of wherever I work."

"Jesus!"

I say, "You asked around, Darley. You did not put a small ad in some local news-sheet. You asked around—you knew the terms, before you sent...so, cut out the song-and-dance act."

He swallows the rest of the whisky, stands up and walks to the bar. As he is fixing himself more booze, he says, "I coulda got somebody a damn sight cheaper. I coulda..."

"Sure you could," I agree. "The nearest all-night cafe. The nearest doss-shop. Wave a five pound note around, and one of those jerks would oblige. They are around, friend...I know that. They will also end you up in stir. They will make a very messy job of it. They will put the black on you until steam comes out of your stupid ass. But, go ahead...do not let me influence you."

As he drops ice into the whisky, he mutters, "It's a helluva lot of money."

"Sure." I grin and say, "The car, out in the street—the blue Merc...yours?"

"Yeah. How d'you..."

"Status," I explain. "The keys are in it. Somebody who figures it won't be used for joy-riding—a car which is known around here...who else, but you?"

"Oh! Yeah. Yeah, it's..."

"You could," I say, "get around on roller skates. They would get you there. Maybe not as fast—maybe not as comfortably...but cheaper."

"I don't see what..."

"You pay for the best, Darley. Always. Machines, or men...you always pay more for the best."

He tastes the whisky on his way back to the table. He has decided...he was never *un*decided. It is there—it was always there—mixed with the greed and the viciousness in his eyes. Because what he wants, and how he wants it, is not for sale in any five-and-ten-cent arcade. It is special ... which means it needs a specialist.

And specialists do not come cut-price.

I know ... I am a specialist.

It takes him half the second whisky and ice to work it out.

Then, he says, "Okay. It's pricey, but ..."

"But you want it."

"Yeah." He nods.

I say, "Fine. We have a deal. Ten G—pounds sterling—deposited in a Swiss bank, within four days. The hit, within one week of me knowing it is safely in the vaults."

He has booze in his mouth, as I say this, and he almost chokes.

I say, "I will tell you the bank. I will tell you the name it is to be credited to and the number of the account. Okay?"

He stops choking, and gasps, "How the hell ... How the hell do I know you'll do it? What guarantee have I that you won't ..."

"None," I say, in a very hard tone. "You don't *need* a guarantee ... any more than you need a receipt. What you need, friend, is a corpse. That is what you will get."

"Meaning I have to trust you?" He glares as he asks this very stupid question.

"Meaning just that," I say. "Which is one hell of a lot safer than me trusting you."

Lewis speaks for the first time. He answers Darley's question, before Darley asks it.

He says, "Ed, look at it this way. You pay him, and he does the job. Fine—you're both happy ... and he's still in business. If he *doesn't* do the job, his reputation goes. And, without a reputation, what is he? It's what he needs—what he must have ... a reputation. You don't need it ... bilk him, and the others will think you're smart."

"And," I growl, "it would mean knocking *you*...for the reputation."

Lewis says, "It makes sense, Ed. You could, perhaps, hook him out of his money. I'm not saying you would...but you *could*. He can't. He daren't...it's part of what he is."

Darley argues. He tries that part-payment offer...but, in my business, we do not do things on the knock. He screws around a little; prepared to part, but not wanting to part. The routine is so old, it has a knee-length beard. I let him talk. All I do is sip tomato juice and say "No" at regular intervals.

Eventually, it comes. It is like drawing a tooth...but it comes.

He says, "Okay...Okay." He finishes the booze in his glass. He waves the glass around, and snarls, "Okay...so the deal's on. You're a hard man, Fletcher. You're a hard bastard...did anyone tell you?"

"I have a birth certificate which calls you a liar, Darley."

He thinks I have made a funny. He makes a smile with his lips...but it is pre-packed and straight from the deep freeze.

I say, "Right. The details...basic. Where?"

"Up in the sticks."

"Why not down here?"

"He won't come...can't come."

"Why not?"

"He can't...it's out."

"Okay." I shrug. "What's his racket?"

"Eh?"

"His racket," I repeat. "How does he earn bread? I need to know...it helps eliminate stupid mistakes in the planning."

Darley moves his lips, and this time the smile is genuine...genuine, but not nice.

He says, "Like you...only ex."

The shivers hit me as he says it. Spiders, with wet feet, crawl around my spine, and the hairs around my nape sit up and beg.

I say, "Details, Darley. This is not some ball game. Give with the details."

Darley watches my face, as he says, "He's a cripple...okay? He lives in a wheelchair. But, before that, he was one of the top hatchet carriers around. And clean, y'know...the cops knew, but couldn't prove. I used him...once. Years ago. I wanted a guy— y'know...he was in the way. I wanted the top, and this guy was in the way. So I used him. Paid him...like I'm paying you."

He pauses, still watching my face.

"And?" I say.

"He knows...that's all." Darley's voice is ugly. "He could black me...like you'll be able. But he *needs* the coin. That's what I hear. He was a wild spender...and now he's broke. He'll put the squeeze on. Sure he will. That, or starve...and he won't starve."

I say, "You would," and I put meaning into the two words.

"Yeah. So will he. So will..."

"I know his name," I say, in a flat voice. "Gawne. He carries the same first name I carry...David. David Gawne."

"Yeah." Darley nods.

I say, "Gawne wouldn't black you, Darley...ever."

"I ain't prepared to take the risk."

I take a deep breath. It is almost a sigh.

"So, the deal's off?" sneers Darley. "Just because..."

"Did I say that?" I rasp.

"You don't sound too happy."

"Do I have to crack jokes, too?" I snarl. "Who the hell are you buying, Darley? Me?...or Jack Benny?"

In a soft voice, Lewis says, "The reputation, Ed. Remember?"

"Why don't you..." I kill the explosion, grab my voice and speak to Darley. I say, "The kid here knows, Darley. He is wiser than you are."

"I want Gawne outa the way. I want the bastard buried... see? He could worry me. He could be a bleedin' nuisance... a *real* nuisance. I've given it thought... a lotta thought. And I want him taken out."

And this is the man; this is Darley. It is there... in that last speech. In the way he talks, and what he says. The way he thinks. The way he figures things. It is what makes him lower than the soles of a snake. It is what makes him scum.

I growl, "You get what you pay for, Darley."

"Just so long..."

"What you pay for."

We talk the details. The cash, and how I want it delivered. The bank and the deposit box number. The name it has to be made out to.

We talk about alibis. Darley needs one—it is part of the deal... and it needs setting up with some care. Me? My alibi is already fixed; it is part of the racket—what separates the pro from the flash-boy... but this is something Darley does not need to know.

We talk through two more whiskies, and until I have half-swallowed that which Darley calls tomato juice.

Then, I say, "Okay. Last thing. I need a finger-man."

Darley frowns his dumbness.

"A marker," I explain, in a tired voice. "Somebody I can trust. Somebody who can handle a getaway car... supposing it becomes necessary. Somebody who can fetch and carry, while I stay out of sight."

"Oh!" Understanding dawns.

"I do not provide my own army," I say, sarcastically. "Not even for that dough."

Darley says, "I'll alert Tipp. He's my man up..."

"Yeah. I know who Tipp is. His beef met me, yesterday."

"Okay. I'll..."

I take a chance. I say, "Lewis. I would like the kid, here, as finger-man."

Expressions chase each other across Darley's face. He looks surprised...almost shocked.

I say, "I need somebody who knows how to take orders. The kid, here, has yet to argue with what I tell him..."

Then comes doubt; doubt which nudges close to suspicion.

"...But not just a dumb-bell. Somebody with brains. Somebody who can obey orders, but knows how to add to those orders if necessary..."

Then comes the dawning of a grin; a sly grin, like he has a secret which is likely to kick some poor jerk right in the guts.

"...And somebody who knows how to handle a car. Really handle it. Not just go like his ass was on fire all the time. Somebody who knows when we need speed, and when we do not need speed..."

The grin grows up and becomes a chuckle; it develops muscles and moves his shoulders as the secret joke explodes inside him.

"...And somebody with a hot line to your ear. In case of trouble. No rep. Not some hick muscle-man you might not believe when you *should* be believing him. I need a guy I can trust. Things do not go wrong—not if you plan them right—but, if they do, the finger-man becomes a very important character. He can blow it...or the other thing. I want Lewis. Okay?"

"Sure." Darley allows the chuckle to escape as a laugh. "Sure...why not?"

"Thanks." Lewis speaks, and the word carries meaning. He looks like he is a kid holding his first puppy.

He say, "Thanks a lot, Fletcher. I won't let you down."

"Just one thing." Darley controls his mirth long enough to deliver the punch line.

"Yeah?" I put on a bored and not-too-interested look.

Darley says, "Lewis—take him—sure... but watch him. His old man was a cop."

Sometimes...

I stretch out on the bed, on top of the covers, and stare at the ceiling. And I think.

And what I think is this...

Jesus Christ and all His saints... *sometimes*!

This is a rough profession. Like everything, it is ruled by the law of supply and demand; and the reason guys like me make a good living is because the demand always outstrips the potential supply. Most people—and I do mean *most* people—have some jerk they would like to present with a wreath. They hate his guts—maybe her guts—and, although they rarely say so, they would dearly like a quick stiffening job performed. Most cases, it is a dream and, most cases, people are satisfied to hang around and hope they live long enough to see the dream come true.

Sometimes, they try for a personal, do-it-yourself corpse. If they are stupid, they try poison... and they are stupid, because poison can always be detected, and traced. If they are only a little less stupid, they try some other way... and they are only a little less stupid, because *any* way starts the cops sniffing around, and the first things the cops earmark are "means," "opportunity" and "motive"—and the greatest of these is "motive." Give a good cop a motive, and he is half way towards solving any damn crime you care to mention.

And the only way to stonewall motive is to have an alibi... and by that I mean the real thing, and not some cooked up tooling around with time and distance which, when it is unravelled, will smash any plea of innocence to hell and back. To be someplace ... and to really *be* there. To have witnesses ... and witnesses who do not *know* they are witnesses. To stop the cops, dead ... to make even *them* admit that you couldn't have done the hit.

Then—and only then—you are safe.

And that brand of safety depends upon men like myself.

Objective men, who perform a very objective, and very dangerous, service ... but whose objectivity costs coin.

But, sometimes ...

Sometimes that objectivity is very hard to come by ... maybe even impossible.

I wouldn't know. I am not yet sure.

I stare at the ceiling of this room, at this motel, and I remember things. And some of the things I remember play hell with objectivity.

BERLIN.
SEPTEMBER—1945

Sergeant David Fleischer, of the Second American Armored Division wondered what the hell he was still doing in Europe. The war was over, the Third Reich was one big heap of rubble and, any minute now, the Ruskies would trample on one too many tits and another war would be on the start-line.

Meanwhile, he'd seen it all.

He'd seen men crushed under tank-tracks, he'd seen men hosed with fire from flame-throwers, he'd seen men unstitched with automatic weapons and with their innards spilling around their boots, he'd seen men decapitated by shrapnel and the headless trunk staggering forward a few more yards while the life hosed out of the severed neck.

He'd seen enough.

He'd seen the camps and, having seen them, he'd puked ... and, for days thereafter, whenever he'd remembered the sight and the smell, he'd puked again, and again. He'd seen what the Ruskies had done—were still doing—to the Berliners ... not the Red Army—not the men who'd done the fighting—but the "occupation troops;" animals; bastards from the Siberian backwoods, deliberately brought in to rape and pillage, to foul and humiliate a civil population already dishonored.

Everything! He'd seen it all ... he'd seen enough.

And now he wanted out and, because this was the one thing he could not have, he was settling for getting good and plastered.

And he was working at it ... brother, was he working at it! He was sitting at a table in this goddam bistro—this room, in a bomb-broken hotel dump on the outskirts of the city—and he was pouring liquid past his tonsils as fast as he could raise his drinking arm.

And this damn Russian gink was making a nuisance of himself.

The booze-parlor was something the high-ups had worked out ... which meant it was so much crap! A sort of "United Services Club." A place where comrades-in-arms (so-called) could get stinko together. The Yanks, the Limeys, the Ruskies, the Frogs—everybody happy—everybody stoned out of their minds, and all pals together.

Up a coconut-tree!

There was more naked hatred—more needle—per cubic foot in this goddam room than anywhere else on earth. An evening with only one fight—with only one blood-letting—was a little like a Bible-class, by comparison with normality at this particular drinking-house and, less than a couple of months ago, one evening session had seen the record of seven full-weight smash-ups start ... and end with the arrival of the Military Police.

In short, it was a nice place ... but, sometimes, a little rough on the nerves.

And now this crazy Rusky wanted to start something.

He was mouthing away in his own lingo and, if the look on his face was a pointer, what he was saying was not nice.

Sergeant Fleischer thought he caught a name somewhere in the gibberish...thought he recognized the name as "Betty Grable."

Fleischer waved a hand, and slurred, "Yeah—a great kid...beautiful legs. She married Harry James. Right?"

The Rusky stepped up the tempo, leaned across the table and scowled.

"Harry James," insisted Sergeant Fleischer. "The trumpet player. Okay?"

The Rusky smashed his fist on the table-top, leaned closer and threw language Fleischer didn't understand into Fleischer's face.

Fleischer eased away from the friendly-allies gag.

He eyed the Rusky warningly, and growled, "Back off, Joe. Your breath ain't too sweet."

Then the Rusky hit him. It was a glancing blow, aimed across the table, with a not-too-tight fist. It grazed the side of Fleischer's mouth and Fleischer moved his head a little too late, and the combination of the blow and Fleischer's own movement toppled the chair and Fleischer rolled on the floor and tasted the salt flavor of blood mixing with the spittle on his tongue.

The Rusky rounded the table and came in with the boot, and Fleischer rolled clear and aimed an upward kick at the Rusky's crotch. The kick wasn't true; Fleischer's booted toe smacked into the hard thigh muscle and, although it momentarily stopped the Rusky, it also drove him to a frenzy of anger.

Fleischer scrambled to his feet and, as the Rusky rushed in, aimed a punch at the dished face; at the broad nose, below and beneath the slightly slanted eyes. The punch landed, and it hurt; it even hurt Fleischer's knuckles so, sure as hell, it hurt the Rusky. But it didn't stop him. He still came forward, arms outstretched and fingers reaching for a hold, and Fleischer knew that these Soviet bastards could wrestle like bears and danced away from the seeking hands.

The overturned chair touched Fleischer's legs and he bent, scooped up the chair and, in the same movement, ducked sideways and clear of the Rusky's dart forward. Then he held the chair, like an animal trainer, and watched and waited.

The Rusky came in again, and Fleischer jabbed with the chair, and the Rusky swept it aside and still came on.

Fleischer did some more quick footwork and, as the Rusky turned, raised the chair and aimed for the Rusky's skull. The Rusky saw it coming, swayed back and, instead of the edge of the seat smashing into his dome, the legs and the cross-pieces landed across the Rusky's raised forearm and Fleischer was left holding what had once been the back of the chair.

Fleischer threw the splintered wood aside, breathed, "Okay, bastard. You want it rough . . . you can have it rough," and settled down to fight.

It was a fool thing to do. With a Yank—with a Limey, or a Frog—it would have worked . . . but not with a Rusky. It was like hitting a locomotive, and the locomotive kept coming forward.

For the first few minutes, everything was Fleischer's. He used his feet and he used his fists, and punch after punch exploded into the Rusky's face; into the mouth, into the nose, onto the eyes. The bastard was bleeding by the gallon. The front of his loose-fitting uniform was saturated with the stuff . . . but he wasn't slowing and, if facial expression meant anything, he wasn't feeling a damn thing.

Fleischer felt something he wasn't used to— something he'd only felt once in his life before...rock-bottom fear. This Russian animal was a killer. He was some sort of sub-human rogue male, and he wouldn't stop until he'd butchered that which stood in his way, and that which stood in his way was a certain Sergeant David Fleischer of the Second American Armored Division.

Fleischer took time off—a single slice of a second—to glance around the room, and what he saw didn't help the fear. The damn place was crawling with Ruskies. Ten—twenty . . . maybe more. And they were all watching their pal; willing him to win; blood-lusting for the life of a man who represented an enemy as real and as hated as any damn Nazi.

And Fleischer knew this was where he was going to end the war. Here, in a crummy booze-parlor, long-gone from his native soil and surrounded by finks who loathed his guts.

He fought...and this time he knew he was fighting for his life.

Which is maybe why he lost his cool and fought stupid.

He moved in for some fast, close-quarter work and, suddenly, he was in a vise. his arms were clamped to his ribs and his whole body was being squeezed until the bones creaked.

The Rusky had him in a bear-hug and, behind his back, muscled fingers held a muscled wrist and the arms from those fingers and that wrist were straightening and, as they straightened, the breath was being driven from his body and there wasn't any way of replacing it.

Fleischer knew this was not just one more punch up. Not one more inter-army brawl...albeit a particularly bloody and vicious one. This one was for keeps. This one carried death as its curtain line.

He twisted, and felt as if the jerk of his body in the hug of the Rusky was tearing ribs from their moorings. Nevertheless, he twisted and, as he twisted, he brought his knee up, hard, into the Rusky's groin. Once—twice—three times... and, each time, the Rusky hissed with pain and sprayed blood into Fleischer's face.

And an arm was free!

God only knew how—or even when... but, suddenly, Fleischer had a right arm he could use. He had a weapon he could fight back with.

Maybe it had wriggled loose in the general wrestling and heaving. Maybe the Rusky had relaxed his grip a fraction when Fleischer had kneed him in the cobblers. Maybe...

Just that the arm was free and, with it, Fleischer could croak the Rusky before the Rusky did the same to him... maybe.

Fleischer forced himself to forget everything except that arm. To forget the agony which radiated out from his spine and made a furnace of the middle part of his body. To forget the grayness, moving to darkness, which was playing around the outer edges of his vision. To forget everything—everything in the world—except that arm, and the hand at the end of that arm, and the fingers which were a part of that hand.

He rammed the heel of the hand into the Rusky's blood-washed face; under the flattened nose and hard against the short upper-lip. Then he curled the fingers and felt for the eyes; made them crawl up the cheeks until they found the sockets, then move over the closed lids and drive in and down, behind the eyeballs.

The Rusky moved his head back, and sideways, as he tried to escape the blinding claw of the fingers. He opened his mouth and gnashed yellowing teeth at the wrist... but couldn't quite make it.

And this was it... two brutes, fighting to the death.

And there was a throat—exposed and stretched above the high-necked tunic—and the throat was

within reach of a man (a brute) who knew damn well
that he was within touching distance of the grave.

What happened brought nightmares, but it had
to happen, because Fleischer wanted to live.

He dropped his face to the exposed throat and
drove his teeth into warm flesh; forced his jaw
muscles to tighten until he could feel the gristle and
cartilage of the windpipe. And his mouth filled to
overflowing with blood—blood which threatened
to drown him—blood which he had to swallow
before he could gulp what little air the pressure on
his ribs allowed . . . the blood of his present enemy.

And then the blood wasn't there any more. And
the pressure was gone. And his right hand was
clawing at air. And his left arm was free.

And there, in front of him—in what grayness
remained in the core of spinning blackness—was the
Rusky, and the Rusky was bent forward, clutching
at his throat and coughing gore into what looked
like a great pool of gore in which they staggered and
which still dripped from both their uniforms.

And Fleischer knew he had to finish him; finish
him, before it was too late . . . before the Rusky came
in again, and broke him into two pieces.

Fleischer dragged every ounce of strength and
concentration left in his wracked body into his
half-conscious brain. He linked the fingers of both
hands together to form a double-handed fist. He
stepped forward, paused, then brought his right
knee up into the Rusky's face and, at the same time,
smashed the double-handed fist down onto the nape
of the Rusky's neck.

And everybody in the room heard the crack;
knew that the neck had gone; knew that one more
good comrade would never see Red Square
again . . . and that the fight was over.

Fleischer backed off, away from the body. He
gulped breath and grabbed slipping consciousness
with every fiber of his mind. He felt behind him with

his hands and, when the fingers touched the wall, he leaned back, weak-legged, slump-bodied and with his arms hanging loose at his side...as near defeated as any victor can be.

He drew air past his throat in great, rasping lungsful and shook his head to clear the mist and, as he shook it, sweat and blood droplets cascaded out, like water from a wet dog's coat.

He began to think coherentiy, and he asked questions of himself. Where the hell was the goddam patrol? Why hadn't the goddam-blasted Military Police muscled in, long ago? Where were the sodding Snowdrops? Where were the rot-gutting Redcaps? Why the hell hadn't they arrived to break the thing up, before it went too far?

Then he looked up, from under his eyebrows, and he saw the reason.

The damn place had been taken over by the Ruskies. The barman, a couple of Limeys and a Free French pilot were being held; a thick-muscled Rusky stood on each side of these guys and held an arm each.

And all the other Ruskies—eight, maybe ten— were going to finish the job started by their buddy.

They were moving in on Fleischer, in a concave line of unrelieved hatred. Three of them had knives out; blades thrust forward and ready to bite into Fleischer's agonized body. One held a bottle, by its neck, and another held a stave...a broken piece of timber from the endless debris which was part of the building and part of Berlin.

They were going to kill him—as certain as sunrise and as sure as the tide—they were going to kill him...cut him up, and feed him to the rats which lived fat on the undiscovered dead of this foul city.

Fleischer spat and cleared his mouth of blood. He straightened, pushed himself from the wall, closed his fists and made ready for one last suicidal gesture.

He growled, "All right. You louse-bound commie bastards! Come on—all of you... and, by Christ, I'll mark some of you, before I go."

He tensed his aching muscles, raised his weary arms...

And the Sten blew the silence to hell and back in a short burst of chattering explosions!

He was a big man. Four inches over the six-foot mark, with about two-hundred-and-fifty pounds of correctly distributed muscle hanging from his broad frame. He wore the khaki battledress of the British Army, with the three pips of a captain at the shoulders. He handled the Sten like he'd nursed one in his cradle; easily, and without conscious effort; without looking at it and without even aiming.

He had a grin on his face... as if what he was doing amounted to a short spell of light relief.

The first burst from the Sten had gone over the heads of the Ruskies—no more than twelve inches over their heads—and had gouged plaster and chipped stonework from the wall opposite the door.

The man glanced at Fleischer, and said, "Trouble, sergeant?" and the voice went with the build; a voice which was unhurried, but very certain; a voice which carried authority over, and above, any insignia of rank which might be sewn to clothing.

Fleischer said, "Yeah—trouble... you could say that."

One of the line of Ruskies figured somebody was bluffing. He was one of the knife-carrying trio. He slipped a sneer of disbelief across his mouth and moved forward, at a crouch.

Fleischer tensed himself, ready to meet another threatened attack.

The big man tilted the snout and squeezed the trigger of the Sten in another short burst. The explosion once more smashed the silence of the room. Wood chippings flew as splintered holes suddenly appeared in the floorboards, ahead of the advancing Rusky.

The big man cocked an eye, and rumbled, "No more tonight, Boris. Not unless you want your balalaikas shot off."

The Rusky skipped back, away from the holes in the floor, tripped over the man Fleischer had killed, and sprawled.

"Clumsy!" murmured the big man. He eyed the corpse with amused interest, glanced at Fleischer, and said, "Is he the loser, sergeant?"

"Yeah." Fleischer nodded...and the movement of his head almost brought back the spinning blackness.

"Dead?"

"Yeah...dead."

"War," remarked the big man, mildly, "can be very indiscriminate. All sorts of people get killed...all the time." He looked across the room, at the two Limeys and the Frog. He said, "You three...out of it. And, don't forget, you've seen nothing. You haven't even been here."

One of the Limey's gasped, "Not likely. We 'aven't been near the bloody place."

"Good man." The big man chuckled.

The three eased themselves away from the Ruskies who had been holding them and, keeping to the wall, ducked out of the door and into the darkness.

"Behind the counter, Fritz." The big man spoke to the barman. "And keep your head down...unless, of course, you want to be a dead hero."

The barman declined the invitation. He scurried to the bar counter, and ducked behind its protection.

"And now..." The big man eyed the Ruskies with sardonic amusement. He spoke to Fleischer, and said, "These runts were getting quite nasty sergeant . . . right?"

"Check," grunted Fleischer.

He moved to a position alongside the big man; carefully keeping himself from getting between the Sten and the Ruskies. Despite all his will-power, he stumbled a little; his legs were rubbery and his head felt like it was filled with helium. The pain didn't help, either . . . and the pain was just about everywhere.

"Y'know," mused the big man, "I think the Red Army are getting a mite too cocky. Wouldn't you agree, sergeant?"

Fleischer gasped, "Yeah . . . I'd go along with that."

"You've killed one . . . right?"

"Yeah. But . . ."

"I don't think one is enough."

And the language was so quietly off-handed—so conversationally matter-of-fact that Fleischer had to force himself to realize that this big bastard was talking about murder. Nothing else, and nothing less . . . murder!

Before Fleischer could think of a reply, the big man said, "There's a jeep outside, sergeant. Tell the corporal at the wheel . . . I'll be out very shortly."

And Fleischer didn't give a damn. And why the hell should he? . . . minutes previously these bastards had had every intention of knifing him to death. So, why the hell should he?

In the Jeep, he heard the stutter of the Sten. Heard a man scream. Heard a second burst of shots from the Sten.

Then the big man closed the door of the bistro, hurried to the Jeep and vaulted aboard as the corporal gunned the engine before letting the clutch grab and spin the wheels into the road-adhesion.

They were less than fifty yards away when the bistro exploded outwards; when the windows and the door whoofed out in a billow of shattered glass, broken woodwork and smoke... the end-product of a carefully lobbed Mills hand-grenade.

The big man turned to Fleischer.

He said, "Introductions, sergeant. My name's Gawne... David Gawne."

I stretch out on the bed and stare at the ceiling of this motel room, and I figure that objectivity—like truth—has no absolute. That it is a quantitative thing. Some truths are more true than others. Some conclusions are more objective than others... and some situations, because of what they are, preclude any hope of objectivity.

It is dark, and I have not switched on the light, but the glow from the outside neons wash the room with multicolored reflections and, from outside, I can hear voices calling and laughing—cars starting up and arriving—and somewhere, beyond the walls of this room, people are too busy being happy to worry too much about abstract things like objectivity... which must be very nice for them!

The motel is not too far from Epping Forest—which means it is not too far from London—and is a combined motel-hotel which provides good service and excellent meals.

I know the place from a previous visit... which is why I chose it. The motel side of the set-up ensures as near complete privacy as it is possible to get in this crowd-oriented existence. You are given a key, and the key fits the door to your own quarters, and the door is an outside door which does not lead to a corridor... leading to stairs... leading to a hall... leading past a desk, with a nosey porter watching everything. Here, you have a place which is peculiarly *yours*. The door is a good door, and the lock is a good lock, and what is beyond that door is a little pricey . . . but well worth it. What is beyond the door is, first of all, a short passage and, on the left, a well-equipped bathroom, and the equipment includes as many good towels and as much hot water as any man could need. To the right of the passage is a built-in wardrobe and a shelf and, on that shelf, there is an electric kettle and crockery and all the things needed to make tea or coffee, supposing you do not wish to wander to the hotel in order to have such a drink served by a uniformed waiter.

At the end of this short passage is the main room. Strictly speaking it is a bedroom . . . but it is more than a bedroom. It is a large room, with a picture-window which is fitted with good drapes and, among other things, what you pay for includes thick-pile fitted carpet and a central heating system which really works. The furniture is good furniture; big, without being clumsy; polished, without being glossy. There is a bed, and it is a good bed; double and spring-interior comfortable. There are two arm-chairs; invitingly cushioned and deep enough to make relaxing a pleasure. There is a color T.V., a wall-plaque V.H.F. radio and a bedside telephone.

This place is not "home-from-home" . . . it is what a lot of people *wish* their homes were like.

The boy is impressed.

He looks around and says, "Nice place. *Ve-ery* nice indeed."

"Not what the movie-makers figure a hide-out should look like," I murmur.

"Is it a hide-out?" He asks the question with an impish grin on his face.

I pull the bathrobe sash tighter and towel my hair. I have just had a shower, and I am ready to look a new day in the eyes.

I say, "This is a very respectable dump, kid. And I am a

very respectable guy...name of Stanley Hemmingway, if anybody asks."

"If anybody asks."

"If they don't, don't offer."

He perches his rump on the unmade bed, and brings me up to date on what goes.

He says, "Darley says to tell you the money is being fixed. To give it three days...four, at the most."

"Uhu."

"He says I have to move in...if that's what you want."

"That is not what I want." I drape the towel around my neck. I go to the bedside table, pick up my pipe and start to charge it while I talk. I say, "You're in the city, Lewis. Stay there. Come up—say—this afternoon...maybe this evening. I need more clothes than we'd time to collect yesterday. Half a dozen shirts, three pairs of pants, a couple of jackets, underclothes, socks...the usual junk. Nothing flashy. Nothing too expensive. You know the sort of stuff...and a suitcase. Shop around the multiples. I need something the cops can't trace."

"The cops won't get within a million miles," he says. "With you...not within a million miles."

There is hero-worship—or something not too far off—in his voice, and I do not like it. He needs rocking back a little, therefore I rock him back.

Very pointedly, I say, "You should know, kid. If what Darley claims is true...you sure should know."

His face loses color and, in a low, harsh tone, he says, "You don't believe that...surely."

"What?"

"That I'm not safe."

"Your old man was a cop...okay?"

"Sure, but..."

"Okay. That means, without proof, you are not safe."

"He was a bastard," he rasps.

"Yeah—could be... but I am more interested in *his* bastard."

His face goes a whiter shade of white and, in what could be called a whisper, he says, "He's dead—long dead... if that satisfies you."

"Sure," I crack. "Which, at least, means *he* is safe." Before he bops me, I add, "Cool off, kid. Precautions... okay?"

"They're unnecessary."

"Oh, no."

"You have to trust somebody. You have to..."

"Nobody!" I drop into one of the armchairs, fire a match and stroke the tobacco in the bowl of my pipe with the flame. This kid has to learn. He has to be told... and no fairy-footing around. He is good—he has real potential—but he still has floss under his skull... floss which must be burned out if he is ever to be as good as he wants to be. I say, "Kid, there is not one sonuvabitch in this whole damn world that you can trust. Not *trust*. They have a price—okay, sometimes the price is high... but it is always there. And there is always somebody ready to meet that price. The coin is always there and, if it is offered... you are left with dynamite up your ass.

"You, kid—the name is Lewis... and that is the guy you trust. Nobody else. No other guy. No dame ...especially no dame. And, you know why you trust Lewis? You know why he is a one-off? I will tell you. Because he is the only guy alive you cannot turn your back to. The only guy who cannot slice you open, from behind... and, if he could do that, you would not even trust *him*."

He looks a little hurt, and says, "That's a hard philosophy."

"Yeah," I say, "but work at it... it will get easier."

The hurt look turns to one of sadness, and I let him live with his little piece of misery while I enjoy pipe smoke.

I say, "We need a car."

"Sure." The interest chases away his temporary blues.

"I ain't gonna buy one," I murmur.

"No . . . of course not."

"So? What sort of a stable does Darley own? Not counting that flash Merc he leaves alongside the hydrants."

The kid grins, and says, "He wouldn't let you borrow that."

"I would not *want* to borrow it. So, what else is there? Something fast, reliable . . . but not too eye-catching."

He ponders a moment, then says, "A Volvo?"

"Which?" I ask.

"A Volvo 164. Six-cylindered, around three-thousand c.c. She'll touch a ton—well past the ton mark—on the flat. Good acceleration . . . from a standing start to fifty, in eight seconds."

"You know cars?" I ask.

He nods.

"Not just behind the wheel?"

"I know cars," he says.

"What goes on under the bonnet? What makes them tick?"

He says, "Give the go-ahead for the Volvo, then leave it to me. I'll tune it—check it . . . I'll guarantee it."

"Okay. A full tank, tire pressures perfect—including the spare—new plugs, new battery, fresh oil, spare bulbs and a spare fan-belt. Do that . . . and have it ready."

"When?"

"I'll let you know." I stand up from the armchair, swing the towel from my neck and unsash the bathrobe. I walk to the bed—to the chair, alongside the bed, where I draped my clothes, last night—and I dress as I talk. I say, "The car. The gun. The gun I will tell you about, later . . . when I have given it some thought. Meanwhile, the car—the Volvo—get it, and get it ready—a minute's notice, if necessary. And the clothes . . . get them out here, for this evening. Then, sit tight until I contact. Leave a phone number. When I call, do not use names . . . yours, or mine. Do not give even a hint as to the location of this place . . . I shall not be calling from here, anyway. And watch Darley. Darley I do not trust . . . not even a little. You are his man—but you are also mine . . . and I am a little more dangerous than Darley. Never forget that, kid. I am here to do what Darley dare *not* do . . . so, if you must cross somebody, be sure it is the right guy."

We talk . . . about this, and that.

He is like a pupil, eager to learn. But I am not yet eager to teach. At this moment, why should I? What would I gain? Other, that is, than a rival?

Lewis (I have already said) is a smart boy. He would learn fast. He might learn a damn sight *too* fast; might figure that he could approach Darley and, with the know-how, offer a cut-price service. He might just do that . . . and Darley might just accept.

I have my future to think about. I learned the hard way . . . so why should not Lewis?

Which is why we talk—but only about this, and that . . . which adds up to just so much gum movement.

Then he blows, and I settle down to kill one more day.

It has been one of those days; a day as dull as a lead nickel. The snow stopped, sometime after I arrived at the motel, and rain and thaw took its place, and now the world looks about as pleasing as a wet cat.

But shiny . . . because, early this evening, I figured I rated better things, took a cab to Woodford and a tube into the city, and now I am walking along Victoria Embankment, past Waterloo Bridge and going towards The Temple and the Thames, on my right, does not look much damper than the tar-mac surface, on my left. They both reflect the lights—one the lights of the south bank, the other the lights of traffic zipping along between Blackfriars and Waterloo.

So, now—I am here... but *why* am I here?

I jerk up the collar of the mac Lewis has provided for me, stroll to the parapet, and try to work out some sort of an answer. Some sort of an answer that makes sense... sense to me, if to nobody else.

I do not need friends—I do not even need acquaintances... but, sure as hell, I need people. I need to know that the rest of mankind has not abandoned this planet; that, although I am a lone-wolf, the pack is still around.

That, I figure, is about the size of things. That my fellow-men give me a pain, but that their absence hurts even more. I do not want to know them. I do not want to talk with them. But I want to see them, and hear them... I want to watch them, and sneer at them, because my contempt for what they are is maybe a little less deep than the contempt I have for myself.

There is an old guy, on a form, behind me. I know he is there, without looking round and checking. I know he is there, because I passed him as I walked to the edge of the river, and I saw what he was and what he was doing.

He is old; maybe not as old as me, in years—maybe older—but he is a centurion as far as hardship and misery are concerned. He has damn-all. No home... or he would not be as dirty and as ragged as he is. No money... or he would not be getting the bench ready to sleep upon. No hope... or his actions would not be so utterly resigned. His clothes would shame a scarecrow. His bedclothes are a couple of newspapers. His body is so bone-wracked with poverty and disease, it should have been buried years ago.

He is a bum... and, goddam him, I both love him and hate him.

I love him because, somewhere inside him, there is the will to live. Somewhere, under those crappy rags, there is the seed of personal immortality; there is the refusal to go under; there is the guts to fart in the world's face and make the rest of humanity catch the stink. For these things, if for nothing else, I would embrace him and call him "brother."

I hate him because of his outward appearance. Because he shambles around, and allows himself to be used as an ultimate in failure. Because he has reduced the life his mother gave him to nothing; to shoving muck into the hole in his face, and expelling it through the hole in his ass; because he is so damn dumb that even charity has turned its back upon him. I hate him for his bottomless stupidity and, for this stupidity, I would spit upon him.

And why does this guy—this person—this animated thing—get under my skin? Why does he flip all my gears out of mesh, and make me wish I had never seen him?

Because he is mankind. Which means, he is *me* . . . what I might have been. What I still might be. What I maybe already am . . . but cleaned up a little.

Jesus!

I turn from the river. On an impulse, I walk up to this bum and hold out a fifty-pence piece. He takes it . . . without even moving his head in a nod of thanks. He takes it, as if it is his by right; as if he has earned it . . . and maybe he has, at that.

I catch a close-quarters smell of him. Meths and dirt—bodily filth and rotting teeth—lice-heavy clothes and unwashed skin . . . I get the full mixture, right up my nostrils. I want to puke in his face.

The poor bastard! He has to live with it . . . he has to sleep and wake at the very core of it.

I walk away from him, and along the embankment and towards Blackfriars. Across the road from me—on my left—I see the half circle sign of the underground. The Temple tube station. I cross the road and buy a ticket which will take me back to Epping.

And, when I am aboard, the damn train does not go fast enough for me.

It is a repeat performance of last night; a staring up at the ceiling of an unlit room, in the motel; a worrying—a haunting—a remembering.

And why?

What the hell is there so different about Gawne? What the hell is so special? Ask *him*—he would be the first to admit the truth...nothing!

Nothing is special. Nothing is different.

He is a guy called David Gawne...period.

MAGDEBURG.
NOVEMBER—1945

"The war," said Gawne, "is over. What is left is the pickings. The loot, if you like...the only things which makes any war worthwhile. The only justification for civilized slaughter." He tipped the can of beer to his mouth, lowered it, wiped his lips with the back of his hand and said, "You've done house-to-house fighting...right?"

"Yeah." Fleischer nodded.

"The truth, then. You risked being shot—you dashed across a street, knowing you might be a target for some rifleman—you broke into a house, knowing that you might be met with a burst of automatic fire...why? Not because some bloody fool with rank on his shoulder told you to. Not because some other bloody fool, miles away—and with even higher rank on his shoulder—signed an order...scrawled his name on a piece of paper. Not for these reasons, Fleischer. You rushed that house, for the same reasons that dogs fight. For food, or for a bitch. For loot, which might be in that house...or, if there isn't loot, for a woman who might be hiding there. Any other reason, and you're a fool."

Fleischer didn't argue. He'd already learned that, to argue with Gawne was so much ill-spent conversation.

He'd argued about going A.W.O.L. and the argument had been shot with genuine worry...he wouldn't be the first guy they'd shot for going over the wall.

Gawne had chuckled, and said, "You're not going over any wall, sergeant. You won't be A.W.O.L. ...except on the records. You're—er—'transfering units.' The Reds know we're around. So do the Yanks. And the British, and the French. They all know we're here...but they close their eyes.

"The killing has stopped. That's what they all say. 'Unconditional Surrender'...the end of the war. No more shooting. But there are still people who need taking out of circulation. And not just Germans. People here, in Europe—Europe's crawling with 'em—people who are in the way...people who should have been killed, but weren't.

"And that's where we come in, Fleischer. We provide something the official armies can't provide...daren't provide. An international execution squad. We're tolerated, because we're necessary. We're approached by all sides...and we provide a service. We're officially outlawed—again, by all sides—but nobody wants us caught because, if we didn't do it, they'd have to do it themselves, and then it would be 'semi-official'...and that would never do.

"God knows how long it'll last. A couple of years, perhaps—three—four, at the most...but that isn't important. The important thing is that we do a good job and charge a high price. We go home rich. We're the only people who've made this blasted war really pay."

And it was no less than the truth.

They were an "execution squad." Six of them. Gawne and a couple of Limeys. Another Yank and

himself. And Igor, the Rusky. They had uniforms
and they had equipment...they could each wear
whichever uniform and whatever rank a job
required. They had papers—the real thing—papers
to get them anywhere...anywhere!

And they killed, for money. Big money. Their
employers were not individuals...they were gov-
ernments, and a government's pocket was bottomless.

Their headquarters—if such a roaming group
could be said to have anywhere deserving of the title
"headquarters"—was the upper floor of this cafe in
Magdeburg, and here they enjoyed some of the best
food, best drink and finest bed-linen at that moment
available in the western world.

Gawne opened a fresh can of beer. He eyed
Fleischer quizzically, and asked, "Have you ever
killed a man, sergeant?"

"Sure. I've seen action in..."

"Not 'the enemy.'" Gawne waved a hand at a
carton, alongside his chair. "Have a beer," he
invited.

"Thanks...no."

"Not 'the enemy,'" repeated Gawne. "I mean a
man—an individual—somebody you can see—
somebody you can watch, as death hits him.
That...have you ever done that?"

Fleischer shook his head.

"It has," mused Gawne, "a certain macabre
attraction. The god-like feeling...if not the creator
of life, at least the creator of death."

"Yeah...I can imagine."

"You'll soon know." Gawne poured beer into his
mouth. "Ten days from now. Paris...just outside
Paris. There's a Canadian. A major. He's organized
a neat black market in antibiotics, but neither the
military nor the police can come up with enough
proof to nail him. He starts a leave—a furlough, as
your people put it—a week from today. He has this

female . . . this place, just outside Paris. The French authorities don't want him to report back to his unit."

It is odd. Self-delusion is a strange thing. It is crazy . . . it can make a liar of a saint.

That time—in the Magdeburg cafe—I'd told Gawne I'd never killed a man. And I'd meant it. I'd told what I thought was the truth—what Gawne had accepted as the truth . . . even though we both knew I was lying.

The Rusky, in the Berlin bistro . . . he didn't count. I'd killed him—I'd killed him, with my bare hands . . . but he was a zero. He did not count.

God, in His high heaven, knows the cockeyed working of any man's mind . . . but I *still* do not count that first Rusky.

Why?

Maybe because his killing was not a deliberate thing. It was not planned; it was what the lawyers might call "chance medley." It may be because this was the one killing I committed before turning pro; the one killing I have not been paid for, therefore, the one killing without cash incentive.

Count them . . . they add up to six. Six contracts. Six hits. Six times I have met a man, and left a corpse . . and, six times, I have been paid to do just that. No feeling. No regret. But, at the same time, no animosity—no hatred or anger . . . just a job at which I happen to be skilled.

A timber-man chops down a tree. Does he dislike that tree? Does he swing the axe with fury in his heart, rejoice when the blade bites into the trunk and exalt when the tree topples?

Nor do I.

He chops trees—I chop men . . . and, for my money, trees are often the more dignified of the two!

But that first killing—the one I never add, and the one

which makes the true total seven... of that one, I am ashamed.

It was done for all the wrong reasons, and for no reason at all. I could have walked away, and all it would have made me was a coward... and, even that, only in the eyes of a bunch of Red Army louts whose opinions I did not give a damn about. Instead, I killed, because those louts forced me to kill; maddened me, until I lost control... and killed in passion. A long, drawn-out killing—a messy killing—an unnecessary killing... therefore, one of which I am ashamed.

Which is, maybe, why I never include it in the total.

Or is it, perhaps, because *that* killing triggered off all the others?

I awaken to a new day, and today is the eighteenth of December. One week from today, it will be Christmas... one week after that, and another year is dumped into the ash-can of history.

I have not slept too good, despite the comfort of the bed and the coolness of the sheets. I have spent too much of the darkness tooling around in that hinterland of half-sleep and half-wakefulness; that condition which allows the mind to stroll, unhindered, across acres of memory... which is only pleasant if the memories are pleasant.

I shower, and decide I will enjoy a cooked breakfast, for a change; that, this morning, I will extend my first meal of the day to something a little more substantial than a couple of cups of tea and a pipe of smouldering tobacco.

I stroll across the paved surround, towards the hotel proper.

For the season, it is not too cold. The snow has gone, and so has the rain, and the lightweight suit which Lewis bought for me, from one of the chain-store outfitters, fits warm and fits well enough.

In the dining room I order tomato juice, followed by scrambled eggs and lightly cooked bacon, followed by toast and lemon marmalade. I ask that a pot of tea be provided, while I wait for my order.

The waiter is a young guy; a kid with a round face, a cheerful grin and an anxiety to please.

I look around me, as I wait for the tea. Bunting and balloons have been strung across the ceiling and up the walls. In one corner of the room, a Christmas tree holds a pyramid of baubles and tiny lights. There is an air—an atmosphere—of expectancy about the place; as if Saint Nick might arrive at any moment, even at this time of day; as if the mummers are already at the door, ready and eager to start their show. It is an atmosphere of smiles and nods and "Good-mornings," from stranger to stranger.

It is a little intoxicating . . . and I do not mind it too much.

The young waiter asks, "Will you be going, sir?"

"Eh?"

I move my eyes, look up at him, then realize that I have been gazing at a poster on the wall of the dining room; not consciously looking at it . . . but which I do, now.

It is a very merry-looking poster; it shows a cartoon fox, guyed up as Santa Claus, driving a sledge which is harnessed to cartoon hounds. There is a surround of holly and snowmen—bells, ribbons and robins—and, at each corner the head and neck of a comic horse grins out at whoever happens to be reading the poster. The wording tells about a Hunt Ball . . . scheduled for this evening, here at the hotel.

The waiter positions the pot of tea, pot of hot water, jug of milk and basin of sugar.

He says, "They hold it, about this time, every year . . . before the Christmas rush."

"It makes sense," I say.

"They let us have a few tickets—to distribute among

the guests . . . if any of them want to have a night out."

"Yeah?" I make-believe I'm interested.

He says, "I could get you a ticket, sir. If you'd like to go."

The word "No" is half way to my lips . . . it is the word I would say, nine-hundred-and-ninety-nine-times for every thousand.

This (and, goddam it, I do not know why!) is the thousandth time.

I say, "Yeah. That would be a good idea."

The waiter beams—I have allowed him to do his good deed for the day—and says, "I'll leave it at the desk, sir. Mr. Hemmingway, isn't it?"

I nod.

He says, "Collect it when you arrive, sir. I'll see it's waiting."

I mutter, "Thanks . . . I'll do that."

He blows, and hurries through the swing door leading to the kitchen.

The tea is brewed just right, the tomato juice is of good quality, the chef knows how to scramble eggs, the bacon is thin, streaky and fried to a T, the toast is just that—toast, and not burned bread—and the lemon marmalade has just the right tang.

It is a very nice breakfast.

Could be, it is going to be a very nice day . . . which would make a very nice change!

I spend most of the day regretting my impulse.

I have broken a basic rule . . . the rule of near-invisibility.

The object of the exercise—the object of every exercise of this nature—is not to be seen; not merely not to be known, but not to be noticed. Because the cops are not mugs; they have the talent of a crossword artist . . . they work backwards, from something which means nothing and, from what means nothing, they build a correct solution. They do not need names and addresses—they do not need talking pictures . . . all they need is a hint. Give them a shadow and, from it, they will create a substance. Give them an echo and, from it, they will resurrect a Wagnerian opera.

The guy with brains knows these things . . . and the guy without brains does not last long enough to pose any serious problems.

To pull a good hit, then, means that the person at the receiving end does not even know *when* he is hit; it has happened, and he is daisy fertilizer, before anything jells. The guy doing the hit is a nobody. As far as the victim is concerned, he does not exist—has never existed—therefore cannot be talked about or described. Nor (on a good job) is the hit man ever noticed by any other person; he is faceless—nameless—one of an unidentifiable crowd . . . seen and, a second later, forgotten.

You, who are reading this—if you are important enough, or if your enemies hate you enough—you, too, could already be the subject-matter of a contract. You, too, could already be lined up for a hit. But, if the man approached knows his job, you will never be sure—you will never know . . . because you will be stiffening before certainty has time to reach your brain. Nor will you know the man responsible—or speak to him, or even see him . . . because this cloak of absolute anonymity is his only warranty of freedom.

And I have blown at least a part of that anonymity. By breakfasting in the dining room . . . by not going out, and to a different cafe or restaurant, for every meal. By letting other guests see me . . . and, more than see me, make seasonal gestures of goodwill towards me. By allowing the waiter to ease me into conversation . . . by giving him some peg upon which he can hang a memory.

And the Hunt Ball boob is the biggest boob of all. Either way, I cannot win.

If I go, I screw the anonymity routine to hell and back. If I do not go, I attract attention... if only from the waiter, to whom I must make some sort of excuse for *not* going.

I must be nuts!

I spend the rest of the day, in my room, telling myself that I am just that... nuts. Trying to figure out some third, and less dangerous option, but there is no third, or less dangerous, option. I therefore decide to give it a quick whirl; to collect the ticket, wander into the ballroom, stay as short a time as possible... then beat it.

Like I say... I must be nuts!

It is climbing towards eleven o'clock, and I am still here, at the goddam Hunt Ball. I arrived all of ninety minutes back... and I am still around.

There are reasons; screwy reasons... but reasons, nevertheless.

Let me spell them out.

It was raining, when I arrived; not when I left my room but, within the time it took me to walk the fifty yards, or so, between my motel room and the hotel entrance, the heavens opened and David figured Mother Earth needed a quick hose-down. It was not cold, therefore I was not wearing a mac. I made the last few yards at a dash, and arrived with dollar-sized splashes across my shoulders.

I collected the ticket, walked to the ballroom... and saw the refreshment bar. I also realized that I had not eaten since breakfast, and that I was good and hungry.

I figured a quick, buffet snack would not do too much harm, and would not waste too much time... except that I did not count on two things. The contents of the buffet, and the band.

Open sandwiches of smoked salmon, goose-liver pâté, spiced asparagus... that brand of food is there, for the taking. The coffee is not of the "instant" breed, and there is genuine cream to go with it.

And, when I got around to listening to the music, I found it was as good as the food... and as rich.

It is a small outfit; trumpet, trombone, clarinet-doubling-tenor-sax, piano, guitar-doubling-banjo, string-bass, drums. A perfect three-and-three; three front men, three rhythm and a pianist who knows how to bridge the two sections; a seven-piecer, and they play New Orleans music in a way which would not shame New Orleans itself.

Which is why I am still around; standing at the bar-alcove, off the dance floor, sipping bitter lemon and listening to the jazz... which is also why I must be nuts.

They are playing *Alligator Crawl*, and the man at the keyboard is doing a fair imitation of Fats Waller. The gobstick boy is following the melody line, with the two horns playing soft counterpoint and the slide man doing some neat gliss work. The string-pluckers are keeping the chords and the bass progression in line with the melody, and the percussion boy is sending out a skinbeat as steady as a heart-throb.

I am half-leaning against an upright of the alcove, and the fingers of my right hand pass the beat onto the surface of the plasterwork.

The dancers are shuffling around a little. They would maybe prefer Victor Silvester, and a more orthodox slow-slow-quick-quick-slow jig. This number has them worried; it is not quickstep—it is not slow foxtrot... it is maybe foxtrot, but not even really that. It is jazz... meant to be listened to, until the feet cannot stay dumb any more and, at which time, the dance fits the music instead of the music fitting the dance.

I like it... and the hell with the dancers!

They are goons. Never having been to a Hunt Ball before, I do not have experience along these lines, but I figure that they are the normal "Hunt Ball" type ... goons. Some are in hunting pink, some are in evening dress, some are in dinner jackets, but most of them are like me ... in pretty somber suits over which, it necessary, it is possible to spill booze without provoking an international incident. Most of the dames have ankle-length dresses; some are backless—some are damn-near frontless ... and, so far, I have not seen a back, or a front, which merits public exposure.

What they lack in beauty they more than make up for in noise.

Okay—they are enjoying themselves. This is a matter of opinion. Ask them, and they would tell you ... that they are "enjoying themselves." Ask *me*, and *I* will tell you ... they are a crowd of high-class oafs who would not know a good musician if he rammed his instrument up their collective ass. They should be listening, and they are kicking up hell's own din. They are yelling and screaming, and making like this is a communal rape session. One fink has a hunting horn, and he keeps blowing it ... and I wish he would swallow the damn thing, choke to death, and make everybody happy.

I try to tune out the racket and concentrate on the stuff coming from the rostrum.

A voice says, "Aren't they a shower of absolute shits."

The voice gets me; it, and what it says, flicks my concentration away from the music. It is a woman's voice—a very peignoir-and-hockey-stick voice—and the drawling pronunciation of every word has "public school education" signs attached.

I turn towards the voice.

She is a little drunk ... and more than a little sad.

I look at her, and she looks back.

She raises her glass, and says, "Let's drink to them.

Let's drink a toast to all the monumentally boring bastards who think a horse between the legs is the ultimate in virility."

I grin, and sip my bitter lemon.

She takes something which is more than a sip.

She is no chick. She is, perhaps, a few years younger than me—but no more than a few—past the half-century mark—but only just.

Which does not mean she is either a hag or ugly.

Her hair is the color of mid-oak and, in the grain, there are fault-streaks of silver, and the streaks add to its attraction. It is cut fairly short, and without frills, and its top reaches to a height a couple of inches above my shoulder.

She has a figure which is compact, but complete. It is the body of an athlete, which has not been allowed to go to seed; there is a smooth grace there, which is both powerful and supple.

The face is round and full. The mouth is half a size too large; the shape of mouth which should have upturned corners but which, instead, has level corners which give the expression a grim, sardonic expression. The expression is carried to the eyes; gray-green eyes whose shine owes as much to cynicism as they do to booze. And, between the eyes, there is a pert little nose, with slightly flared nostrils; nostrils which look as if they might quiver very easily.

It is a nice face. Not beautiful, but with character... and nice.

She is wearing a full-length dress; royal blue, with a flared skirt and baggy sleeves which are cuffed tight at the wrists. The dress is high-necked and, around the neck a single string of pearls vie with the blue of the dress to catch the fancy lighting of the dance floor and the bar-alcove. Her only other jewelry is earrings, which match the pearls at her neck.

Like I say—no chick... but I have known chicks who

would give ten years to be as attractive.

She says, "You obviously like the orchestra."

I make an affirmative grunt... and wonder what sort of kook calls a seven-piece jazz outfit an "orchestra.'"

"Not quite the L.S.O.," she remarks, and there is mild contempt in the observation.

I let it pass.

"The London Symphony Orchestra." She makes the explanation as if I am as dumb as the goons gallivanting around the dance floor.

"Yeah?" I make with the mock-surprise. "I figured you might mean the Lichtenstein Sewage Organ."

The crack amuses her. She giggles.

Then she says, "Yank?... right?"

"Uhu."

I turn my head, and focus on the rostrum once more. What I do not want, at this particular moment of my life, is a pick-up.

She says, "Are you with somebody, Yank?"

I keep watching the rostrum, and say, "Yeah ... myself."

"That's not very exciting company... surely?"

I say, "Speak for yourself, lady. I find me pretty fascinating."

"You're lucky."

It is the way she says it. Soft and whimsically sad; like a broken figurine boxed carefully away in wool padding... that is what it reminds me of. Could be, I heard all that in those two words; something broken—something which has been hidden away, someplace, to prevent it from being completely smashed.

The seven-piece change tempo. They do not wait for applause—I know the type... they play for themselves more than they play for the morons who hire them. They move into a smooth and smoochy arrangement of *Beale Street Blues*.

I turn to the dame. Two tears are building up, one at

each eye corner. She grins, blinks the tears out of existence and tosses what remains of her drink down her throat.

She holds the empty glass at waist-height.

"What?" I ask, and ease the glass from her fingers.

"Gin and orange. But I'm not..."

"Don't go far," I say.

When I get back from the counter, she is smoking. Fancy cigarettes; black ones, with gold tips. They smell like something from under a ferret's tail.

She takes the drink, says, "Thanks," and opens a miniature handbag. She takes out a fancy case, springs it open and offers me one of the black cigarettes.

I say, "I go for pipe tobacco...but not here."

She returns the case, closes the handbag, sips at the drink and eyes me with her head tilted a little.

She says, "Joe."

"Eh?"

"That's what I'll call you...never mind what anybody else calls you. I'll call you 'Joe.' It's a nice, Yankee name. During the war, we called all the G.I. boys 'Joe.' They didn't mind."

I try to be gallant, and say, "What the hell can *you* remember about the war?"

"Everything." Her voice is wistful. It saddens a little more, and her eyes go dreamy, as she adds, "I can remember every minute of it...and parts of it were wonderful."

I should see a nut doctor. I swear...I should be certified and locked out of harm's way.

At a time like this, I am sitting here, within feet of the band, surrounded by howling, tanked-up finks of both sexes, trying to draw jazz diagrams for the benefit of some dame who has memories of G.I. Joes.

Some of it she is understanding.

That the two horns—the trumpet and the trombone—must do the slow standards in unison; that thirds are a nice close-up distance, when two horns are moaning a blues number and that, if they share both melody and volume equally—and if their tones work well together—the result is good music.

That, on the bouncy numbers, the clarinet can hit the high register and spin around up there as fast as its player can finger the keys and that, while this is happening, the trombone can do slide licks down in the basement; that, while these things make for the fireworks, the trumpet man should not stray too far from the melody line, and the rhythm boys should hammer out a steady beat.

That the percussion man is the heart of an outfit such as this. That, like a sportsman can do wonderful things with his limbs, but only if his pump is working okay, so a jazz combo can only hit the peaks if the skins keep up a regular four-time... that the front men would go haywire, if the drums began to trick around, as the sportsman would also go haywire if his ticker skipped a few knocks.

That the bull-fiddle is an extension of the pianist's left hand, and the guitar is an extension of his right; that chords and base progression are what all and any number is built upon, and that the piano provides the cement which holds that foundation together.

All of this she listens to, and some of it she understands... I hope.

But that does not alter the argument that I am a nut case; that I should be strapped in a straitjacket, for my own good... that I have screwed the anonymity thing to all hell and a cactus bush.

She says, "You like this sort of music, don't you?"

"It is a nice sound," I admit.

"No." She shakes her head, and tries to get through to

me. "I don't mean just that. I mean you like it—really *like* it... enough for it to be important."

"I like good jazz," I say.

She swirls the booze in her glass; a gentle, circulatory movement which has a musing, thoughtful quality. Strange, but she is not as stoned as she was when she first spoke to me—not as stoned as she was, or not as stoned as she pretended to be... maybe it was an act, or maybe she just wanted to get drunk, as quickly as possible, and was meeting the gas-out half way. She is not stone-cold, you understand. She is happy-boozed, but with her wits about her. I figure she is relaxed and enjoying herself... maybe for the first time in years.

She watches the liquor in the glass, and murmurs, "It's very basic—very primitive... I think that's why you like it."

"Jazz?" I cock a cynical eyebrow.

"It *is* basic," she insists.

"It is simple," I say. "It is uncomplicated. It does not take too much thought... therefore, it is my sort of music."

"You're a very uncomplicated man." She looks up from the glass, and meets my eyes, head-on. She says, "You're a very nice man, Joe. You're basic—honest... it makes a change."

"I'm a nice guy," I crack. "Ask anybody. Give me a good-looking woman, and I'm a nice guy."

"Don't sell yourself short, Joe. She is deadly serious.

I say, "Skip it... eh?" I taste the bitter lemon. It is my fourth... and the taste is getting a little monotonous. "We have had a couple of hours. Okay—now run home to hubby... explain that now you know a lot more than you did, about jazz."

The seven-piece is playing another standard. *Lullaby of Birdland.* They are moving it along at a slow-bounce tempo, with the drummer doing wire-brush work on a sizzle-cymbal and the piano-player fingering out a soft, barrelhouse background. The front men are easing it along, as if they have forever and, if forever is not long enough, a day extra. There is no hurry—no rush...just quiet soothing, soft-shoe jazz.

She says, "Do I look it?"

"That you know something about jazz?"

"Married? Is it so damned obvious?"

"You are married, honey," I say, gently. "You are...or you have been."

"That's not quite what I asked."

The waters are getting deep. I am no longer dipping a toe into the shallow end; I am no longer paddling around, at a depth where I can scoot if the waves look like they might dampen my pant cuffs. Any minute now, they will surge up, above my head. Any minute now, I will have to swim for it—and swim fast and hard...because there is a very mean current!

I pick my way through the words slowly, and carefully.

I say, "Honey, with a dame like you—with a dame with your looks, and your personality—it has to be. Figure it out. When she reaches your age, she is married...or has been married."

"And *looks* married?" The question is not a true question; it is a comment—bitter...directed against herself, and away from her own sex.

I say, "Anything else, does not make too much sense. Anything else means that all the guys you have met are deaf, dumb, blind or stupid...and that I will not buy."

The trumpet-player is making the second chorus a vocal. It is one way of giving his lip muscles a quick rest. He has a bullfrog voice, and it does not have much reach, therefore he sings with the mike within an inch or so from his mouth. Nevertheless, he can sing jazz...and he knows the words.

She is talking.

She is (and I know this) talking to herself, but hoping that I am listening; some of it is booze, but a lot of it is bitterness—and I listen, because I know she wants me to listen...and (goddam it!) that is a better reason than any reason I can think up for not listening.

"James," she says, softly. "That's his name...James. Not Jim. Certainly not Jimmy. He's the last person on God's earth anybody would dream of calling Jimmy. James—always James...even from me. He imports things. Fruit. Citrus fruits, mainly. Lemons, limes, oranges and grapefruit...that's what he does for a living. Imports lemons and limes—grapefruit and oranges...and you've no idea how bloody *boring* lemons and limes and grapefruit and oranges can be! You've no idea how bloody *devoted* a man can get to them. How much of his *life* they can claim."

She takes a mouthful of booze, then continues, "That's where he is now. In Italy, somewhere. Arranging shipments. It's Christmas—a time for parties—a time when normal people enjoy themselves...but not James! Not good old, fruity James. He's rushing around Italy buying lemons...or something. Business before pleasure—that's what they say...that's what James *always* says."

"He will maybe be home for Christmas," I murmur.

"Mid-January—that's when he'll be back...that's what he says. Sometime in mid-January. When he's organized all the grapefruit."

I move my shoulders. What the hell is there to say when you are at the receiving end of this type of talk.

"I wouldn't mind," she muses, "if he had some little Italian dish hidden away somewhere...if he was human enough for *that*. I really wouldn't mind at all. I think I'd admire him a little...if he was man enough to have even *that* sort of a weakness."

"That," I growl, "is crap...and you know it."

She smiles, and the smile calls me a liar, and tells me I do not know what the hell I am talking about.

She takes time off to light one of her snazzy cigarettes, then she blows smoke, and asks, "Do you have memories, Joe?"

"Eh?"

"Memories? Things that happen, that you remember? Happy times?—even sad times? . . . times that you remember?"

"Sure. Everybody . . ."

"Not everybody," she says, sadly.

"That," I say, "is crazy talk. Things happen . . . you remember them. A laugh here—a little pain there . . . sure, you remember them."

"And what if there's no laughs, and no pain? What if it's all one flat, gray wall? Nothing! What then?"

"Nobody's life is that dull," I insist.

She draws on the cigarette, and her words come out smoke-wrapped.

She says, "My memories ended with the war. Good memories, too. I enjoyed the war. I was sorry when it ended. I mean that . . . I was truly sorry. Then—less than a week after V.J.—I married James . . . and I can't even remember the damned honeymoon! The hotel—the date—the weather . . . I can remember those, if you want to count *them* as memories. But, if my life depended on it, I couldn't remember one thing that should matter. Not one thing I *should* remember. James—the man I slept with—the man who changed me from a virgin . . . and, I was that. And I'm damned if I can remember how, or exactly when, or exactly where . . . or exactly *anything*! And—damn him to hell!—it's what he was, and what he still is. And—and . . ."

She stops. The tears are not too far beneath the surface. Nor are they drunken tears, because she is not asking for sympathy; she is not putting on an act for the sake of schmaltz. What she is is a very lonely dame—a good-looking dame, and a dame with feelings, like every other dame...a dame with a dumb monkey for a husband.

The goons who are making all the noise are raising the decibel-rate around us. The fink with the hunting horn is pratting around like a runaway elephant. Every other dame in the room seems to be shrieking like somebody has just dropped an eel in her bath-water. All the guys are hooting and yelling like it is a football game.

The band hits the first note of something they all know—*When the Saints Go Marching In*—and the noise becomes part-organized into an off-key sing-song.

I watch her grab herself, and push her grief out of sight.

Then, when she talks again, her voice is a little stumbling...like it has not journeyed along this path before.

She says, "I'm—I'm not cheap, Joe."

"No. Nobody figured you as a..."

"Not like some of these." She moves her head, and takes in all the howling, screaming females. "Some of these would sleep with almost anybody...almost anybody."

"Yeah. I know."

"I'm—I'm not like that."

"Sure you're not. You're..."

"I'm not a tart."

"For Christ's sake, honey..."

"That's what you thought I was, at first...isn't it?"

"No," I lie. "Of course I didn't..."

"A pick-up."

"Look..."

"At first you thought I was a pick-up. Didn't you?"

"Yeah...maybe," I admit reluctantly. "But..."

"I'm not."

"Okay. But..."

"I'm a respectable married woman."

"Sure you are. And..."

"I've—I've never done this before... never anything like this before."

"Okay. I believe you, but..."

"Even during the war. I didn't throw myself at men. I—I enjoyed life. Y'know... enjoyed dancing, and having a good time. But I was never a prozzy. I wasn't a camp-follower. I was never anything like that."

I say, "Listen, honey. It is Christmas. People let their hair down a little... okay. This is a party... maybe a little wild, but that is what it is. So, sit back, listen to the band..."

"Sleep with me, Joe."

"...and relax, eh?" What she has just said, in a soft, pleading voice, registers. I blink, stare, and say, *"Eh?"*

The look is one of confused defeat. It is the look kids put on when they have just taken a beating for something they did not do; when they are helpless against what they know is a gross injustice.

She whispers, "Give me one wonderful memory, Joe. No questions. No strings. Just something I can really remember... something to make this a special Christmas. Sleep with me... *please!*"

And, out there—a million miles from where we are sitting—the fink with the hunting horn goes marching in with all the other crappy saints.

The train is making good time through the evening darkness and, about thirty miles ahead, the Big City is waiting for me to pick up the pieces and, beyond the Big City—at the end of another train journey, which will dump me not too far from Epping Forest, and a motel where I have left vacant a room I should have occupied for the last three days—there is a telephone. And I must use that telephone and, having used it, I must then kill all recollection of what I have just left. I must kill the immediate past. I must kill it as surely, and as completely, as I kill the conversation when I return the receiver of that telephone to its prongs.

I must never remember.

I must never *ever* remember...

That first night, when she gave to me everything her damn fool husband should have been glad to take; when she opened herself and offered what had been rejected for years... offered it all, as if one man could take, in a single moment, all those years of pent-up passion.

The madness that kids do not understand; the madness of the middle years, when glorious heights can still be scaled... but are savored the more, because experience and age also brings true appreciation. When the coupling of a man with a woman is less a thing of lust, and less a thing of appetite, and more the sharing of a journey—a journey of exploration, to be taken slowly and tenderly, with pauses for ecstasy *en route*.

I must never *ever* remember...

The unspoken agreement that this thing could not be worked out in a single night. Not even a night like that first night... when she'd smiled at me, across the pillows, and said, "Joe—darling Joe—there must be a law against what we've just done... don't you think?" and I'd said, "Sure. There'll be a law against it, someplace."... and she'd laughed happy laughter, rolled until her mouth was touching my ear, and whispered, "You're positively obscene. Positively *obscene*. And I should be out-raged... but I'm not."... and I'd grinned, and she'd grinned back. And the unspoken agreement had been there; that this thing could not be worked out in a single night.

Then, Bristol.

Hell knows why Bristol... except she said she'd once

visited Bristol, and had liked the place. Which was a good enough reason. A damn good reason, as far as I was concerned.

We'd taken her car—a Triumph Vitesse—and she'd handled the wheel, and she'd said, "Bristol? I stayed there, once—a weekend, years ago... it's a delightful place," and I'd said, "Sure. Why not?"

Then, three days...

None of which I must remember.

None of which I must *ever* remember...

That, as a return gift for jazz, she had introduced me to another kind of music. Music, with a beat as eager and regular as jazz, but not as raucous as jazz. Music by Mozart (of whom I'd heard, and whose music I'd listened to but, until now, had never understood) and music by Bach (a guy with a heart bursting with melodies, and a mathematician's mind, who had also the genius to combine the two to make fantastic sound) and—last night—Handel... Handel's *Messiah*.

Okay—I hadn't wanted to go... the word "oratorio" scared the hell out of me. Like the word "opera" and the word "ballet." They were all labels given to music which wasn't my style; music with a big noise and a lot of unnecessary puff. Music hard to understand. Music hard to listen to. Music for the intelligentsia... not for slobs like me.

And—okay—how wrong can you get!

Those choruses were something out of this world. They did things to the muscles at the nape of your neck. They played upon tiny nerves behind your eyes, and damn near brought the tears. They cleansed... I swear, you felt *cleaner* because you'd just heard them. Those damn choruses! And, especially that last chorus—what's its name?... *Worthy Is The Lamb*.

Let me tell you, friend. If Handel hadn't written

another note of music—just that one chorus, and not one more note—it would have been enough...he'd still be immortal.

We'd walked from the hall and into the night air. Clear, again—crisp, again—with a hint of frost and a promise of snow. And it was closing up to Christmas, and a Christmas the like of which I'd never known before; a Christmas Handel must have known and understood, else he'd never have been able to pen that oratorio. And we've walked—in silence, except for the echoes of those choruses inside our skulls—and we'd held hands, like a couple of teenage kids out on a first date. Walking slowly, out across the Avon on Brunel's bridge, under the swing of fairy lights fixed to the suspension cables, then back and through the streets to the hotel.

We'd stopped a couple, or three times...and I'd held her...and I'd said things to her...and she'd answered...and we'd both meant every word we'd said...every damn word!...and every word had been like a knife in the other's ribs...

And (goddam it!) none of these things must I ever remember.

Not the music—not the words—not the love-making...*nothing*.

None of them must I *ever* remember.

I have checked with Amsterdam, and they have had word from the Swiss bank...the money is already lodged. Darley can work fast, when he is nudged a little.

I have talked and, just supposing we have been listened to (just supposing somebody has fixed a tap to this wire), that does not mean a thing. We have talked ordinary talk, but our words do not have dictionary meanings. And, as from now, I have an alibi. Cast-iron and unbreakable. As of now, I am in Amsterdam...and can prove it in any court in the whole damn world.

And now I am talking, over the wire, to this kid Lewis, and he is making noises like he is some breed of hotshot... which is all I need to finish off the pie!

"Where the hell have you been?" he asks.

"Come again?" I say, gently.

"I've been trying to get in touch."

"Is that a fact?"

"I've been..."

"Why?"

"Darley told me to ring you, and..."

"As I recall, I told you *not* to ring me."

"I know. But Darley..."

I say, "Lewis, do me a great big favor. Okay?"

"What's that?"

"Blow." I slip teeth into my end of the talk. "Make for the hills, junior. Lose yourself, in the canyons, with all the other trash."

"What the hell is that..."

"And, on the way, make smoke signals to Darley. The deal is off."

There is a pause then, in a quieter voice, he says, "You can't do that, Fletcher."

"You have led a very sheltered life, kid... as this guy 'Fletcher' would have told you, had he been holding this receiver."

"Darley's paying good money for..."

"Wrong tense," I snap. "Late... as always. He has already paid."

"Yeah—I know. That's why..."

"Experience does not come cheap. He has bought some. Tell him—next time, he says 'what'... but he does not say 'when' or 'how.' He is not hiring a performing seal. Tell him that. It is information he has just bought. And you too, kid... help yourself to a slice, on the way."

I slam the receiver onto its rest.

I undress, take a shower and crawl between the sheets.

I try to relax—try to blast the last three days from the calendar . . . and the only way is to remember other things.

The flat was within a kilometer of Route Nationale Number Two; on the south of the Avenue Jean Jaures, and just about midway between the city limits and Le Bourget. It was one of those nice, typically continental flats. It was part of a tree-ornamented cul-de-sac; a first-floor flat, with a neat "Romeo-wherefore-art-thou" balcony leading from the french windows.

Fleischer figured that this flat was one of the stinking aspects which are part of every war; he figured that maybe German brass had also used this flat as a love-nest . . . and maybe (who knew?) with the same sparrow sitting on the same eggs. It was possible—and a damn sight more than possible . . . because the whole district was unsullied by war, thanks to some Frog fink declaring Paris an open city.

And now some maple-leaf bastard was also using it as a private tailing alley. And the maple-leaf bastard was paying for the upkeep of this zingy flat, and all its zingy contents, by letting decent guys rot to death for want of antibiotics.

But not for much longer, buster!

Fleischer fingered the bell-push and, when the Canadian jerk answered the ring, Fleischer went into the spiel.

It was like taking candy from a sleeping child. Fleischer ("Colonel Fletcher" of the Canadian Military Police) was accompanied by a sergeant and a corporal (Gawne and the other Yank from the outfit). They all wore correct uniforms and correct rank-badges. Everybody had documentary "proof" of identity. And the hard-spoken line of patter washed the Canadian major's face clean of all color.

There was a certain amount of cross-talk. The

French dame did a short, but pithy, oo-la-la routine. Then the Canadian jerk capitulated, struggled out of his pajamas and into his uniform, the dame dumped herself on her fanny and looked sulky, and the four men marched out to the waiting Citroën.

The "corporal" drove. The "sergeant" sat in the front passenger seat. Fleischer shared the rear with the Canadian jerk.

...She'd said, "Mozart always reminds me of a stream. Clear. Bubbling. Happy and always in a hurry. Some of the others—Beethoven, Brahms, Tchaikovsky—they're more like a rip-tide...they're more destructive. They tear you to shreds, emotionally. Every time I hear Tchaikovsky's Fifth, I die a little. Does that sound silly? I hope not...because it's true. But Mozart—dear old Wolfgang—he's like a happy uncle. He pats your head, chuckles, does a little jig and makes you well again. I like Mozart. I think he's..."

They stayed clear of the Route Nationale.

Ten kilometers out, where the road ran between deserted fields, the engine of the Citroën died. Fleischer delivered his lines to the "corporal" and the "corporal" returned the agreed come-back talk. Then the "corporal" climbed out of the car, in order to shove his nose into the engine.

Fleischer suggested that they might stretch their legs; that they might enjoy some of the dawn-fresh air.

The Canadian jerk agreed.

"Sergeant" Gawne held the door open for the Canadian, and the Canadian turned his back on Fleischer.

Fleischer bent and scooped the Colt automatic from under the seat. The Canadian stooped to duck out of the door. Fleischer leaned forward, touched the cloth of the tunic, between the shoulder-blades, with the snout of the automatic, swallowed and squeezed the trigger.

Gawne jerked the door wide, to allow passage for the body to pitch from the car and land, face downwards, on the verge.

There was no need to check ... the Canadian was way beyond any magic his antibiotics might perform.

The "corporal" closed up, returned to the wheel, worked the ignition and started the engine. Gawne climbed in, beside Fleischer.

The Citroën moved off, and headed back, towards Magdeburg.

... "An oratorio," she'd said. "For God's sake ... it's only a *word*. It has to be called something. Why not 'oratorio.' You like Glenn Miller—Tommy Dorsey—you like the big bands ... what you call 'section work.' That's all this is. 'Section work' ... but with voices, instead of instruments. You don't have to believe the words—you don't even have to *listen* to the words ... just the music. Joe, darling, believe me. The choir is the orchestra. A perfect— beautifully balanced—orchestra. The principals ... they're the soloists. And that's all it is. A great orchestra, with wonderful soloists and superb 'section work.' And the result—like your Glenn Miller, like your Tommy Dorsey—is magnificent music. Just give it a try. Just ..."

Gawne passed the hip flask to Fleischer.

Fleischer took the flask, without a word, unscrewed the top and poured a double measure of Cognac down his throat. The brandy hit his guts, rebounded to his brain and chased the oncoming heebie-jeebies to hell and gone. He wiped the mouth of the flask with the heel of his hand, replaced the top and handed the flask back to Gawne.

"Better?" growled Gawne.

"Yeah...thanks."

"You almost muffed it."

"Was it so goddam obvious?" Fleischer's question was shot with self-disgust.

"Everybody." Gawne grinned, and returned the flask to his pocket. "The first one gets everybody...or, if it doesn't, he isn't part of this outfit. We're executioners. We're not psychopaths."

"That," said Fleischer, "is nice to know."

"After this," Gawne assured him, "it's easy. I know what I'm talking about. After the first, it's easy. Like riding a bike. Like swimming. At first, you think it's impossible. It's difficult...but it gets progressively easier. In time, it's a job. Just that...a job. Like any other job."

Fleischer blew a valve.

He snarled, "Knock it off, Gawne! I have just killed a man. That, and nothing else. Nothing less. I have just ended a man's life. So, let us not make noises like I have just swallowed my first oyster. Let us not pat me on the back like I have just screwed my first broad. What I have just done is one hell of a lot more serious than that. I have just committed my first murder...and, if I am honest with myself, for no damn-good reason."

"Five hundred reasons," said Gawne, calmly. "Five hundred very good reasons...and in pounds, not dollars."

"I would like to tell you where to stuff those five hundred 'reasons,' but..."

"But you won't," Gawne chuckled. "You've more sense. You know you've earned it. In this outfit, the man who pulls the trigger always gets the biggest cut. In your case—this time—five hundred. Tax-free pocket money."

"At least I come a little more expensive than Judas."

Gawne said, "Sweat it out, Yank. It'll wear off. It always does. And, for the best reason in the world ... because however you approach it, the bastards we handle could never do stand-in duty for Jesus Christ. None of 'em!"

We'd stood on the bridge. We'd gazed down, into the gorge, and watched the lights reflected upon the surface of the Avon. We'd stood there, in silence, for a few minutes.

Then, she'd said, "Well?"

I'd nodded my head a couple of times. Slowly, and without turning to look at her.

After a silence, I'd said, "Tomorrow," and she'd known what I'd meant.

She hadn't answered. There'd been no need for her to answer ... we'd been close enough to communicate, without the hindrance of words.

And we'd stood there, on the bridge, gazing down into the gorge, watching the lights reflected upon the surface of the Avon, and we'd touched fingers, and the fingers had clasped and, for a moment, that moment had been the reason, and a good enough reason, for all eternity ...

On the way back to Magdeburg, Gawne explained the finer points of professional slaughter to Fleischer.

Fleischer listened, but only for one reason ... because he couldn't not listen. He couldn't stop his ears to what Gawne was saying. He couldn't escape the words ... and the truth was that, at one and the same time, the words disgusted and fascinated him.

Gawne said, "One thing, Yank. Never let the victim take over. Out-rank him, like we did this morning. Or, if you can't out-rank him, dominate him. Make him feel inferior. More than that, make him show his feeling of inferiority. Think about it. If you don't make him feel inferior, it can play hell with your ego ... make the job that more difficult." Gawne chuckled quietly, then added, "Logically, it must play hell with his ego, too . . . to be chopped by somebody you despise."

. . . That last night, she'd asked. The question guaranteed to throw me. The question I'd dreaded. The question I'd almost prayed she wouldn't touch.

In the darkness of the bedroom, she'd said, "Tell me, Joe. What do you do?"

"Uh?" I'd made-believe not to catch on.

"For a living? What's your job?"

"No questions," I'd murmured. "Remember?"

"Sorry."

"Okay . . . no questions."

She'd touched my arm with the tips of her fingers, and whispered, "Is it something outrageous? Something shocking?"

I'd said, "Yeah," and she'd thought I was joking.

"Something really and truly disgusting?"

"Yeah. I make love to lonely dames . . . specifically lonely, middle-aged dames."

And she'd laughed, quietly, and said, "And you do it wonderfully, darling. Believe me, you're an expert."

And (goddam it!) I'd nipped my lip between my teeth to stop myself from telling her the truth . . .

Gawne said, "The trick is to do it when it's least expected . . . like this morning, when he was getting out of the car. He wasn't ready for it. He wasn't ready for anything. It came from an unexpected direction. It also saved us the trouble of dragging him from the car . . . and didn't plaster everything with gore.

"Little things, Yank. But they're important. They're the difference between art, and a botched-up mess. Without them, he'd be no less dead . . . but it might have taken longer, and been more messy."

...This morning we'd left the hotel, and walked. Where the hell we'd walked I couldn't say...nor, I think, could she. We'd just walked. Happy to be together. Miserable in the knowledge that it was ending.

We'd finished up in the market—in All Saint's Lane—and mooched into the *Rummer Inn* for lunch.

Ten bars...but we hadn't the interest to count them. The oldest hostelry in the West Country...but we hadn't the time to admire the atmosphere. We hadn't the time for anything. We hadn't much time...period.

And then the time had run out.

I'd left her sitting at the table. Sitting there, smoking one of her crazy black cigarettes. Touching the coffee cup with the tip of one finger. Silent—pensive—staring through the window...at a guess, watching the events of the last three days.

I'd left her, like I was going to the john, but we'd both known. We'd both known...because that's how near we'd become.

I'd settled the bill, walked out into All Saint's Lane, then headed for the hotel to collect my suitcase.

Finished!

Smashed!

Curtain!

No last good-byes, because that is not how it should be done. No big talk. No soul-searching. No explanations, no excuses, no lies.

Nothing...

"The one thing you mustn't do," said Gawne, "is prolong the agony. Apart from showing a sadistic streak, it makes you vulnerable. He isn't interested in reasons...would you be? A man shoves a gun in your navel. Can you think of any reason which might justify him squeezing the trigger? We-ell ...nor can he. You're paid to do a job, Yank. You do it. As quickly as possible. As neatly as possible. Because, the longer he stays alive, the better chance he has of ducking."

I am jerked out of some sort of sleep by the sound of hammering on the door. I climb out of bed, slip into my robe and paddle along to investigate.

Darley and Lewis are standing there.

Darley is annoyed. Part of it may be booze—I get a whiff of his breath, as he steps close when I open the door—but much of it is genuine heat. His saffron-tinted skin is flushed, his slanted eyes are slit and his mouth is working a little at the corners. Any minute, now, steam will squirt from his ears.

So, Darley is annoyed . . . big deal!

Lewis is something not too far removed from amused. He is not actually smiling, but damn near . . . like he has just seen the gag-line of a particularly subtle joke.

Darley starts the talk with a very loud voice.

He bawls, "What the hell's all this I hear, Fleischer? What the hell sorta . . ."

He stops bawling when I hit him in the mouth.

While he is wiping the blood from his lips, I say, "That name, bastard. You were warned, last time. From you, it is out . . . out! Use it once more, and I will scratch it across your eyeballs, letter at a time."

I turn and walk into the room.

Darley follows. Lewis follows Darley, and closes the door . . . he closes the door very softly and very deliberately.

I swing to face them and, as I do so, I drop my hand into the pocket of my robe. I put meaning into the movement; I make damn sure Darley sees the bulge as my hand folds itself around what is inside the pocket. He sees it all right, and what he sees dries his lips and backs some of his temper into a hole.

He says, "You wouldn't dare. Not here. Not in front of witnesses."

"Lewis?" I sneer. "Does he have armor plating across his belly? Something like that?"

"You—you wouldn't..."

"It would," I assure him, softly, "be easy. Like a plumber fixing a washer to a faucet...as easy as that. And two washers would be just as easy."

He takes a deep breath as he weighs what I have just said. He believes me—which means he has brains—and, because he believes me, he lowers his temperature.

He says, "You make me mad, Fletcher. Y'know that?—you make me mad."

"Yeah. I effect people that way."

"Sending a message, like that, with the kid, here."

"I meant it."

"Oh, for Christ's sake!"

"The deal is off, Darley."

"I've already *paid*. The dough is..."

"I know."

"For Christ's *sake*!"

"The deal is off."

I use a cold voice and, at this moment, I mean what I say. At this moment, I would not touch Darley's proposition with a vault-pole. It stinks, because too many grubby fingers have already stirred the mix. Darley and Lewis—some fink called Tipp and one of Tipp's muscle-heavers called Bishop...these I know about, and there could be more.

I say, "You play this game, like it was pin-ball. You have boulders for brains, Darley. You, and this young punk who fancies himself as a zip-kid. You want I should make Gawne coffin-meat—okay...if the price is right. But not with an audience, friend. Not with invites to all the dumb bastards you figure might like to watch the show. I do not work that way, Darley. Not for you. Not for anybody! Therefore, the deal is off."

"Okay." Darley waves his arms and moves his shoulders. "We've done it wrong. We've done some damn stupid things..."

"Yeah. Too many. One is too many, and you have crowded in more than one."

"But no more...eh?"

I say, "The deal is off, Darley," and I still mean it.

"Your way. All along the line."

"No dice."

"You say, Fletcher. Whatever it is. We even breathe at your tempo...if that's what you want."

"That is what I wanted. Now, it is too late."

He stares at me and does more deep breathing exercises through his nose. A thread of blood from his split lips trickles from the side of his mouth and down, towards his chin. The red of the blood makes a nice color scheme against the golden-yellow of the skin. He wipes the blood with the back of his hand and, instead of a scarlet thread, there is a smudge...not as neat, and not as nice.

"'Professionalism! Professionalism!'"

The kid makes his play. He speaks for the first time and, from the tone—from that first word—I know what he is going to say. There is soft contempt in his voice, and he knows (as I know) that he has found what Darley could never find. The soft under-belly. The weak spot. The one hole through which I might allow an argument worth listening to.

He says, "Is that what you call this, Fletcher? 'Professionalism?' Is this what earns all the bread? A couple of things slip the rails—no noses skinned, nothing like that...but the starting-blocks are out, ready for the getaway. And you call *that* 'professionalism?'"

I growl, "Stuff it, Lewis. I have lived longer than you. I know the..."

"You'll live forever," he cracks back. "What you do

isn't dangerous... you see to that. It should be. It carries enough coin to be. But you make damn sure it isn't. Not the way you work."

"I know the score." I finish the sentence he interrupted.

"The score," he sneers, "is that you have a reputation you don't deserve. You're supposed to be hot property... you aren't even luke warm."

"Watch it, kid," I warn.

"Why the hell should *I* watch it?" He smiles, and the smile is twisted and unfriendly. "Why the hell should *anybody* watch it? You're not going to do anything, Fletcher. You haven't been paid, and it might go wrong—there's a million-to-one chance it won't, but it might—and you aren't the man to take chances... so curl up, buster, and cut out the bluff. That, or shove your reputation where your mouth is."

Odd...

Anybody else—any other guy I can bring my mind to—and I would belt his brains loose for half that speech. I have made nurses and quacks work overtime on goons who had said far less.

But not Lewis... which is odd.

That what he is saying has enough truth in it to hurt is not what I am getting at. It is something else. It is something to do with Lewis himself. There is about him that which leaves no doubt that he is a man who does not give a damn, and a man who does not give a damn—who does not *truly* give a damn—is a man not often met with.

Maybe this is why he is getting away with mouth music which would earn any other guy a hospital bed.

I say, "Kid, I could do it. Even now. Even after the cow-up Darley and his finks have made... I could still do it."

"If you wanted to," mocks Lewis.

"Yeah... if I wanted to."

"Which is not an easy boast to make... right?"

"Right." I nod, slowly. I have been gaffed . . . but, what the hell! I say, "Therefore, I will make good the boast."

"Y'mean . . ." begins Darley.

"What I say," I snap. I turn to Lewis, and say, "Okay—tomorrow . . . late morning."

"Today," he corrects me.

I check my watch. It is a quarter after one . . . well past midnight.

I say, "Yeah . . . today. The car. Ready for off. I want a shotgun—Winchester Model 12—twelve-gauge, pump action . . . new and unused. I want a handgun—Smith and Wesson, nine millimeter, Model 39—semi-auto-matic . . . again, new and unused. I want shells for both . . . one unopened box of shells for each shooter. I want two dark track-suits . . . one for you, one for me. Dark plimsols—heavy duty . . . a pair for you and a pair for me. Lightweight surgical gloves—four pairs . . . two pairs each. Leather gloves—lightweight . . . two pairs. I want everything new, everything unmarked everything untraceable. Get them here, and be ready to move."

Before Lewis can do more than nod, I turn to Darley.

I say, "From you, I want co-operation . . . which means you stay pinned to your ass until you are told to move. Then, move fast. No questions. No discussions. Just *move* . . . okay?"

Darley says, "Sure. Whatever you . . ."

"Great. Now, beat it. I have some sleep I wish to catch up with."

I see them to the door, then walk back into the room. I remove my hand from the pocket of my robe and, with it, the pipe I have been holding. Darley thought it was a piece . . . which is what I wanted him to think. Lewis? Christ only knows what Lewis thought . . . but he was wise enough to keep his thoughts to himself.

Meanwhile . . .

Meanwhile I have been contracted to bury David

Gawne, and David Gawne is no patsy. Time was, he was
top man in the trade. Until he tripped over a cliff... and,
even then, the cliff was no ordinary cliff. The North Face
of the Eiger, no less. A hunk of rock most men dare not
even *look* at. Talk has it that Gawne figured he could tame
it—that mountaineering, rock-climbing, that brand of
crap, was one of his hobbies—and that the rock punched
back... hard enough to smash Gawne's spine. But what
the hell does that prove? That he is sitting on his ass, in a
wheelchair... that is all. Not that he is now dopey. Not
that he cannot use his trigger-finger. Not that he does not
still know all the moves in this particular game.

David Gawne is still David Gawne... and I am no
North Face of the Eiger!

I pack my pipe, light it and settle down to some very
heavy thinking.

The Volvo rides well. The engine has a sweet, well-tuned
hum and the suspension eases out the rough spots and
straightens the corners. Within the first fifty miles I have
already come to like the car. To trust it. To realize that it
has a certain Swedish flair—properly finished and made
to give lasting pleasure... like their furniture and their
blue films. If things go wrong—and this is always a
possibility—the fault will not be with the Volvo.

Lewis drives and, in doing so, substantiates what I
already know... that he is a class driver. His fingers
caress the wheel and the gear-stick like a lover caressing a
too-long-absent mistress. He plays clutch and gas-pedal
with all the skill of a concert organist.

He can drive.

Without taking his eyes from the road, he says,
"There's a better way... y'know that?"

I make a noise which means nothing from behind
closed lips.

"A quicker way," he amplifies.

"More arguments?" I say, softly.

"Sorry. No more arguments."

From my eye-corner I catch a look at his mouth as it bends in a quick grin.

We are moving north, along the A.10. We are reaching out towards King's Lynn. Cambridge is a couple of miles behind the rear fender, and the Isle of Ely is all around us in the shape of flat, dark-soiled fields.

He wants to ask questions.

I decide to answer some of the questions he will not allow himself to ask.

I say, "The A.1? Maybe the M.1? Right?"

"They're quicker," he agrees.

"More obvious."

He hesitates, then says, "Are we expected?"

I move my shoulders, and murmur, "We pre-suppose the worst. Then, if it happens, it does not come as a surprise."

"Okay. But who the hell..."

"Darley." I speak the name gently. "*He* knows. Maybe a fink called Tipp...a fink I have not yet met."

"I know Tipp."

"So? Are you hinting that earns you some sort of certificate?"

"No. Just that that's what he is. A fink."

"That, too, follows."

"But Darley wouldn't..."

"Darley," I interrupt, "is a slippery bastard. He is the breed of bastard who is ready to pay heavy bread, in order to double-cross a guy who once did him a service. Which makes Darley very unreliable. Do not tell me what Darley would not do, kid...because there is *nothing*."

The car eats its way through a few miles of silence.

I continue the kid's education.

I say, "There is also the small matter of cops."

"Coppers?" There is mild surprise in the question.

"Yeah." I nod. "You will learn. Supposing you live long enough... you will learn. The *polizei*. The *politiet*. The bulls. The fuzz. Whatever... some are dumb, and some are smart. Most of the smart ones patrol the autobahns and the motorways. It follows. They are eager-beavers. They can remember car numbers. They can remember faces. What they do not see, they cannot remember... okay?"

"Okay," he says, quietly. And one more tiny piece of know-how is filed away inside his skull.

"You should know," I say, slyly.

"Eh?"

"Your old man."

"Oh, Christ... not *that*."

"I would like to know," I insist.

"It's not important."

I say, "I never take another man's opinion... not when I can check."

He sighs, and says, "He was a copper—a city copper... a detective."

"And?"

"A detective chief superintendent. Detective Chief Superintendent Lewis."

"Big man," I murmur.

"Top plain clothes in the force," he agrees, reluctantly.

I say, "Tell me."

"Why? What the hell..."

"Because," I interrupt, flatly, "I am riding alongside his son... and I like to know who is handling the steering wheel. That is as good a reason as any. So, tell me."

"He was a bloody animal." There is hatred in the kid's voice; deep zero-qualification hatred. That any guy should hate one of his parents so much, is a little puzzling... but that this kid *does* comes pre-packed with every word. He says, "The other coppers loathed him. There's a man called Raff. Another man called Ripley.

Collins—another copper ... they all detested him. And with good reason. Every bloody bobby he ever worked alongside."

"You, too," I murmur.

"Eh?"

"Like them ... did not subscribe to a fan club."

"He wasn't human." The kid's eyes shine, as they stare at the road and, at the same time, see other things. "My mother ... he led her a dog's life. I've seen her heartbroken. Too many times. So has he ... but he didn't give a damn."

"And you?"

"He believed in the big stick. At home, as well as at work. He had weight. He threw it around."

I turn a little in my seat, and watch his face as I ask the next question.

I say, "Okay ... he was a hard man. A red-necked cop. But that answers nothing. Why *you*? Why the jump to the other side of the line?"

He considers the point. Maybe he has not tried to figure out the answer before—maybe the contradiction has not floated through his brain until this moment— maybe ... but I doubt it. My guess is that the question is one he has asked himself many times but, so far, without any clear-cut answer.

He says, "A psychiatrist would argue that it's a case of over-reaction. That I'm getting back at him by being the thing he hated most ... a criminal."

"And?" I encourage.

"It's possible." He twists his mouth into a cynical grin. "On the other hand, it's also possible that I like money ... and this is the only way to make it in large lumps, without heavy weather."

"And?" I insist.

He takes a deep breath then, very softly, he says, "Coppers. I think that's the real reason."

"You do not like the law?"

"No more—no less—than the next man...but I *know* coppers. And too many are too bent. Not all...but a bloody sight too many!"

"One is too many," I remind him.

"Yeah...I've heard the argument. Like all perfections, it doesn't meet at the edges. Okay...as long as the bent ones don't rise. But some do. Some go way up."

"Your old man?" I ask, softly.

"He hated crooks so much, he was prepared to be more crooked than they were...just so long as he smashed 'em."

"Nice guy."

"A pig...in the real sense."

There is another length of silence, and the Volvo eats up the miles, like it is a spool and the road is a tape.

Then the kid says something. Quietly. Grudgingly...as if to put the record straight.

He says, "He was a bastard, but he was tough."

"Your old man?"

"Nothing scared him. Nothing! He took on a couple of Mafia hatchet-men...the Majuri brothers. Jack and Joe Majuri. They were over here after a guy called Rossetti. They got him—and his wife—then the old man lost his temper, and..."

NEW YORK.
APRIL—1972

Dave Fleischer listened, and said little. But what he said had meaning; every word, because, with these people, a wrong word—an unintentional hint which might be picked up and misconstrued—could mean trouble...lethal-sized trouble.

They were in the rear room of a Brooklyn restaurant. Three men—Fleischer, Tommy Ernst and Frank Ferriano. Ernst was doing most of the talking, Fleischer was doing the listening and Ferriano was doing the scowling.

Ernst said, "We've got the boys. I don't have to tell you, Fleischer. We're having trouble holding them, since what happened at the C.R.L. meeting. We know damn well who fixed Joe Colombo . . . we ain't dumb."

Ernst waited, and watched Fleischer's face. The pause was for a reaction and, from the reaction, an assessment.

Fleischer said, "Word gets around."

Ferriano made growling noises from the back of his throat.

Frank Ferriano—on paper, a janitor from New Jersey—on the files of the New York Police Department, a "fixer" for the Profaci "family." When necessary—when the heat was too high for anybody else—a Profaci "soldier."

Now, a double-crosser . . . because what they were discussing was the murder of Crazy Joe Gallo, head of the Profaci mob.

Ferriano looked the part. He was a bad man to meet on a dark night. Under the thatch of black, curling hair the narrow forehead stopped at the overhang of the thick eyebrows. In the caves, under the brows, the eyes were savage, and a little mad. The nose sprawled across the center of the face and, from each side of the nose, deep creases ran down, alongside the heavy moustache, to end at the corners of the thick-lipped, sneering mouth.

Fleischer waited.

He guessed what was coming, and what was coming scared him a little.

It scared him . . . but, at the same time, it engendered a warm feeling of pure satisfaction. Because, what was happening—the proposition he was about to be offered—made him top man in his profession . . .

Lewis is saying, "The old man wanted me to follow him. Y'know... into the force. My aching back! Following a bastard like that. Being the son of a swine everybody hated to all eternity. What the hell sort of life would it have..."

Fleischer knew the score. He was not alone... everybody in New York City knew the score.

The New York "families" were feuding. Since 1961 the Profaci mob, with the three Gallo brothers at their head, had claimed top place... and always the Colombo outfit spitting in their eye.

Then, in June of 1971, Joseph Colombo had been gunned in Central Park.

It had been the greatest single hit of modern criminal warfare. The boss-man of one of New York's top "families" smashed into a state of permanent comatose, while surrounded by cops and thousands of enthusiastic followers, at an Italian-American Civil Rights League rally. Flap-mouths had said it was a Profaci set-up—and the Gallo brothers did nothing to quieten the rumor—but those in the know had few doubts.

Gambino had been behind the Joe Colombo shootup. Carlo Gambino... the quiet guy, with influence, who planned to be the final czar when all the guns had been holstered and all the gore hosed off the streets.

And the actual hit itself? The cold-nerved bastard (or bastards) who had sent slugs into Joseph Colombo at the one moment when that man had felt supremely safe?

The Majuri boys... who else?

The top freelance guns in the whole world; the duo willing to stiffen anybody, anywhere... if the price was right.

Then some time later, they'd tripped to the U.K., tangled with some hick Limey cop, and...

"It's a small world," I muse.

"Eh?" Lewis does not know what the hell I am thinking about, therefore he does not know what the hell I mean.

"Jack and Joe Majuri," I say, quietly.

"You knew them? The two killers my old man..."

"Of them," I say. "Not personally. But everybody knew the Majuri brothers were around. And available."

"Yeah...I suppose." He is still not completely sure of which way my thoughts are pointing.

"The world," I say. "It is small...but small! Your old man clobbered them. And, kid—this will kill you—except for the Majuri boys, and something they did, I would not be what I am. I would not be here, sitting alongside you."

He still does not understand.

The hell with him!...let him stay ignorant.

Fleischer said, "Gambino." He spoke the word softly, but very deliberately. He wanted the other two to know that he, too, was wise. Not that he objected...merely that he knew. He said, "Let us not horse around too much. Let us name names. Like...Carlo Gambino."

Ernst frowned.

The frown sat uncomfortably on the face of Ernst, because the face of Tommy Ernst was the face of the typical "all-American male;" it could have been used on a propaganda poster. It had everything. The rounded, slightly chubby cheeks. The wide-spaced, spaniel-worried eyes. The pert and slightly humorous nose. The mouth, with the hint of a pout at the lower lip. The high forehead. The crop of neatly trimmed hair. The "all-American male," in person...who just happened to be a Staten Island mobster, supposedly on the side of the Profaci "family," and who was busy angling a sweet double-cross against that same "family."

He hesitated, then said, "The Gallo boys are

crazy. They want a mob war...like twenty, thirty years ago. They don't call him 'Crazy Joe' for no reason."

"And Al and Larry?" asked Fleischer.

"Larry goes along. Al we can handle."

"But not Joe!" Fleischer let a tight smile touch his lips.

"An outside job. None of our own soldiers...see?" Ernst opened up. He was asking something important. Important enough to deserve some degree of explanation. He said, "Joe is looped...y'know that? He has no brains. He figures himself as Capone...and Capone wouldn't work these days, anyway. Guns...that's all he wants. The Colombo contract. That was stupid. Okay— Gambino fixed it...but it was still stupid. Joe Gallo didn't think so. He figured it a great hit...up my ass it was a great hit! And now he wants to take the pieces along and wipe out the Colombo team, before they can get organized to hit back."

"And Gambino?" Fleischer pushed the question which Ernst was ducking.

Ferriano spoke for the first time.

He growled, "Hey, Fleischer. Keep the questions buttoned, eh?"

It was a warning and, from this man, a warning was something to heed. He could be rough...and more than rough. He could break a bone—an arm, a leg, a neck—as a warm-up for the real thing. Frank Ferriano had a name—a rep...and he'd earned it.

Fleischer turned to face Ferriano. His voice was cold and without tremor.

He said, "Wop, if Gallo could have been talked to death, they would maybe have hired you. That what is needed is something you cannot deliver is so goddam obvious that even you should be able to grab the gist. So-o...any mouth-zipping around here is strictly your scene."

Before Ferriano could come back, Ernst snapped, "Okay...cut it!"

Ferriano held himself...just.

Fleischer said, "We are wasting time. On the table...okay? You are anxious to buy something. Maybe I am willing to sell. Just answer the questions. Who? What? How much?"

Ernst lighted a cigarette, returned the book of matches to his pocket, removed the cigarette from his lips, and drawled, "Ten G. Gambino is the pay-master. We want Joe Gallo...retired."

We are eating.

The eating-house is the *Globe Hotel Restaurant,* a neat grill-shop in King's Lynn Tuesday Market Place and, although the food is not fancy it is nicely cooked and served well.

Lewis has retired into himself a little. He is not sulking, but I figure he is slightly worried by the silence of the last few miles before we hit the town. He has chewed his way through a mixed grill.

I pack a pipe, glance around the room to check that nobody is within hearing distance, then put him out of his misery.

I say, "Okay, kid. Now we go up the coast."

"Yeah?" He pretends an unconcern which I know damn well is false.

I say, "Cleethorpes, with luck."

"We can get a lot farther north than..."

"After dark," I interrupt.

"Early evening. We could..."

"But, after dark," I insist. "Say four—thirty after four—then, it is dark."

"So?"

I wave the stem of my pipe at him, and give him

another short lecture upon the finer points of what we are about.

I say, "Kid, it is Christmas...okay? This means turkeys...okay? This means booze and cigarettes ...okay? This means many things which are there to be lifted...okay? Now—come on, kid—you tell me what *that* means."

"Road blocks," he says, gently.

"Yeah. Police checks...and, kid, you should know! They are not dumb-bells. They, too, know. They will be out, and about, checking motor cars. Stopping motor cars. And we have things in the Volvo which we do not want the coppers to see."

He gives me a twisted grin, says, "Point taken," and his mood disappears out of the window.

"And another thing." I shove the pipe in my mouth and talk around the stem as I hunt for matches. "Again, it is Christmas. That means boozed-up goons behind steering wheels...and they are around after dark. What we do not need is a smash-up. Not even a small one. We take our time. We slide north, without being noticed. We arrive, and nobody knows about our arrival until we are *there*...check?"

"Check." He lifts matches from his pocket and hands them across the table. He says, "The little things. It's nice to have them pointed out."

I take the matches and, in a very somber voice, say, "There are no 'little' things in this game, kid. They are all big—they are all important...and the 'little' thing you have missed is the one which is going to smack you right in the mouth."

Cleethorpes...wet, windy, cold and miserable.

They are all the same—these so-called "seaside holiday resorts"—once fall has moved into winter and the crowds have shuffled back to the monotony of their humdrum lives; once the candy stalls have put up their clapboard shutters and the cheap cafes have closed their doors; once the barkers have closed their mouths, till next season, and the cheapjack traders have crawled back under their stones.

They are all the same...like half-smoked cigars, dropped into a rain-washed gutter; tatty and coming apart around the edges; a reminder of something which was once expensive and enjoyable, but which is now soggy and damn-all use to any man.

Cleethorpes...like all the rest.

The wind coming in from the North Sea has fangs which snap their way through normal clothes, touch the skin and bring up goose-flesh. The tide is low and the gusts of a squall, which is building up to something bigger, whip the rain across the deserted sands and smash into one side of my face with an insistent fury which numbs the flesh. Along the waterfront the hotels stand, like square shaped skulls with sightless eyes; some still have their bars and part of their restaurants open...booze-rooms and eating-houses, surrounded on all sides, and above, by empty cubicles in which are empty beds without sheets or blankets.

A ghost town, in which to wander alone and think about ghosts.

David Gawne—a ghost from my past...the bogey-man of my immediate future.

Make no mistake, I am not scared. I can take the man; I could take him, if he had both legs—if he was not anchored to a wheelchair...and I can certainly take him, now he is a cripple. I can take him quickly and painlessly, and he will not feel a thing and this, at least, I owe him. He made me what I am and, although I have no great pride in my profession, that does not mean that I am not proud of being top man in that profession.

It is just that...

Let me put it this way. Gawne is a man; even without legs, he is a complete male. That he is amoral, I do not give a damn about. That he has killed his fellow-men, is of no importance to me. I care not what he is, or how he has behaved. He is a *man*... and that is enough.

Because the bastard who wants him dead—the bastard who has given me the contract—is considerably less than a man. Darley is a louse and, six times, I have exterminated men like Darley... and, more than once, for money provided by other men who were also like Darley. Lice fight lice and, when the fighting gets rough, they employ men to eliminate their fellow-lice. And the men they employ are men like myself... and men like Gawne.

We are a select company and, very soon, we shall be one less... because the lice require one of the men to eliminate a fellow-man.

It is a sobering thought and, as I walk along the sea frontage, with cold air blasting in from the east, carrying with it slivers of ice-water, the thought makes for poor company.

Back at the hotel, I re-check the security. The guns and the equipment are in a locked case. The case is locked away in the boot of the Volvo. The Volvo, in turn, is behind the locked doors of one of the hotel's garages.

Three locks... whereas, had we carried the gear into the bedroom, it would have been behind only two locks. A further point which had to be explained to the inquisitive Lewis.

In the foyer of the hotel I ask around and, eventually contact the guy who operates the hotel switchboard.

I question him, and learn that he has been on duty since six o'clock this evening, and is on duty until six o'clock tomorrow morning. I proposition him and, at first, he makes outraged noises like I have suggested that he rape his maiden aunt . . . which is a big laugh because, like all of his ilk, he will play footsie if the grease is thick enough.

A ten-spot buys him.

Yeah . . . he knows which room Mr. Lewis is occupying. No . . . no telephone calls have been logged into, or out of, that room since Mr. Lewis arrived a couple of hours back. Yeah . . . he also knows which room I am occupying. Yeah . . . he will let me know of any calls to, or from, Mr. Lewis's room, between now and six o'clock tomorrow morning. And, yeah . . . he will balls-up telephonic communication between Mr. Lewis's room and the outside world, before he checks off duty at six.

Which is dandy, and an arrangement which I do *not* explain to the whiz-kid.

Follows a late dinner, which is moderately well prepared, moderately well served and moderately well enjoyed . . . after which the kid and I wander into the lounge, sprawl in armchairs, chew about this, that and the other, but nothing important, then crawl off to bed.

I sleep well because, last night—thanks to the lunacies of a fink called Darley—I slept little.

And now we are moving in upon Ground Zero.

It is late afternoon and, away to the west and across the Vale of York, the Pennines reach high to make a summit, like the one we are on, in a great, geological switchback. I know this territory; a couple of times, while we worked together, Gawne and I visited this district. Once to iron out the difficulties corporate with a certain R.A.F. flight sergeant who figured he could make a quick buck by hawking top secret radar know-how to interested parties and, the second time, because Gawne liked the place and the rock-climbing potential it offered . . . and still offers.

This is maybe the last of the untamed parts of the U.K. They tell me Scotland, too, is pretty wild . . . I would not know. But (from what I hear) slabs of it have been taken over, and are now doing duty as makeshift ski-runs; the haggis has lost its mystery and what goes on under the kilt is no longer a secret; the sharks have moved in and made a killing...the crofter's cottages are now fitted out with chrome-and-glass furnishings and are hired, complete with antlers, at a throw which would make a millionaire blanch.

I wouldn't know...but this is what I hear.

But here, my friend—here, where the Clevelands and the Hambletons and the North Yorkshire Moors add themselves together to make a damn great rectangle, whose corners are Pickering, Helmsley, Guisborough and Whitby—the speculators and the get-rich-quick boys do not have a prayer; they would have their nuts frozen off at the roots before they had time to get themselves noticed.

Which is nice to know.

Which makes me figure that mankind is maybe not quite as goofy as it sometimes acts.

I check the map, and say, "There is a dirt road, to the left. As I read it, we are almost at it."

"A couple more miles," says Lewis.

"Is that so?" I put meaning into the question.

"Beechwood Brook," he says, smoothly. "It used to be Ripley's patch."

I say, "Yeah?" and wait for more to come.

"Beechwood Brook Division...when my old man was around it didn't include Pike Top. It does, these days. A large acreage. Beechwood Brook and Pike Top...all Beechwood Brook."

He closes his mouth and concentrates upon the driving.

Maybe he figures he has said enough—all that is necessary—and that, from what he has said, I can guess the rest...but, like hell he has and like hell I can!

"Ripley," I murmur.

"Chief superintendent—he was only superintendent when he worked with my old man—boss-man of Beechwood Brook."

"You—er—you *know* him?"

"Certainly I . . ." The meaning penetrates. He moves his head for a quick glance at my face, and the spitting disgust of his expression comes through on the words, as he says, "For Christ's sake! You don't still think . . ."

"Yeah . . . but *always*." I jerk out the plug and let him have full flood. I snarl, "Always and forever, junior. Night and day, and at all time. And especially when I am with some young punk who is on name terms with half the stinking cops in the United Kingdom."

"My father was . . ."

"You keep telling me, and I am not too interested. Screw your father. Up your father's ass. *You* are the bastard who is worrying me."

"He was known. He was . . ."

"His son, too, is known. That is what worries me."

"And Ripley—both of them—they were both well known. They hit the headlines when they . . ."

"Junior—get this—I do not give one sweet-scented fart about your old man, or this Ripley goon you keep mentioning . . ."

". . . smashed the Majuri brothers. Between them. My old man and Ripley . . ."

". . . Just give me one half-good reason why I should trust you to even hand me a ready-wrapped candy bar."

". . . Together—they did what the whole of your bloody F.B.I. couldn't do. It was headline stuff. So, they got the headlines."

I breathe, "Sweet creeping Jesus, and all His goddam saints!"

"In these parts Ripley's a bloody legend."

"Is that so?" I say, harshly.

"I'm trying to tell you. It's no good . . ."

"And you know him...right? You are on buddy-buddy level with this zing-a-ling cop, inside whose patrol area we now are? Inside whose patrol area we are due to stiffen a certain citizen? You know the bastard? He is a friend of yours?"

"The devil he is!"

"I get this feeling, kid. That..."

"You're a bloody fool," he rasps, and the way he says it lifts the remark well clear of friendly banter. "I needn't have told you. I could have kept my blasted mouth shut...kept you in the dark about possible opposition. But, I thought you should know. I thought you'd have sense enough to *want* to know. The hell with Gawne—you worry yourself sick about Gawne—but Gawne is only a man. One man. Ripley—the cops... they're a damn great machine. They're an organization. *They're* the ones you should be worrying about. The law. The Ripleys. Okay—if you like—the Lewis-types. The big boys. The men who can take the Majuri team, chew it up and spit it out. Y'know what, Fleischer—Fletcher, Hemmingway, what the hell else you want to call yourself—give *those* boys a chance, and they'll boil you for four minutes, and serve you for breakfast. Gawne won't need to worry... all he'll have to do is sit back and watch."

It is a long time—so long, I do not remember when—since anybody last threw talk like this in my direction... and it is a damn sight longer time since I sat back and caught it!

But...

We-ell—maybe the kid has something worth saying, and something worth listening to... maybe I am looking under the bed too much, and not paying enough attention to the closet.

I give things a few minutes of no-noise.

Then, I growl, "The next dirt road to the left, junior. Do not miss it."

• • •

Because (looked at from my angle) the kid is right.

Cops—that brand of cops—can be very nasty...cops who are capable of ploughing hatchet-carriers like Jack and Joe Majuri into the nearest furrow.

NEW YORK.
APRIL—1972.
FRIDAY—APRIL 7th—5:15 a.m.

Fleischer turned into Mulberry Street and realized that this street—this corner of Manhattan's Little Italy—might well be the last place he saw before sudden death blinded his eyes. The thing was that big...to smash Crazy Joe Gallo here, at the very heart of Profaci territory, was a little like taking dough for committing certain suicide.

Because—like it or not—Gallo was no patsy.

He (and his brothers Al and Larry) had been the top hit trio for Joseph Profaci himself, when there had been no need to argue about who was top Mafia man. Profaci...who else? When Profaci had put the finger on his only near-rival, Albert Anastasia the Brooklyn waterfront hoodlum...until Anastasia had been rubbed in the Park Sheraton Hotel barber's shop. And the guns which had removed Anastasia had been carried by the Gallo boys...again, who else?

And now—after heaving Profaci himself from the switchback—the Gallo boys headed the "family," with Joseph ("Crazy Joe") Gallo undoubted top-kick.

A bastard—bigger than Anastasia, bigger than Profaci...and he, David Fleischer, had been given the contract to hit him.

And had accepted.

A lot of men had been certified for less.

He walked along Mulberry Street, forced his legs to move at a moderate, not-too-fast-not-too-slow rhythm, and checked the various—the almost

unlimited—hints and lessons he had received from
Gawne. Remembered them, and added to them the
few tricks he had learned for himself.

Not to look, or act, like a killer. To make it
sudden and absolute. To send it from an unexpected
quarter. To have the guy dead, before he even
knows what is happening. To use as few slugs as
possible. To ignore the victim, once the victim is a
corpse, and concentrate upon what might snarl up
the getaway. To...

He turned into Umberto's Clam House.

Despite the pre-dawn hour, the place was busy.
All-nighters, calling in from some party or some
dice game or poker session. A handful of sightseers,
anxious to view "gangland" and maybe spot some
notorious "gangster"... and, this time, they were
lucky.

They were all there—sharing a group of tables,
half way down the room—enjoying Joe Gallo's 43rd
birthday party. Joe and his wife of less than a
month, Sina. And Sina's ten-year-old kid, Lisa.
And his mother; podgy-faced, tinted-haired Mary
Gallo. And Gallo's sister, Carmella Fiorella. And all
the others—thick-limbed hoods and mobsters and
their over-dressed broads—living proof that the
bigger the bastard the fatter the bankroll. And
there, on the next table to Gallo, Pete "The Greek"
Diapoulas; fat-gutted, fat-faced and the most feared
gun in all New York... and Joe Gallo's personal
bodyguard.

They were all there. Twenty—maybe thirty. And
every man—and every woman—would have hap-
pily killed him on the threshold had they even
suspected he was there to stiffen the big man.

Fleischer walked into the room. He glanced at
the eaters. He looked directly at Gallo, smiled and
nodded... as if to a passing friend. And Gallo—
because he was a bum, and a self-opinionated bum

who figured he was as well-known and as well-respected as the president himself—grinned and nodded back.

Gallo... of the high forehead and the receding hair-line. Gallo... of the curiously level eyebrows and the wide-eyed emotionless eyes. Gallo... of the razor-slit mouth and the battleship chin.

Gallo... the man Fleischer was there to bump.

But Diapoulas did not grin. Diapoulas did not nod. Diapoulas did that which he was paid to do—that at which he was an expert—he watched... he watched everybody. His eyes were flickering, living things which had a life apart from, and independent of, the man himself. They missed nothing. They saw everything.

They saw, and watched Fleischer... and Fleischer was aware of their scrutiny.

He walked towards the far end of the room, passing the Gallo tables on his right and, as he passed, he unbuttoned the loose-fitting overcoat and began to peel it from his shoulders. Less than five yards beyond the tables, the coat-rack had an empty peg and Fleischer removed the overcoat and hooked it onto the peg. He took off his hat and hung that, too, on the peg. Then the scarf... pulling it from around his neck in a smooth, natural movement and looping it over the hat.

He turned—turning left—and, as he turned, his right hand brushed the overcoat and slipped the Colt .45 automatic from the overcoat pocket. For a second—for less than a second—his body hid the Colt from the eyes of Diapoulas and, as he continued the turn, he brought the snout of the automatic up and into line of fire. He took up some of the trigger-pressure as he turned.

The trigger-pressure was a little out, and the damn gun was too heavy. Little things... but they wasted the first slug. It took Gallo through the left cheek of his backside.

But the quick, second squeeze finished him; it ploughed in, throught the left shoulder and found the pump.

And Fleischer was yelling, "Freeze, Greek! Touch anything, and you're with him in hell."

And Diapoulas was motionless, but piano-wire tense. And the dames were yelling and screaming. And the hoods were crouched on their chairs, ready to explode. And the customers were diving for cover. And general hades was erupting inside Umberto's Clam House.

But Crazy Joe Gallo was spilling the last of his life-blood on the carpet...which was the reason for it all.

Fleischer sprinted for the exit and, as he hit the starting-blocks, Diapoulas moved. The Greek jerked his piece free of its holster and pegged a triple burst after Fleischer.

Fleischer reached the door, grabbed the jamb to help in a fast turn-round, dropped to one knee and returned the fire. Four shots—two bursts of two—and Diapoulas yelled, dropped his gun and grabbed at his hip.

Then Fleischer was back on his feet, diving for the sidewalk and reaching for the already opened door of the Chev as it braked to receive him. Then away...fast! Out of Mulberry Street. Clear of Manhattan. Long-gone from New York. Beyond the U.S. boundaries and into Canada.

And Fleischer was richer by ten thousand dollars...which was also the cost of Crazy Joe Gallo's funeral!

I murmur, "I will tell you, kid. The Majuri boys were punks, both. They were amateurs."

"Eh?" Lewis frowns. He has not heard me too good. I sigh, and say, "Forget it, junior. One day I will draw

you some diagrams. Meanwhile...first turn left. Okay?"
They are around.

The guide books (supposing these places ever reached
the pages of a guide book, which they do not) would call
them "inns." Okay...they are inns. But they are inns
from the Dark Ages. Their walls are anything up to
twenty-four inches thick, and made of rough stone with a
concrete holding mix in which the glitter of powdered
granite can be seen. They are squat, scowling places and,
inside, their rooms are correspondingly squat and
low-ceilinged, and their interior walls are, again, of rough
stone—sometimes plastered and sometimes thick with
accumulated color-wash, but never smooth. Their
furniture is of solid, no-nonsense oak, beeswaxed and
stained, and uncomfortable as hell to flesh which is not as
hard as tanned leather. There are rafters...thick,
adze-marked and seasoned to a point where they bend
driven nails as easily, and as surely, as steel girders. There
are windows...small-paned and wide-mullioned, with
the glass tinted green and brown by impurities in its
make-up. There are fireplaces...ingle-nooked and with
box-shaped fire-baskets which burn logs, or cobs, or peat
and which are rarely allowed to go out. There are
lights...the incandescent brilliance of pressured and
mantled paraffin, or the yellow, dancing-shadowed glow
from wick-drawn oil or, in rare cases, electric bulbs
boosted into life by means of a generator throbbing away
in a lean-to at the back.

And there is a smell. It is a smell peculiar to these inns.
Not an unpleasant smell...but a strangely masculine
smell. It mixes age-old tobacco-smoke with the tang of
well-used harness; the smell of carbolic with the smell of
the soil; the trail of the oil lamps with the whiff of heavy
tweed. These, and many more scents, with the base smell
of booze. Beer and cider, perry and stout, whisky and
rum, brandy and old port. But rarely sherry and rarely

gin ... and never anything as exotic as vodka.

Because, you see, these places are the last of the true drinking houses. They are where men (and, very very occasionally, a woman) sit and smoke and *drink*. They talk ... because not to talk to a fellow-drinker would be impolite. But they want no distractions such as music, or darts, or even dominoes. They are there to booze ... period. And, to get there, they have come a long way, therefore the booze had better be good and well worth the journey.

And they *have* come a long way. Every customer. Because (and this is the real means of identifying this class of inn) there is no surrounding village, beyond the low-porched door. There is no flash car-park, or neon-spelled name above the door.

There is a dirt road, and moorland ... and that is all.

Originally, they were the smugglers' inns dotted, dozens of miles apart, on a zig-zag route which led from the east-coast caves to the men who bought the brandy and the women who bought the lace. They are isolated and hard to find, and no revenue man could approach without being spotted a mile away. They are part of the history of an island race—part of the history of a people who have always thumbed a nose at unpopular laws— and, because of what they are and what they once were, they are still around ... and God help the lunatic who figures he can bulldoze them clear of the path of some proposed motorway.

They are around.

And one of them is *The Plough*.

Tomorrow will be the day of Christmas Eve. And, even here—in an isolated inn which belongs to another age—there are signs galore that the big festival has just about arrived. The holly is real holly—wild holly, hacked from open hedgerows—heavy with berry and dark-leaved; it is thrust in great bunches, without care and without arrangement, behind faded pictures and into huge, pot-bellied vases; the townies would give their eyeballs for such holly and the dames who go in for floral decoration would have a great time... but what the townies and the floral decoration dames would do to it would emasculate it and turn it from the rip-roaring defiance of winter which it is into a weak-as-water fantasy of red and green. The mistletoe, also, is the mistletoe of this neck of the woods; bright green and with tallow-white fruit as big as peas; hung in bunches, not to be kissed under but—as was its original purpose—as a charm against the evil things which crawl around dark corners at the year's end. There is also ivy—star-leaved trailings of this feminine evergreen to match the masculine holly—which, despite the carol, is not too often found as part of the seasonal decoration, except in wild places such as this.

And it is all that—this place called *The Plough*...it is certainly a wild place, surrounded by equally wild country.

As Lewis arrives at the table, dumps a pewter tankard of newly-drawn ale alongside his plate and settles himself down to eat, I mention this fact to him.

I say, "Some dump you have come up with, kid."

"Here?" He grins across at me, past the glare of the hissing Tilley.

"Yeah...it only needs Dracula to complete the decor."

"I rather like it."

I shrug. I, too, "rather like it"...but, as always as the time of a hit moves in on me, I have a sour temper.

He says, "I've known it for years. Last time I came here, I was a kid...we used to ramble these moors and, if we were thirsty, we always called in here for a quencher."

I say, "Yeah," pick up the knife and fork and join him in the eating routine.

It is good food; not fancy, but the best any frying pan

could ever come up with. Ham...home-grown and home-cured, and served in slices thick enough to need pressure to saw through. Eggs...a perfect pair which, this morning, were still inside hens. Mushrooms...wild, and with a taste the cultivated kind do not have. And, with this fry-up, bread—home-baked and newly-baked, crusty and with the clean taste of yeast to the tongue—and butter—churned not many miles from here, buttercup yellow and thick and rich as clotted cream—and tea served in solid, half-pint cups; tea which has been "mashed" (not "brewed") and with new milk and as much good sugar as the palate can take.

Suppose such food could be served at the center of a city, the guy serving it could retire within a few years...and every other eating-house would be out of business.

Lewis chews, nods at my plate, and says, "Okay?"

"I have eaten worse," I growl.

"Better?" He grins as he asks the question. I have the feeling he knows my mood, and is not taking my belly-aching too seriously.

I say, "I would not know. I eat...I do not keep tally."

The grin grows big and blossoms into a quick chuckle.

We are in the eating-room of *The Plough*. It is a fairly large room, long in proportion to its width, and with a square-shaped alcove at the end near the fire. Imagine an "L" with a very short lower stroke. That is the shape of this room, and we are at a table placed in that miniature lower stroke. The rest of the room is empty—it not being any sort of season for ramblers, walkers or even motorists—and, as sure as iced drinks are not served in hell, this room is not bugged...with a place like *The Plough*, electronic crappery will, if pushed, arrive with the twenty-first century.

We are safe to talk.

I say, "Okay...what?"

"There's this farm house." He waves an empty fork as he talks; like he is conducting some damn orchestra. "It's called 'Diasc Farm'... along a road leading to nowhere."

"Where is 'nowhere?'" I ask.

"Just that... *nowhere*. About a mile beyond the farm it stops. Becomes a sheep track, and disappears into the moors."

"Isolated," I say. "Is that what you are telling me?"

"Very isolated." He stops conducting and loads his fork with ham and egg and mushroom. "There's one way in—one way out... and, if that's blocked, we've had it."

"Is it likely to be blocked?"

"I can't think why it should be."

"Then, why the hell..."

"Unless there's a sudden heavy snow."

"There is also," I say, nastily, "the possibility of a sudden civil war. Or maybe an earthquake. Or maybe—who knows?—there could be a goddam volcano around here, someplace... and it might start erupting, any minute now."

"You asked." He buries the loaded fork in his mouth, chews and talks through a barrier of food. "And it's winter. And, in this country, in winter, it sometimes snows... and, in these parts, when it snows it *snows*."

I grunt and join him in chewing for a few moments.

Then, I say, "Isolated... okay. What sort of a place?"

"A farmhouse. It's..."

"What sort of farm house?"

"Big... pretty big."

"'Buckingham Palace' big?"

"Christ Almighty! Not *that*..."

"Okay—be specific... what is 'pretty big'?"

"As big as..." He looks around him. "As big as this place... about the same size, in ground space. But taller. Higher."

"Two stories? Or three?"

"Two . . . I think."

"You've looked at the damn place," I snarl. "It is why you went. It is what you have been tooling around at, most of this day. Goddam it, kid . . ."

He comes back with, "I didn't know you wanted me to ring the bell and ask for a conducted tour. I took it for granted you'd want a quiet examination. From a distance . . . far enough away not to be noticed. However, if you want the wallpaper pattern included in the bloody . . ."

I snap, "Skip it," and reach for his beer.

He watches me, and surprise takes over from the spurt of sudden annoyance.

As I replace the tankard, he says, "I thought . . ."

"I don't. Not often." I wipe the back of my hand across my lips. I say, "It is nice booze. It has a kick."

"Why don't you . . ."

"No." I treat him to a smile, and say, "Just the one mouthful. It looked good . . . it tastes as good as it looks. But that is enough."

"Sure." He moves his hand in a tiny, couldn't-care-less gesture and slips his attention back to what is on his plate.

I give him a few minutes of quiet; time for him to cool off a little . . . time, too, for me to cool off.

Then, I say, "Okay, kid. The house—this 'Diasc Farm' place—tell me about it. The layout. The approach—The grounds . . . supposing there is some grounds. What cover we can use. Anything . . . everything."

He tells me, and this time I do not interrupt.

The place (according to Lewis) is called "Diasc Farm"; it is one of those farm houses which do not have a farm attached; it stands in its own grounds—uncultivated, and with plenty of tree and bush cover—to one side of this dirt road which leads to nowhere. It is three—maybe four—miles from *The Plough* and, from what some talkative local sheep-tender says, it is where Gawne and his wife, Belle Gawne, live alone.

This follows... Gawne, being what he is and what he once was, is not the type of guy to invite too many guests. It also follows that, unless an elevator is installed (which seems doubtful) Gawne, if not his wife, must sleep on the ground floor; a cripple in a wheelchair—especially a cripple with as much meat on his bones as Gawne had, last time I saw him—is not a thing for a woman to muscle up and down stairs each day.

All these things I weigh, as the kid tells me and as I listen to him tell it.

Then...

The kid looks awkward, and says, "There's—er—there's one more thing I think you should know."

He stares at me, and I have this feeling. Everybody knows the feeling I am talking about—it is as near a sixth sense as any guy can truly lay claim to—it is like miniaturized ants are crawling around, under the skin, above and behind the ears.

I say, "Yeah?" in a very soft voice... and wait for the bad news which I know is on the way.

"About four years ago." He talks quietly, and a little more slowly than he has talked up to now. "About this time of the year... Christmas time. There was a big snow, and a couple of groups were snowbound in Gawne's place. Some sort of pop group, and a bunch of villains... bank robbers, on the run. There was some trouble. A lot of trouble. And the cops had to sort things out. Y'know... they would, wouldn't they?"

He pauses, and waits for a reaction.

In a very deadpan voice, I say, "Yeah... they would."

"Ripley. Y'know... Ripley."

"You have mentioned Ripley. You have mentioned him, more than once."

"He was... He led the cops."

"It follows."

"So..." He shrugs. "He knows Gawne."

"Which means?"

"He knows him. *Knows* him."

"Spell it out, kid," I growl. "I am dumb—I am the world's biggest dumb-bell, when it comes to riddles... spell it out."

He takes a deep breath—it is almost a sigh—and says, "There was a shoot-out. There *had* to be. A man like Gawne... and some bloody money-snatchers trying to shove him around. So-o... Ripley must know Gawne. That he handles guns. That he can kill a man, when he wants to. That... Y'*know*..."

He fizzles out, like a wet firecracker. He waves his arms a little and looks worried. For a moment—and, for the first time since we met—he looks a punk... and a very helpless punk, at that.

I give him a lopsided grin which carries no humor whatever, and speak in a low-temperatured voice.

I say, "Kid—I have not made this speech before... so listen carefully. I am the best. Not the best around. Not the best in the U.S.A.—or the best in the U.K.... not just that, *The* best! Which means I can take Gawne, or any other goddam jerk, supposing there is a whole wall of 'Ripleys' in the way. I can do it easy, or I can do it hard. I can hit and run, or I can hit and stay and watch. I can send it from the front, or I can send it from the back. You name the way... that is the way I can deliver. With, or without, frills. Knife, gun or strangle-wire. Quick, or slow. Asleep, or awake. Sitting down, or standing up. I do not give one single, spit-in-the-eye damn. I deal in corpse-meat, kid. It is my speciality... and I *specialize*! Okay?"

"Yeah... okay." He swallows, and nods. And I get the

feeling that he is only half-convinced.

I say, "I need the guns upstairs. Get them from the car. Use the rear door... I will walk to the bar and keep tabs on the landlord, and anybody else who happens to be around."

"Whatever you say." There is relief in his voice, and he pushes himself away from the table.

"Do not rush things, kid," I murmur. "Nice and gentle... eh? Nothing zingy, nothing stupid."

He smiles and says, "Of course. Nice and gentle."

All of which is very hot talk... but a neat bundle of pre-packed garbage.

Because, you see, this thing has been screwing itself into reef knots since the launch-pad. Things have gone wrong. Not big things, and not too much wrong... but enough. Enough to let me know that something about this particular pool game annoys the nostrils; that the balls are a little elliptical.

Okay... a killing is on the time-table. But it is a special type of killing. It is a polished killing. It is that, or it is nothing.

What it is not, is a killing which ends a spell of cross-screwing, when some husband finds his ever-loving wife performing between the sheets with his best friend; when the cork pops and hubby smacks and keeps smacking until lover-boy is only a nasty smear on the bedclothes.

It is not that kind of a killing.

Also, what it is not, is a killing which writes "finis" to a boozing friendship; when two jerks soak themselves stupid in tonsil-tonic, then grow muscles they never had before, go into a dark corner and slug each other to find which is going to buy a wreath.

It is not that kind of killing, either.

It is not a muscle-killing... a hoodlum's smash-out,

where the whole countryside is sprayed with slugs, in the hope that one of the slugs might hit what is meant to be hit.

Nor is it a snatch-killing... the unwished for clobbering of some fink who stands in the way of a group of gang-oriented bank-busters, and who must be flattened if the cops are not going to make a very easy arrest.

These killings, and their various permutations, are what this killing is not. It is the opposite to all these killings, in that it is a quiet killing. A secret killing. A very polished killing.

This is what it is—correction... this is what it *should* be!

It should be a very smooth—very simple—execution job.

And that it is working up to be not quite what it *should* be tends to worry me a little.

I stroll into the bar parlor.

The bar parlor is genuine Olde Worlde English, complete with flagged floor, beamed ceilings, wooden forms around the walls and enough horse brasses to make a Clydesdale buckle at the knees. The light is from three hanging Tilleys and four glass-chimneyed oils positioned about the room on shelves and window alcoves; the effect being a mix of eye-scorching white, soft yellow and dark-shadowed corners... something to make any avant-garde Hollywood film-man rhapsodize for hours.

I order a tankard of what Lewis used to wash down his meal and the landlord—a pot-bellied, morose-looking man—bends to fill a pewter mug from the wooden tap which has been knocked into the end of one of a row of benched barrels behind the bar. The liquid leaves the tap thick and brown—the brown of good and well-cared-for saddle-leather—and, as it climbs up the inside of the tankard, it grows a topknot of a million baby bubbles.

It looks what it is. Good ale... expertly brewed, and straight from the wood.

A voice says, "If it's convenient, there's somebody outside who'd like a few words with you."

It is a woman's voice and, at first, I do not realize that the remark is addressed to me.

The voice says, "It might be advantageous to both of you."

I get the message... that she is talking to me. I turn, and look at her.

She smiles, and says, "If you don't mind."

She is a woman... and (okay) that does not tell much. But some women are easy to describe, and some women are hard to describe. With this one, it is impossible. Even to make a guess at her age would be stupid; she is maybe ten years older than I am... equally, she is maybe ten years younger than I am. She is ageless; she looked as she looks now, the minute she left girlhood, and she will look the same until the day she takes her last breath. She is thin—almost angular... but she is not without shape. She is not beautiful, but she has poise.

But (and this above all else) she is *peaceful*. It is the only relevant word... "peaceful." She is more than relaxed... she is at rest. She personifies tranquility and, just as it is comparatively easy to describe a raging storm, but near-impossible to describe the sense of stillness which follows that storm, so it is almost impossible to adequately convey the aura of quiet amity which is part of this woman... and the part that hits you the minute you see her.

She smiles, again, and repeats, "If you don't mind."

I nod, and say, "Yeah... sure."

The landlord puts the tankard on the bar-counter and, to him, I say, "Thanks... I'll be back."

Then, I go outside.

It is mid-evening and the thermometer has dropped to

a couple of degrees below freezing. There is a mean breeze coming in, across the moorland, from the east and, with it, the first flakes of what could build up to a blizzard.

Outside, parked on the verge, there are a couple of Land Rovers, a van, the Volvo and a Rover saloon. The lights of the Rover saloon are switched on and, in the combined backwash from the dashboard and the glow from the windows of *The Plough*, I can see him sitting in the front passenger seat.

David Gawne. A little grayer about the temples, a little more lined about the face . . . but, apart from these small things, the same guy.

David Gawne!

LONDON.
MAY—1948.

Gawne raised his glass, and said, "To memories . . . the good and the bad."

Fleischer sipped the Cognac in reply to the toast.

It was the end of . . . we-ell if not of a "beautiful friendship," at least of a very successful partnership. It had started, almost three years previously, in a bomb-smashed booze-room on the outskirts of a defeated capital, and it was ending here, in the plush American bar of another capital which also carried its marks of bomb-bruising and, between the two—between the meeting and the parting—a lot of money had been made across the bleeding corpses of men who had deserved to die.

It was a consolation . . . of a sort. But, good or bad—sufficient or insufficient—it was the only consolation available.

Fleischer had earned a reputation . . . a reputation which was almost on a par with that of Gawne himself. Not merely as a killer; in hard statistics, he'd only squeezed a trigger three times. But his reputation was that of a "frightener." He represented "the final warning," sometimes merely

spoken but, more often than not, accompanied by
pain. His visit was always the last "or else..." and,
with it he had learned to bring terror. Not the
blustering, extrovert terror of the average heavy.
Not the sneering, self-indulgent terror of the sadist.
But, instead, a terror which was peculiar to himself;
a quiet, unemotional terror, which stopped its ears
to pleas and was unaware of agony-induced
screams. Fleischer's reputation was built firmly
upon an ability to terrorize...to be without
mercy...to be devoid of all humanity.

Some goddam reputation!

"Where now?" asked Gawne.

"Home...where else?"

"Home?" Gawne raised a quizzical eyebrow.

"The States," said Fleischer.

"There should," observed Gawne, "be pickings
enough there. They know you. Word gets around."

"Yeah."

Gawne tasted Cognac, hesitated a moment, then
smiled, and said, "Advice...are you past it?"

"Not from the right person."

"Good." Gawne nodded, slowly. He said, "In
that case—for what it's worth—don't commit
yourself to any one employer. Be freelance. If you're
good enough, they'll come to you...and the harder
it is to come, the more they'll be prepared to pay. It
also gives you freedom of choice. To accept, or to
refuse. Stay freelance...always."

Fleischer twisted his lips into the beginnings of a
cynical grin.

He said, "Yeah...that way, I can chop anybody
in the whole goddam world."

I walk up to the parked Rover and, as I approach, Gawne
winds down the window.

I move my head in silent greeting. I say nothing; it is *his*
ball game, therefore he makes first play.

He looks up at me, and says, "Thanks."

I look him a question, but stay quiet.

"For coming out. Belle said you wouldn't."

"Belle?"

"My wife."

"Oh . . . yeah."

"She was wrong."

"Yeah . . . she was wrong," I agree.

"I was sure—damn sure—you'd come out. You'd be curious. You'd have to know who . . ."

I begin, "If she'd said . . ."

"Naturally." He nods his head and there is sardonic sadness in the movement. "That's why she didn't say."

I grunt something which means nothing . . . a noise which, in the wind, I doubt if he even hears.

"Caution," he muses. "Caution and curiosity . . . they make one hell of a combination."

I wait and, as I wait, I grow colder The wind comes like it is from an open fridge door and (maybe I am imagining it) the flakes seem to be coming faster by the second.

"Life?" he asks.

"It goes on," I admit, carefully. "And you?"

"From the navel up." He glances at where his knees are wrapped in plaid blanket. There is no bitterness, but a soft underflow of cynical humor, as he adds, "South of the navel, it stopped some time ago."

"Yeah . . . I heard."

"You, too. People bring me news."

"About me?"

"About a character called Fletcher . . . David Fletcher."

I relax a little of the deadpan expression from my face.

Gawne says, "He travels. And, when he travels, he travels for a purpose."

"Is that so?"

"That's what people tell me."

I growl, "People make mouth noises."

"Agreed."

"So?"

"He has a reputation. That much, at least, is true."

Again, I wait for it... whatever "it" is. Something is easing its way to the surface but, as yet, I do not know what. Therefore, I wait and, as I wait, I grow colder. I jerk up the collar of my jacket and push my hands into the jacket's pockets.

"I won't keep you." Gawne smiles, and the smile has an odd, innocent quality. "Winter, in these parts, can be rough."

"Yeah... you can say that again."

"Christmas?" he asks and, in the question, the eyebrows raise politely.

"It will be soon here. Soon gone," I admit.

"See it in with me," he says, softly. "For the sake of old times."

The proposition rocks me. It is so unexpected... so goddam stupid. I figure some of the shock must have worked its way into my expression, because he watches my face and a slow smile grows around his mouth.

"Why not?" he says. "I've few friends. Only Belle ... and she leaves, tomorrow morning, to visit her family for a few days."

I watch his face. I watch his eyes and the tiny muscles around his mouth and jaw. I search for something—anything!—which might hint at what goes on under that graying wig.

There is nothing... only apparent friendliness. Only what looks to be pleasant honesty.

He murmurs, "Unless, of course, you've made other plans. If you've already..."

"No." I shake my head. "Nothing. I have nothing fixed."

"Well?" He raises his eyebrows, moves his shoulders and tilts his head to one side as he waits... and the bend of his lips form a smile which has "Welcome" written all over it.

Between my ears, a lot of work is going on. I am adding things up; I am making two and two come to four . . . and, sometimes, a little more than four. I am remembering things about this guy. What he once was, and what he now is. His strength and his weaknesses. His advice and cunning.

"Well?" he says, again . . . and it is a reasonable question, without push and without guile.

I make up my mind.

I say, "Okay. It might be interesting."

"To talk about old times."

"Yeah."

"Shall we say nine o'clock?" He looks a polite enquiry. "Will that be convenient?"

"I'll be there," I agree.

"Good. I'm already looking foward to it."

There is nothing else to say. The goolie—supposing there is one—has been dropped and is not too hot to retrieve. I have said "Yes" when, maybe, I should have said "No" . . . but, on the other hand, maybe "Yes" was the right answer, and "No" would have been the wrong answer. It happens that way, sometimes. A choice . . . and only time decides whether the choice is a good one, or a bad one.

As now.

Time will decide.

I turn and walk back to the inn. The woman is coming out, and we pass each other at the door, but do not speak. She does not even look at me.

Inside the inn, I turn down the collar and shake the dusting of snow from my jacket before I walk into the bar. The pewter tankard is waiting for me, on the counter, and I drain half its contents in a single swallow.

It tastes good ... and I needed it.

God, did I need it!

I finish the booze more slowly, and mix its taste with the taste of good pipe tobacco. I keep clear of the handful of customers, use the bar-counter as an elbow rest, and set my mind swimming around in deep waters.

I do what I should not do; what, with men like myself, unstitches the seams and spills out much of the stuffing. I take a long, hard look at myself.

Understand me, it is not self-pity. I regret nothing. We-ell—maybe that is not quite accurate ... I regret the effect a little, but I do not regret the cause which has led to that effect. Take any one moment in my life and, for what it has given me, I would re-live it. At the time, I may have hated that moment but, in retrospect, each moment was necessary—each moment was vital—if I was to become what I wished to become.

What I *am*.

It is the "what I am" part which throws me a little ... and not even wholly "what I am." It is the part which is a spin-off from "what I am."

Logically (and, to stay on an even keel I must deal in logic) I am no more—no less—than a slaughterman. I kill animals ... as does any working slaughterman. And (again, logically) that the animals I kill happen to be human animals makes me no worse—no better—than any expert employed by an abattoir. I kill as quickly as he does. I kill as cleanly as he does. My hatred for what I kill is no greater—no less—than is his hatred.

And, if he can slaughter one animal and love another—if he can butcher a steer and keep a hound as a pet, if he can kill and skin a sheep, yet love and have deep feeling for a horse—why, for Christ's sake, can't I? What has he got that I do not have? What is so damn sacred about the human species—about certain members of the human species—which makes their removal a sin? What makes the man who removes them a creature to be spat upon? What makes him, if not ashamed, at least secretive about his trade?

What the hell is this hypocrisy, and why am I part of it?

I am good—I am the best in the world, at my own craft . . . so why the hell should I feel shame?

If, indeed, I *do* feel shame . . . and, even upon that point, I am not too sure.

And, if it is not shame, what the hell is it?

What the hell is this feeling which gnaws at me—this feeling which started when I bedded a dame who taught me a little about highbrow music—which turned me into a sulky, half-scared kid in the presence of a man dead from the waist down . . . what the hell *is* it?

It must have a name, but I cannot put a name to that name . . . and this annoys me.

So—what the hell!—up it . . . whatever it is.

I finish the drink and make my way towards the bedrooms.

And now we are getting things ready; we are in the bedroom—my bedroom—with the door locked and the curtains drawn, and the guns and the gloves, and everything else we need, are out and ready to be fixed for use.

We are each wearing surgical gloves, and the gloves are fixed at the wrist by means of surgical tape; the way—the only cast-iron way—to make damn sure no dabs find their way onto inconvenient surfaces.

We have cheese-cloth . . . two rolls. We have surgical spirit. We have a roll of inch-wide surgical tape. We have gun-oil. And (because this is the sort of place where such things are still found) we even have an open fire in the bedroom . . . a thing I had not counted on, but a thing I am delighted to have.

Lewis does what he is told. Exactly, and nothing more. He knows, because he is no mug, that what happens here in this bedroom could make the difference between freedom, or a long hard lie on a prison cot.

Me? . . . as usual, I am very careful.

There is a triple-layer of cheese-cloth, a yard wide, along the top of the bedclothes; a layer of cloth thick enough to soak up any stain, before that stain can reach the bed linen. This (as I have already explained to Lewis) is where we place things as, and when, they are dealt with . . . and not before.

We start with the shotgun case. We empty it; take out the Winchester, the gun-oil container, the cleaning rods and the magazine plug. Then we clean the case; we sponge the felt lining with cheese-cloth soaked in spirit to remove any dust particles then, using a fresh spirit-soaked cloth, we sponge the exterior of the case to remove all fingermarks . . . not forgetting the metal surfaces of the clasps and locks. Then the gun-oil bottle, the cleaning rods and the magazine plug.

As we clean each item we place that item on the bed.

I say, "Handle it, kid. Every piece. Turn it in your fingers—check exactly where your fingers can go . . . and that spot needs a good rub down. Okay?"

Lewis nods, and works in silence. He is remembering everything . . . every word I say, and every tiny thing we do.

Then the gun; the barrel, the stock, the slide handle, the tubular magazine, the trigger and the trigger guard. Everything! Lewis cleans it thoroughly, then hands it to me and I, too, clean it. I then take a square of cheese-cloth, drop a touch of gun-oil (my own, not the grade which came with the shotgun) onto the center of the cheese-cloth, work it into the fabric and rub over all the metal parts of the shotgun, to counter any effect which the spirit might have upon their respective efficiencies.

Then, the shotgun, too, goes onto the bed.

I say, "Okay. That is one piece made clean. Now, burn all the cloths we have used . . . we start on the Smith and Wesson with everything new. That way, there is no possible connection between the two guns."

With the S and W we take even more precautions. Everything gets burned, except the handgun itself; the case, the cleaning gear . . . the lot!

Having cleaned it—cleaned, and re-cleaned every square millimeter of its exposed surface with surgical spirit—having oiled it and tested its action for smoothness, I place the automatic on the bed and take scissors and cut some surgical tape into calculated lengths and widths.

The kid watches, and does not understand.

He wants to say something; to ask questions.

He gets as far as, "What . . ."

"Just watch." I growl. "It is a trick the mobsters of the thirties thought up. Gloves—gloves are okay . . . but, wear gloves when you should not be wearing gloves, and the other guy gets certain ideas. This way, even without gloves, the gun stays clean."

What I do next takes practice . . . but I have had plenty of practice.

I bind the tape around the stock of the automatic. Single-thickness, in order not to make the gun bulky and awkward to handle. High enough up the stock to make sure that the grip is easy and firm, but without skin touching the metal. Low enough down to bring the tape in line with the surround of the magazine housing.

Then I take some very narrow lengths of tape and bind

the trigger and the trigger-guard.

I re-test the gun's action; checking that the tape is not likely to hinder its smooth working.

Finally, I take a razor blade. Carefully—gently—I slit the tape covering, down the rear of the stock, around the front and side of the trigger-guard, behind the trigger.

I view my handiwork, glance at Lewis, and say, "Get it?"

"I think so," he murmurs... but does not sound too sure.

"It can be used." I hold the S and W on my open palm. "With, or without gloves. With gloves... okay. Without gloves, all you have to do is tear away the tape—from where I have cut it... still okay. The dabs are on the tape, the tape is destroyed... the gun stays clean. There are ways around everything, kid. All you need is to know them." I toss the S and W onto the bed, and say, "Okay... now we fix the ammo."

We open the boxes. Still wearing surgical gloves, we clean all the twelve-gauge cartridges, and all the 9 mm Luger ammunition for the S and W automatic, then we load the guns.

There is (I have already said) an open fire in the bedroom. There is also an old-fashioned scuttle, loaded with coal... coal in shiny cobs the miners themselves use. We build up the fire and, when it is going good, we burn all the boxes and all the packing we do not want, including the box in which the Smith and Wesson was housed. We wrap the guns in cheese-cloth and fix the cheese-cloth into position with more surgical tape. The same with the spare ammunition... we wrap that up, also, in bundles of cheese-cloth. Then we remove the strip of cloth from the bed, and burn that too.

There is nothing left... except two guns and ammunition.

I strip off my surgical gloves, and the kid does likewise.

"That's it?" he says, and the words are something of a question.

"That," I say, "is it. All we need now is a timetable."

"And?" There is suppressed excitement in his voice.

I check my watch. It is twenty after ten.

I say, "The bar is not yet closed."

"We're residents. We can..."

"I could do another drink," I say.

He looks puzzled, then says, "I thought you didn't drink."

"Rarely," I admit. "I figure that the muscle-power needed to lift booze from waist-height to mouth-height does not amount to much. It does not make anybody Tarzan."

A slow grin creeps across his face, and he says, "Y'know what? I do believe you're tightening up. I do believe, as we get nearer the hit, you want a little—just a *little*—Dutch courage...even you."

I eye him coldly, and snarl, "Do not psychoanalyze me, junior. Do not play at guessing what makes me tick...ever! That is a thing I do not like."

Okay...so he is right.

I need a drink. Not because we are nearing a hit, but because we are nearing this particular hit. The Gawne Hit...and, in my mind, I have already given it that title, complete with capital letters.

PITTSBURGH.
NOVEMBER—1939.

To kill a dog...and for no reason, other than that you wish to kill a dog...other than that you wish to illustrate what an unbelievable bastard you are...other than that you wish to break a teenage kid's heart...other than that you wish to hear a

dumb animal scream in pain, and smash a fellow
human being, young enough to be your own son...

I sit at a table in a darkened corner of the bar parlor. I sit
hunched over the table, and nurse the glass which holds
the triple whisky. I nurse the glass in both hands—folding
my fingers around the contours of the glass in a
half-fist—and, at regular intervals, I raise the glass to my
lips and take a mouthful of the spirit. It is neat whisky,
and strong whisky, and it burns as it hits my throat. I want
it to burn. I want it to cauterize everlasting wounds. I
want it to burn away certain memories. I want it to blaze
up inside me, and purify me... take away the bitterness.

Instead, it makes me even more bitter.

It releases the memories. Colors them. Burns them
even deeper.

The freight-yard guard said, "That your dog, kid?"

He had a high-pitched voice—a pansy's voice,
and especially for a man so heavy with muscle—and
he pronounced the word "dog" all wrong. He made
the word a mild obscenity. He pronounced it
"dawg."

"Yeah." Young Fleischer nodded. He was
scared—there was that about this man which was
terrifying . . . a glowering, sub-humanity which
equated with torture-chambers and the evil which
only comes with diseased minds. Fleischer swallowed and, with the spittle, tried to swallow some of
his fear. He said, "Yeah... she's my dog. She ain't
doing anybody any harm."

"You reckon?" The guard moved his lips into a
sneer, and the tiny, piggy eyes gleamed hatred.
Hatred which sprang from no better reason than
that a teenage kid had the gall to defend his mongrel
dog. The guard squeaked, "Seems to me that dog's
trespassing, kid. It ain't no business depositing it's

shit around this here freight-yard. No more than
you have any business lifting things that don't
belong to you from these freight wagons."

"She—she ain't messed nowhere," muttered
Fleischer.

"That's what you say."

"She's a good dog, mister. Honest . . . she's a real
good dog. She's obedient. Y'know . . . obedient. Tell
her to do a thing, and she'll . . ."

Fleischer stopped talking. His words trailed off
into horrified silence as he watched the guard's
hands.

The guard switched his bobby-stick from his
right to his left hand. With his free hand he pushed
aside the skirt of the knee-length storm-coat. He
reached high, to his waist, unclipped the flap of the
holster and brought out the gun.

One hell of a gun. A big gun . . . a big gun, whose
stock disappeared in the curled maw of the man's
big hand. A revolver—a .45 . . . which made it a very
big revolver.

"Hey, mister. Please! PLEASE!"

Fleischer dropped to one knee on the rough,
snow-blown ground. He wrapped his arms around
the neck of the dog and gazed up at the bastard with
the gun. He tried to find words—words which might
release something akin to mercy from this man who
was about to do the unforgivable . . . but what words
he knew he also knew to be insufficient.

The dog raised its head and licked Fleischer's
cheek. Its long, stupid tail scythed the dusting of
snow as it proclaimed its love for its master . . .

The kid walks across. He eyes me uneasily before he
speaks.

"You okay?" he asks.

I growl, "Yeah . . . I am fine." I finish what is left of the
whisky, hold the empty glass out to him, and say, "Same

again...eh? Double the measure, this time. A man's drink. Six whiskies...neat."

Lewis gasps, "For Christ's sake! You'll be..."

"Does it matter?" I rasp. "To you—to any bastard...does it matter? I drink myself stupid. I drink myself to death. Does it matter? To you?...to anybody? Do not con me, junior. There would not be one damn wreath. Not one damn mourner."

The kid hesitates, then takes the glass and returns to the counter. I watch him as he orders. I see the look of surprise on the landlord's face...then the shrug of phlegmatic resignation.

The kid brings the booze and places it on the table in front of me. A new glass—a tumbler—filled with liquid forgetfulness.

I curl my fingers around the glass and raise it to my mouth.

I am going to forget.

Goddam it—whatever it costs—I am going to forget!

To kill a dog...and for no better reason than that you are a bastard...for no better reason than that you are kill-crazy, and that to kill a man—to kill a teenage kid—might give rise to awkward questions...therefore, to kill a dog...and that the dog has done you no harm, and will do you no harm, is not material...merely that something has to forfeit its life for the sake of a reputation which already stinks...therefore, a good enough reason to kill a dog...

The lights in the bar parlor are unsteady; the shadows and the yellows sway, as if in variant wind, but there is no wind in this room and the glass-chimneyed flame which gives birth to the yellows (and also the shadows) sways as wildly and as immoderately as the yellows and the shadows to

which it gives birth. Nor is the white-hot mantle of the
pressure-lamp a thing of restful stillness; it swings, and
sometimes rises and falls as if suspended upon oscillating
elastic and the fat, eye-scorching mantle is no longer
fat—is no longer a mantle . . . it is an imprisoned meteor
which ducks and arcs, leaving a quickly extinguished tail
of elongated light, blue-tinged at the edges and never still.

And, in this restless light, the walls themselves seem to
move. To shimmer and lean a little. The ceiling lowers,
then highers, then rises higher than it was before. And the
flagstones of the floor ripple gently—I can feel them
ripple under my feet . . . like the warning nudge before the
onset of an earth-tremor. And the furniture—and the
barrels—and even the people . . . the landlord, Lewis and
the handful of cronies who have stayed to drink well past
the lawful o'clock.

Everything is movement. Swaying, pitching-and-
tossing movement. Like a slow-motion, storm-caught
ship . . . and only I am still.

Still and hot. I am not hot—stifling hot . . . and for no
good reason.

I slop whisky into my mouth in an attempt to counter
the heat. To quench the dry-mouthed thirst which is a
concomitant to this unreasonable and mysterious heat.

The guard thumbed back the hammer of the
revolver as he brought it clear of his storm-coat. He
thumbed back the hammer with a thumb as thick
and ugly as a blanched gherkin and, at the same
time, threaded a frankfurter finger through the
trigger-guard and around the trigger.

He squeaked, "That dog ain't gonna be no damn
good to you where you're going, kid. The judge ain't
gonna let you come back to no dog, that for a
clincher. You ain't gonna need no dog for a long
time, kid . . . not after what I tell that judge. And you

know what that means? It means that there dog of yours is gonna be a stray... and there ain't but one thing to do with stray dogs."

The guard's lips bowed into a leering, Jack-o'lantern grin as his finger eased back the trigger.

Fleischer hugged the dog and began to scream. "No!"... but the scream was smashed into a sobbed hiccup of silence as the bobby-stick landed on the side of his head and knocked him clear of the dog.

Then the gun spoke.

Its voice echoed around the freight-yard and ricocheted from the freight wagons; its lungs were cordite and its tongue was flame, and its single, roaring word was one of agony which brought a high keen of pain from the wounded dog.

Fleischer pushed himself to his hands and knees, and made as if to crawl to his mortally injured animal... to give it succor and comfort as it died.

The guard kicked him away. It was an off-handed—almost lazy—swing of the heavy, high-laced boot, delivered as the guard tucked the revolver back into its holster; a side-of-the-neck kick which was merely an extra minutia of an overall and terrifying evil.

Then came the beat-up.

Round-arm blows and full-muscled thrusts with the bobby-stick. Kicks in the ribs, and the stomach, and the small of the back. A dragging into an upright position by means of a handful of hair. Forehand and backhand slaps, until his head rocked like that of a broken doll. Then more kicks, and more blows, and more slaps. Pain—an involved kaleidoscope of pain... a million different pains, and every pain a different color.

And, as background music to the pains, the screaming of the wounded dog. And, as the pains increased, the screams became weaker, and moved into the lower key of agonized whimperings.

The beat-up ended and the guard dragged Fleischer off, towards the guard-hut at the entrance to the freight-yard.

Fleischer saw his dog for the last time. It was past voice, and almost dead. Its hindquarters were smashed and caked in blood, but its eyes were wide and, behind the gathering glaze of death, the eyes asked a question...a question which Fleischer knew he could never answer.

I mumble, "Y'know what? He was a bastard. A very nasty bastard indeed...period. He was the first I'd ever met—y'know...the first real bastard I'd ever met. I didn't know they were around. Not his sort...y'know—*real* bastards. He was the first. Like every other cop in creation—eh?...a bastard."

In a soothing voice, Lewis says, "Sure. Sure."

He hoiks my right arm more firmly across his shoulders and grips me around the waist with his left arm. The landlord has my left arm across his shoulders and he, too, has an arm around me at rib-level.

Lewis does not know what the hell I am talking about. He does not know—he does not care...but, one day he will know, and one day he will care. Like me, he will learn the hard way...and then he will know.

The landlord does not care what the hell I am saying. His profession includes minding his own business...and this he does well.

Their present problem is getting me upstairs and into the bedroom of *The Plough*, and it is not an easy problem. The quick consumption of concentrated booze has filleted me. I am a thing of sponge rubber, and without bones; my legs drag behind me and my feet twist and turn at all and every angle.

The stairs are wide enough for two, but not quite wide enough for three. They would have found things easier, had they taken one end each; one at the feet and one at the shoulders. It would have been a little less dignified as far as I am concerned...but ask me whether I give a damn about dignity at this moment in time. However, it is their problem and, if they wish to do things difficult and fancy, let them go ahead...screw them!

On the landing, my right foot hooks itself around a fire-bucket and plays awkward. It will not come loose. It slides up the side, and tips the bucket, and the sand spills out onto the polished wood of the floor.

My eyes focus in on the sand. It reminds me of something...something *I* once did...something *I* should do...something. I stare at the sand and, as we struggle past the overturned fire bucket, I twist my head to keep the sand in my line of vision.

What?

What about the goddam sand?

What the hell is there about the spilled sand that I should...

Lewis gasps, "For Christ's sake!"

I move my head in a series of slack-necked nods, and mutter, "Okay, kid. Don't wet your nappies...everything's going to be okay."

"And shurrup," he growls, warningly.

Like I have already said (so many times) this kid has all his fuses intact. He knows when to sound the alarm bell...when to blow the hooter for a close-down.

I grin across at him, and say, "Lewis, I love you. You are everything I once was, myself. You are so goddam sharp...you are gonna slit your own sweet gizzard one day. You are gonna bleed all over the landscape, and I am gonna be the only punk around who is weeping."

He needs what breath he has left for hauling me through the bedroom door, therefore he does not answer.

They toss me onto the bed, hoist my legs into line with

the rest of me, pull off my shoes, loosen my tie, throw an eiderdown over me, then leave me with my booze.

In five seconds, flat, I am asleep.

It is thirty after four, in the morning.

My head feels like I have traded in my brain for a trip-hammer and, if doom is due to crack within the next five seconds, I must still find time to douse myself under cold water.

I feel my way along to the bathroom, use my lighter to tease flame around the wick of the oil-lamp, then shove my head under the tap and let liquid ice make a new man of me.

I walk back to the bedroom and, in the flame from my lighter, I see the spilled sand, still on the floor of the landing.

Back in the bedroom, I light the lamp, unlock the wardrobe door and take out the guns and ammunition. I pull on the surgical gloves, unwrap the guns and ammo from their cheese-cloth coverings and make a careful check.

The thing is to trust nobody... but *nobody*!

And tomorrow night—correction, tonight—I have a date with a man I am due to chop... and always, at the back of my mind, is the knowledge that the man I am due to chop has, himself, chopped more men than I have. He was once what I am... and, possibly, still is. He is dangerous. As dangerous as Joe Gallo—as dangerous as Pete Diapoulas... and maybe, more dangerous than either.

I check the guns. I fix the ammo. I re-wrap everything in cheese-cloth. I position things in the back of the wardrobe... noting exactly, and to the hair's-breadth, where everything is. I take off the surgical gloves and lock the wardrobe door. Then I undress, turn out the lamp and climb into bed.

From the bed I can see the window and, away to the east, a dirty gray is smudging the horizon...the sun is forcing itself to take another peek at a lousy world.

I turn my back on it, close my eyes and hope I am going to dream about nicer things.

More ham, more eggs—this time with fried bread and tomato—and this time with a liberal spraying of Yorkshire Relish...the thin variety. Yorkshire Relish, because Yorkshire Relish is really Worcestershire Sauce, with an extra kick...and the nearest thing you can get to a Bombay Oyster short ot the real thing. It bites its way through the film of morning-after muck which lines my mouth; it scours my throat and, when it reaches my guts, it will scour them, too.

By the time I reach the home-made bread, home-made butter and home-made marmalade, my taste buds are cleaned and I can enjoy their honesty.

"You were," remarks Lewis, "stoned, last night."

I concede the point; that, last night, I was a little gassed.

"Why?" he asks.

"Because the moonshine they serve at this place has a fair-sized kick."

He says, "I'm serious," and I watch his face as he says it, and I know that that is what he is.

I shrug and watch him chew ham for a few moments.

"I mean it," he insists.

"Okay...so you mean it."

"Look..." He uses his empty fork for a baton, and conducts his own conversation across the table from me. "If you turn up at Gawne's place pissed to the wide—like you were last night...even half as drunk as you were last night. If you do *that*..."

He leaves the rest of the argument unspoken.

I try to look interested, and say, "I have you, little man.

You are my safety net . . . as always."

"For Christ's sake!"

"Okay." I am already tiring of his yap. I say, "If I am stoned, Gawne will do the bopping . . . not me. I will be the one to get bopped. It will, at least, be a novelty."

"Look. What sort of . . ."

"Meanwhile, you will be on hand with the twelve-gauge. He can't shoot in two directions at once. Even Gawne can't do that! So-o . . . one squeeze on the trigger, kid. That is all. You have earned yourself a reputation . . . and Darley's undying love. For what that is worth."

It stops him. He looks worried; like he wants to say a lot more things, but is a little scared of the possible come-back. He is still raw—good, but still raw . . . and words still worry him.

I say, "Eat hearty, Lewis. Then, go to the bum who runs this place and tell him we want a late-afternoon meal . . . when we get back. And to have the bill ready."

"Is this . . ." he begins.

"Yeah. Tonight is the night. And I shall be sober. That I promise. So, quit jawing and just eat. While you are fixing things with the landlord, I will load the gear."

I get this impression. That he is not as hungry as he was a few moments ago; that the falling chips are worrying him more than he thought they would worry him. He puts on a front—he still chews his way through ham and eggs and fried bread . . . but I doubt if he is tasting what he is eating.

And now, it is snowing. Large flakes—like blossom petals caught in the high wind—which swing towards the car, touch the windscreen, stay there for a second then, as the conducted warmth of the glass does its work, change from white to pearl and begin to slide down the surface.

We are parked, some few miles inland from the east

coast and, all around us is open countryside. Bleak—the brand of landscape upon which was built the great novels of the Brontë dames... although *their* country is a few score miles to the west. But that brand of moorland. High and harsh; country which, from a distance, looks rolling—mildly undulating—under a cover of now-dead ling, and bracken, and grass which only a moorland sheep can turn into energy. Like that... from a distance.

But come closer, and you see the ravines. The slopes steep enough to make one-in-four seem like level ground. The outcrops of weather-hammered stone. The coppices... spindle-trunked trees, bent against the force of the prevailing wind.

One hell of a country... untamed, because it is untamable.

I know these tops. I have been here, before—not many times... but I have visited them.

The wind never sleeps around here. It dozes a little, for a few days in high summer, and it becomes a breeze, but no zephyr; it still rustles the air, creeps through light clothing and brings on goose-flesh.

Right now, it is blowing a force seven, or eight, and the snow is travelling sideways as fast as it is travelling downwards and, in the gloom of the early evening, visibility is not much more than twenty yards and, after that, there is an opaque curtain of grayness... then nothing.

It is a little spooky sitting here, in the parked car, with the engine ticking over to keep the heater working. We are both smoking—Lewis a cigarette and I my pipe—and this, combined with the hint of warm oil coming in with the heater, and the windows being closed, makes what we are pushing into our lungs something rather special... not nice, but special. It is thick, like the silence has been for the last few minutes; thick, and filled with things.

Thoughts, for example.

This is what is known as "it." When we move, it is the last move before the big moment. When we part, it is to meet again after I have pulled it—or not pulled it . . . as the case may be. Today is today, and this evening is this evening, but tonight—in the early minutes of tomorrow morning—we shall be belting south as fast as the Volvo, the roads and the weather will allow . . . that, or I will be decomposing fast!

And, good as he is—much as I admire his inbuilt panache—I have never worked with this kid before. I suddenly realize that I do not know him as well as I would like to know him . . . but that it is too late.

And that is exactly what it is.

Too damn late.

So, what the hell!

He says, "Christmas Eve," and he says it softly—dreamily—like he has suddenly remembered something which might be important.

I grunt.

So, it is Christmas Eve. People die at Christmas, too. The gravediggers do not have an understanding with Old Nick. People die—lots of people . . . one more will not throw the schedule to blazes.

"It's a thought," he murmurs.

I say, "Okay. Go ahead. Think it."

"Midnight?" he checks . . . for maybe the third time.

"On the hour," I growl. "On the minute . . . or else."

"As punctual as Father Christmas," he promises, with a quick grin.

Me? . . . I am in no mood for grinning.

Nor is he, after that stupid, unfunny remark. He smokes his cigarette pensively for a while then, in a voice which holds just the right mix of curiosity and worry, he asks the question they all ask.

He says, "What's it like?"

"To kill a man?"

I do not hedge—like I did with Valda—because, to this kid, the question is important. He wants to know, because he has doubts and, to have doubts, means that he is not dumb. The stupid bastards—the finks who have mouth, but no brains—they are the ones most likely to skid everything to hell and gone; they are the hotshots of which to beware. They are the clowns who will make it messy; spray the whole damn area with blood and bullets . . . then take time off to puke their guts out.

I have seen them.

I have watched them curl up in a corner and wait for the cops, because they have emptied themselves; that which they thought was pure vinegar has turned out to be weak piss, and has evaporated.

These punks I do not require, but Lewis is not one of them.

He has a question which he wants answered. It is a serious question, and a sensible question, therefore I answer it as well as I am able . . . even though it does not admit of any answer worth the name.

I say, "To kill a man is easy. It is also the most difficult thing in the world. All it needs is a few ounces of pressure on a trigger . . . plus something no man knows whether, or not, he has until he adds those few ounces."

"Cold-bloodedness?"

"Not that." I remove my pipe from my mouth, gather my thoughts into a tight bunch and try to harness them to words which might mean something. "Cold-bloodedness is nothing. It is not an asset. I figure it to be a liability. The syndicate hoods have cold-bloodedness. They want to chop a man—okay . . . they chop him. But they do not give a half-hearted fart who, or what, gets in the way. They kill everybody—maim as many nobodies as necessary—just to reach the one guy they have a bullet for. They are like the monkey and the typewriter. The egg-heads who claim that, given time, the monkey will experiment—given time, and enough permutations, it will end up with a word—given more time, and one hell of a lot more permutations, it will end up having re-written the whole of Shakespeare...that is what the egg-heads argue. Okay...but there is a world of wasted paper, and a forever of wasted time, before that particular trick is pulled. The hoodlums—the cold-blooded bastards—are like the monkey, kid...they deal in unnecessary waste.

"Cold-bloodedness is nothing. I do not rate cold-bloodedness very high in this profession."

"Nerve?" he suggests, quietly.

"Yeah. Nerve...one sort of nerve," I agree. "If nerve is the opposite of nervousness, okay...nerve. To be nervous is to be dead, if the other guy has a shooter. The brand of nerve that makes a guy drive in the Indianapolis...just so long as he has a good machine and knows how to handle it. Anything over that is not nerve. It is stupidity. Courage is maybe a strange word to use. Courage goes with the Congressional Medal of Honor—your V.C.—that sort of crap. But to cool a man—to do it when you are not half crazy with anger, or jealousy, or some other such wind-up—to do it when you are not pumped full of some sort of dope, or booze—to do it, like you might go out and buy tobacco...maybe like you might *sell* tobacco. To sell that other guy's death...I figure that takes some sort of courage. Some sort of nerve. But no medals attached, kid...definitely no medals!"

"And..." The big question stops short of his lips. He wants to ask it, but does not know how.

"What does it feel like?" I ask the question for him. I ask it quietly, and in a soft voice.

He nods, quickly, and says, "Yes...what's it feel like?"

"Nothing," I say flatly. "Like selling tobacco. What does the tobacconist feel? What he feels, you feel...if you are a pro. You have a commodity for sale. A service. You sell it. You do not do a jig if somebody wants to buy it. Why should you? It is there to buy...it is how you earn bread. And that which they are going to box in a coffin is just that... bread. Without it—without what you have made it—you would starve... therefore, you feel nothing."

"No dislike? Dislike of the man you're killing? If not, dislike of the job you're doing? Not even that?" There is a subtle mixture of curiosity and near-disbelief in the questions.

"Nothing," I growl. "Zero... *nothing*! You use a gun... the gun has all the feeling necessary. The same goes for the knife, the rope... whatever else you are using. They matter. You do not. They are all more important than you are. You are merely what makes them work."

He stares at me for a moment, then blows out his cheeks. He takes a few more pulls on the cigarette, then screws it out in the ash-tray.

He murmurs, "It's not easy. Get down to the buttons... and it's not easy."

"Remember that," I warn him. "At midnight, to-night... remember that, kid. That twelve-guage is the heaviest piece of iron you are ever likely to carry."

Maybe he knows what I mean. Maybe not. Either way, it is now too late. The meeting has been arranged... Gawne fixed the o'clock, himself. Darley has been informed; he knows exactly when to surround himself with more witnesses than would fill Madison Square Garden. The Volvo is topped with gas, the oil and the tires have been checked... and we can make it, with a single stop for gas, to the capital any time the urge arises.

I say, "Okay, kid. Back to *The Plough*. We eat... then we part company for a few hours."

From inside, a voice bawls, "Come in! It's open!"

Gawne's voice. A big voice—a man's voice... a voice which (God help me!) for one micro-second makes me want to turn and run.

"Diasc Farm."

Let me tell you...

It is like, when God made the world, He had some garbage left over. He dumped it, then some damn fool built a square, brooding monument to Death itself. It was planned with set-squares, plumb-lines and spirit-levels; a thing of straight lines and right-angles, without a curve to its name; stone built and solid, with a double row of small-paned rectangular windows...and even the windows are as expressionless as a blind man's eyes.

It is a snow-caked building...but it somehow still gives the impression of blackness. It is up this lane—this glorified cart-track—and the lane leads nowhere, and the narrow road from which the lane turns, leads only to the next place...the next place to nowhere!

Friend—I tell you—I have travelled. I have seen the U.S.A.; looked out upon some of the loneliest places on earth. I have mooched around Canada; moved over the tundra, where the next-door neighbor is maybe a few hundred miles of snow away. I have seen Europe, after half a dozen armies have blasted hell and blue blazes out of every living, standing thing in their path. I have seen these things—I have seen them and not been touched...but this place!

It carries a feeling and, when you touch *it,* it touches you back.

It is Diasc Farm.

And, as I pushed my way along the lane, just now, I saw car-tracks. The snow had not yet filled them in, and they reached to the open gates of the Diasc Farm frontage, then formed a double-row where the car which had made them had turned to go back to wherever it came from. And there are marks in the snow, from the gate to the house; half-filled footmarks—strange footmarks, like they were made by somebody (some *thing*)! not yet one-hundred-per-cent up on walking...and the footmarks go up to the house, and into the house, but do not come back.

Could be Gawne himself made those prints—but I doubt it . . . my information is that Gawne cannot even stand, much less walk.

All these things add up—the house, the weather, the footmarks . . . and Gawne. They add up to a spookiness I have not felt for years. They add up to a graveyard feeing. A stupid feeling. But a very *real* feeling.

Which is why I checked that the Smith and Wesson was snug in the pocket of my mac, before I thumbed the bell-push . . . even though I knew it was there, loaded and ready to go.

And now this voice—Gawne's voice—from inside this cubic, tomb of a house . . . and the flicker of panic which dances across my nerve-ends and makes me want to run.

"Come in! It's open!"

I turn the knob—a knob as big as a baseball—push one wing of the double-door and walk into the hall. I close the door behind me.

It is a little like entering a church. It is a big hall. High and wide. The walls are plastered and color-washed, and the ceiling is criss-crossed with beams. It is a little like a vestry, and the furniture is vestry-type furniture; oak and old, heavy and with the dull sheen of beeswax.

For a moment—like some sort of crazy movie-screen shows a split-second projection, under my skull—I see Manhattan. Little Italy. Mulberry Street. Umberto's Clam House. And, through the walls—the walls of the eating joint, which are also the walls of this hall, and which are suddenly made of glass—I see Pete "The Greek" Diapoulas . . . grinning and waiting, and with his finger already crooked around a trigger.

Sweet Jesus!

Then the voice—Gawne's voice—yells, "In here! On

the passage, then first door on the right."

And I follow the instructions. Cat-walking, and ready to dive. With my hand on the S and W. Not scared any more...just ready!

And I open the door, and Pete "The Greek" Diapoulas is not there...and how the hell *could* he be there?

And I breathe normally again.

David Gawne is there, and he dominates the whole damn room. He is in a wheelchair, with a blanket tucked around his knees but, in some strange way, this does not make him a cripple—nothing would ever make David Gawne a cripple...he is too goddam *big* to ever earn that tag. I will tell you what Gawne looks like. Exactly. The Ghost of Christmas Present. That, and nothing else...at this moment, there is no other way to describe this big bastard. You know your Dickens?—*A Christmas Carol*?—the third ghost to visit old man Scrooge? ...Marley, The Ghost of Christmas Past, then The Ghost of Christmas Present? That is Gawne; sitting there, huge and more healthy than any man has a right to be; extrovert, noisy and boisterous; radiating seasonal good-will and self-assurance like they were beams of light.

The wheelchair is his throne and, although there is no cornucopia around, there is a man-sized table to his right hand, and the table is heavy with booze, cigars and cigarettes, and there are four plates, piled high with sandwiches, fruit and mince pies; therefore, he can surely eat, and he can surely drink...and he always *was* merry.

And the room goes with the man. It goes with the hall...but more expensive. It has fitted carpeting; the sort rarely walked upon, outside top-class cinema foyers. It has a fire, which is blasting away at full-sized logs; with an under-the-floor fan which turns it into a young furnace and sends the flames roaring up and into the black, steel hood. It has furniture which matches the room; big furniture; near antique furniture; furniture made to last forever, and made by craftsmen who would walk under a trolley rather than build emporium-salesroom junk.

This is the room, and this is the man who goes with the room.

He waves a hand, and says, "Sit down—take your mac off—sit down in that chair . . . relax for a while, and we'll talk."

The chair he is waving at is a big chair. A very comfortable-looking armchair. It has a very seasonal gimmick leaning against its back . . . a holly wreath.

Gawne says, "Shift it. Put it on the floor, and sit down."

I do that. I also wonder a little. Okay, it is a holly wreath—they are around at this time . . . but it is still a *wreath*!

So-o . . .

I take off my mac and hang it, carelessly, over the back of the chair. Carelessly—but also very carefully . . . so that the pocket in which the S and W is housed, is not too far away.

Then, I sit down, look around me a little more, and see the other man.

As I see him, Gawne makes the introductions.

He says, "Charlie . . . Fleischer—David Fleischer. Fleischer . . . this is Charlie Ripley. I thought you'd like to meet each other."

Cop!

Never mind the name. Never mind that Lewis has already spewed his guts about this guy . . . about this chief superintendent of the local fuzz. Never mind that Lewis's old man was once a grabber, and that he worked with other grabbers, and that this one was one of those he worked with.

This bastard is trough-man. A pig. A nab. There is that

about him which stands him apart; there is the hard mistrust in the eyes, resultant upon listening to too many lies; there are the lines, etched around the mouth corners, which come only with a sardonic humor which, in turn, is what makes a cop continue to be a cop and stay sane; there is the quiet air of arrogance, which is unconscious and which, I do not doubt, he would deny . . . but which is the brand-mark of every top-line cop who has spent a small lifetime being just that bit better than the bastards who are trying to beat him.

For a cop, he is not a physically big man. But tough-looking and compact. He sprawls in an armchair which is a companion to the one I am using, but which (deliberately, at a guess) is positioned in one of the less brightly-lighted parts of the room. He sits with his legs straight, in a V, in front of him and (again at a guess) the legs are not all they should be . . . and the shoes, on the ends of those legs, made the marks in the snow which worried me a little.

He is smoking a pipe . . . and this is odd because, the fact that he is using a pipe the way a real pipe-smoker uses one, chalks a credit mark alongside his name, as far as I am concerned. I have found that, in descending order of popularity, cops who play at pipe-smoking are better than cops who smoke cigarettes, and that cops who smoke cheroots are the very lice of their breed. The few good cops I have ever met—the few who were men first, and cops second—all smoked pipes, and all knew *how* to smoke pipes . . . as pipes, and not as cigarette-or cigar-substitutes.

He nods a greeting, and I nod back at him.

He says, "I've heard a lot about you, Fleischer," and the words have the open vowels and sandpaper texture of Northern England.

"Yeah." I watch his face, and add, "I, too have heard things...about you."

"From young Lewis?" Gawne asks the question, and the question goes with a deep-throated chuckle.

"From Lewis." I turn my attention to Gawne, and use a flat voice, when I say, "This is Christmas Eve, Gawne. Not April Fool's Day. I do not like jokes, at any time. I am allergic to them...like I am allergic to the law."

"Lewis's father..."

"I know all about Lewis's old man." I jerk my head at Ripley, and add, "I also know all about this guy. He has a reputation, in a profession which does not give reputations away with saving-stamps. I would like to know why he is sitting in."

"I told him you were coming. He showed interest."

Ripley begins, "Talking about reputations..."

"I was not," I snap. "To you I was not talking about one damn thing, copper. If I have a religion, that is part of it...not talking to the law."

Gawne does some more chuckling, reaches a hand towards the table, and says, "Bitter lemon...right?"

I am going to tell him where he can squirt his goddam bitter lemon, but he has the top flipped and is pouring it, before I can speak.

He says, "You'd better come up for it, Fleischer. If not, I'll have to swing this blasted chair around...and Ripley's legs are as near useless as makes no bloody difference."

I glance at the cop, and he is watching me with a twisted grin plastered across his face. It is not a nasty grin—not bitter in any way—just sardonic...the thing I have already mentioned.

He says, "Leg-irons. Another gun-happy lunatic who thought he could shoot his way out of trouble."

I growl, "He should have aimed higher, and a little to

the right," and do not mean one damn word I say.

The grin broadens and Gawne gives it the backing of a full-blooded belly-laugh.

"Didn't I tell you," gasps Gawne. "A museum piece. The best in the business—that's what everybody tells me...and he needs clean underpants every time a policeman looks at him."

"I'm not a policeman," growls Ripley.

"Ex," says Gawne.

"There is," I say, "no such animal. Like the unicorn—like the dodo...there is no such thing as an *ex*-cop. He changes the uniform for a box. However long it takes."

"It's a thought," murmurs Ripley.

I push myself up from the chair and go to collect the refreshment. What else? These two have conned me...conned me bald! Gawne I know; he is as slippery as a greased eel, and the cop is his way of slamming the door on any hit which might have been timetabled for this particular night; he knows—too damn right, he knows!— I do not travel to a dump like this except for one reason...and that reason has to be *him*. Ripley?...hell only knows what, about this cop called Ripley. He knows something—but what that "something" is I can only guess at...but, already, I have realized that he is a very wise guy who does not flash his wisdom around like it is cheap coinage.

Gawne works another fast trick. As I reach the table, he pours a beer and hands me that, too.

He says, "Play waiter for us, Fleischer. Take this across the room. Charlie needs to wet his whistle."

I do just that. I play servant-boy to a nab-man...a thing, I would never have thought possible.

Ripley takes it and nods his thanks. Our eyes meet...and (damn the man!) there is a twinkle there which tells me that, to him, this whole get-together is a little jokey, but not a joke in bad taste. There is no hatred. There is no contempt. There is, instead, a subtle and silent offer; an offer of friendship whose only qualification is that I meet it half-way; the friendship of a complete man for somebody he counts as being different, but equal.

He says, "You smoke a pipe?"

"Yeah," I grunt. "I smoke a pipe."

He moves his fingers towards a four-ounce tin which is balancing on the arm of his chair.

He says, "Try it . . . let me know what you think. It's a Christmas present from my wife. Very expensive. Not the usual stuff I smoke. I'm not yet used to it. I haven't decided. Try a pipeful . . . let me know what you think."

Such a little thing.

Common ground—that is what he is telling me . . . that we are both pipe-smokers. That, in this small thing—if in nothing else—we are alike. That, if we start from there . . . who knows?

I hesitated, but the hesitation is so slight as not to mean anything, then I reach down and pick up the tin.

I say, "Thanks."

I return to my chair, take a first sip at the bitter lemon, then place the glass on the carpet and begin to charge my pipe.

It is after eleven o'clock—closing fast towards the thirty-after mark—and midnight, and Christmas Day is not too far away. The draught-induced fire keeps the room temperature warm and cozy but, beyond the walls—beyond the curtained windows—the elements are having a ball; the gale wind is bouncing itself off the stone walls of the house and making the panes rattle and, if there is still snow (and the chances are in favor) that snow is muscling itself into drifts which might take some getting through.

Ripley is toying with his beer. Gawne is pouring booze down his throat like it was water, and his innards were on fire. Me? . . . I have finished the bitter lemon, and am now taking an occasional sip at water with a hint of Scotch to give it taste.

And we are talking.

Correction . . . Gawne is talking. Ripley and I are listening.

Gawne has been yapping for some few minutes, and he has wound himself up into some sort of hellfire sermon based upon a religion peculiar to himself. The Gospel According to Gawne . . . you could call it that. He preaches it with a voice an organ would not be ashamed to own; a voice which has resonance and carry-power; an instrument capable of playing an intricate fugue of argument and counter-argument, with nuances and assertions.

A voice worth listening to, talking words worth thinking about.

He is saying, ". . . that's what the law says. That murder is murder. That a man kills a man, and that's *murder* . . . and never anything else. That justified murder doesn't exist. Manslaughter? Forget all the forensic ribbons and baubles . . . it boils down to watered-down murder. It's still punishable. It's still a crime. It still makes a man a criminal. Infanticide . . . the same thing. Mealy-mouthed bullshit! Murder is murder . . . and, under English law, neither you, nor I—not even the Almighty Himself—can come up with an acceptable excuse."

He pauses, slops booze down his throat, then rumbles, "And that is pure crap. You both know it. Charlie . . . you know damn well that some bastards shouldn't be allowed to live. They shouldn't have been born. They're not of the human race . . . therefore, why the hell must we wait until *they* kill somebody before we, in turn, can bury them? And, come to that, why the hell can't we kill *them*? What the blazes makes them superior to the poor sods they themselves have chopped? What makes them special? What gives you—me, anybody—the right to cream taxes from every man, woman and child, just to keep these miserable creeps in comparative luxury?...and, with some of 'em, it's *real* luxury, to what they've been used to. They're useless. They're parasites. They need removing...and that's *all* they need. Bury them, like the garbage they are."

He stops, because Ripley is grinning at him. It is a friendly enough grin...but a very knowledgeable grin. It says that this cop has heard, has understood, but has not been impressed.

"What the hell's so funny?" growls Gawne.

"You." Ripley bends the grin into an even wider arc.

"I'm damned if I see what's so..."

"Self-justification." The grin becomes vocal and changes into a quiet laugh. "You...of all people. What you were. What—for all I know—you still are. You're justifying your own merchandise."

"Death?" says Gawne in a flat voice.

Ripley nods.

"It was never proved. Nobody ever..."

"Nobody ever *lived* to prove it." Ripley is still smiling, but the words do not have humor. "Proof and knowledge, Gawne. Two different things. They touch, here and there...but not often. Never, as far as you're concerned."

Gawne watches the cop's face, and says, "And you despise me? Is that what..."

"I didn't say that."

"No-o." Gawne moves his head in a slow nod; like the nod of a Mikado in a Gilbert and Sullivan comic opera...exaggerated, but with an under-surface of absolute power. He says, "You don't despise me, Charlie. You're a little envious...that, perhaps. But you don't despise..."

"Why the hell," asks Ripley, "should I be envious."

And now it is Gawne's turn to smile.

He glances at Ripley's legs, and says, "It took a mountain to shove *me* on my backside. With you, all it took was an ignorant bastard with a loaded gun. With me, he wouldn't have lived long enough to put pressure on the trigger. That's the difference. That's why I think you're envious."

The cop gives his lopsided mouth-twist, tastes his beer, then comes back at Gawne's argument.

He says, "If it's confession-time—all right . . . let's be honest. I've killed men. As surely as you have . . . as surely as Fleischer, here, has. You've killed them, personally. I've killed them in the name of the law—on behalf of an outraged public . . . before topping was a thing of the past. Looked at it, that way, we're three killers. None of us have regrets. But that doesn't mean I envy you. Or would have liked to slaughter the hound who crippled me. He was mad. All right—you shoot mad dogs . . . but not bold men. There's a difference. Gallo was mad—mad as a hatter—and if ever a man deserved gunning *he* did . . . but that doesn't mean *I* could have done it. The law . . . certainly. The electric chair . . . you bet! But not to be gunned down by Fleischer. Because that was Gallo's own way, and . . ."

I turn off the conversation. I stop my ears and freeze my face.

Because, suddenly, this conversation has turned dangerous. Deadly dangerous. It is no longer academic. It is no longer the talk between two middle-aged has-beens about once-upon-a-time days.

It is suddenly very personal.

What should have been a secret is, within the walls of this room, an easy talking-point. It is being bandied around as a means of emphasizing an argument which has no real end. It is spoken of, as readily—as off-handedly— as a mention of the weather which is still beating the hell out of the landscape beyond the windows.

I have visions. Quick flashes of mental imagery. Newspaper photographs which I remember ...photographs of which I was the cause. Photographs which I looked at, and which scared the hell out of me; which punched home what I had done, and what those I had done it to might, in turn, do to me.

Joe Gallo and his new bride, cutting their wedding cake...Gallo with a toothy grin plastered across his ugly puss, and the dame glancing sideways at the camera, to make sure she is giving a good profile.

Photographs...

The wife of less than a month—Sina Gallo—snapped by a newsman as she walked away from Beekman-Downtown Hospital, with her ten-year-old daughter...the new widow, now not giving a damn about profiles and with the hell of mental agony stamped across her face.

More photographs...

Guido's Funeral Home in New York...the five-thousand-dollar bronze casket, lid open and corpse stiff for all to see...the banks of flowers—as if a surfeit of beauty might counter some of the rottenness...Gallo's mother, black-frocked and fat-faced from weeping, being helped down the steps of Guido's Funeral Home, before she joined the twenty-six-strong cortege of limousines which snaked its way to Brooklyn's Greenwood Cemetery...Gallo's sister, Carmella Fiorella, blonde-haired and doped to hell, fur-coated over a mourning dress and carrying a look of everlasting hatred which had been caught and frozen by the camera...Pete "The Greek" Diapoulas, not giving a damn that every news-lens in sight was being trained on him; immaculately dressed, face shaved to a shiny smoothness; black hair beautifully trimmed and groomed; arrogant in the knowledge that every cameraman and every newshound covering the gang-war was busy finding fresh ways to underline the certainty that nothing—nothing short of the casket he was following—would ease the pressure until he'd gunned the man who'd gunned his boss.

Photographs...

They were old. Long-used and long-filed-away. They were no longer news. They told the pictorial details of a gangland killing...the violent death of a man who did not deserve to live.

But I remember them, in detail. Every face on every one of them. Some of them are already dead, but they are all ghosts—ghosts imprinted upon negatives, stored away in newspaper offices...ghosts which have haunted me, and which will always haunt me.

Because...

"What was the price?" asks Gawne.

I blink myself out of Memory-Land.

"Gambino," says Gawne, gently. "How much did he pay? As I recall, you always charged ten thousand...the currency of the country. Did Gambino pay you more? Or was it a cut-price, prestige job?"

"I..." I close my mouth, because my voice is notched too high. I swallow, touch my lips with the tip of my tongue, and regain control of my vocal equipment. I say, "I figure you must mean *something*."

Gawne moves his lips into what might be a smile...but isn't.

I glance at the cop.

The cop is eyeing the froth on the surface of what is left of his beer; he is examining it, like he has just discovered a theory which might make Albert Einstein look a dope.

I shift my eyes back to Gawne and look, not at his face, but at his hands. His right hand is under the blanket which covers him from the waist down . . . and I know damn well what that hand is holding.

"Joey Gallo," murmurs Gawne.

"Yeah . . . I hear he's dead," I say.

Ripley says, "Some time ago. Three years . . . thereabouts," and acts like he is talking to that very interesting froth.

I flick a look at him, and say, "That is what they tell me."

"Which," says Gawne, "would be a hell of a waste of time."

"What?"

"Telling you."

"I don't get . . ."

"Telling *you*. You!"

"That," I say, carefully, "is an opinion."

"It's a bloody *fact*." Gawne somehow makes the words into a shout, but without raising his voice. He snaps, "I'm only dead from the arse down, Fleischer. Above that line I'm more alive than ever."

"So?" I ask, slowly.

"I hear things. From people who don't lie to me."

I move my shoulders, and let things ride. Somebody has to make the next move . . . even if it is only Gawne, moving his trigger-finger. I am in a corner, fenced in by two heavyweights. The only thing I can do is cover up, and wait for an opening.

Ripley ruins the beauty of the froth he has been admiring, by draining what is left of the beer. He holds the empty glass at crotch-level—using both hands—then starts a personal recital. He uses a soft, deep tone of voice . . . as if what he is saying is apropos nothing at all.

He says, "Lewis—young Lewis . . . I knew his father. His father was the most complete bastard I've ever had the misfortune to meet. He was a great policeman, but a disgrace to his profession. They come that way, sometimes. Swine . . . and, the luck of the draw is that they decide to work on our side of the line. Unpopular . . . but bloody effective. He hated crooks. He hated *everybody*. And everybody hated him. His wife—his family . . . everybody!"

He closes his mouth, and there is silence.

I say, "Are you trying to tell me something, copper?"

"Like father, like son," says Ripley, gently. "It's a cliche. But it does happen."

Before I can come back at him, Gawne interrupts.

He says, "Charlie needs another drink, Fleischer."

"Yeah? Well, I'm damned if I'm going to . . ."

"I'm anchored to a chair." There is a pause, of exactly the right duration, before he adds, "And I only have one hand free."

I hesitate then, again, I decide to ride this thing out to the end. And (again) what the hell else? What other options are open to me? Gawne has a bead on me and, supposing I tried for the S and W, he could drop me before my fingers reached the cloth of the mac. Supposing I started to walk out of this room, he could drop me before I reached the door. Supposing anything— supposing I blinked when he did not want me to blink—he could drop me. That is how tightly he has me pinned, and he knows it . . . and he knows *I* know it.

The unknown factor is the cop. But the cop is *not* a cop . . . and, even if he still was, I would not be too sure. Ripley is something I have never met before. Ripley—to be honest, if only to myself—scares the blue hell out of me.

Which all adds up to one large reason for riding this thing out.

I push myself out of the chair, stroll across the room and pour beer into a clean glass. I hold the glass in my right hand, the bottle in my left and, as I turn my wrist to pour, I sneak a look at my watch.

Eight minutes from now, Lewis will come through the door.

And then?

Gawne will start blasting. That is the only certainty available. Everything else is guesswork. Could be I am living the last eight minutes of my life. Could be this cop has a trump card tucked under his cuff. Could be Gawne's first round will not do the trick, and I can make a quick dive for the S and W.

Come to that, could be the damn house will fall down around our ears . . . but I doubt it.

I carry the beer to the cop, exchange the filled glass for his empty one and return the empty glass to the table. I would make a great bar-keeper . . . but it is all killing time.

I go back to my chair, unearth my pouch from my pocket and charge my pipe . . . and, all the time, the other two watch me. I get the tobacco to my liking, give Ripley an enquiring glance then toss the pouch towards his lap.

He catches it, moves his head in a quick token of thanks, then positions his beer on the carpet alongside his chair while he fingers shredded Virginia into the bowl of a well-used Peterson . . . and it is all killing time.

Time is what I need. Time and luck. Not much time, but all the luck available. I can make time . . . but, with luck, it is a matter of taking what is going.

"Darley," says Gawne, quietly.

It is not a question. It is merely a name; a word upon which to peg the undoubted fact that what he does not already know he has long-ago guessed.

"Yeah . . . Darley," I sigh.

"He thinks he's a big man."

"Everybody does," I say. "The whole world is over-populated with pygmies who think they are giants."

"And you?" asks Gawne.

"I have a certain size."

"Big enough—or is it small enough?—to fit into Darley's wallet?"

"You should know," I murmur.

He does not understand.. The crack has flown yards high, above his head.

"You were once his man," I explain.

"Man" And he looks genuinely outraged as he says it.

"He is your friend." I jerk my head in the direction of the cop. "Maybe you do not want him to know. That is your own personal crossword puzzle. But—seeing you brought up the subject—*I* know you have done a freezing job for Darley."

"You miserable bloody hound!" His voice notches up to a steady roar. "*That* orange-skinned baboon! He daren't even *ask*. I picked and I chose...I still do. Not only who I stiffened. But who I stiffened *for*. Not just for bloody money. I had pride. I did what needed doing...and I decided. I *removed* rats...I didn't *work* for them."

He stops for breath.

"That," says Ripley, softly, "is your story. And you're sticking to it."

"If you think, just because you're a blasted copper..."

"I'm not a copper," interrupts Ripley. "Otherwise, I wouldn't be here."

"You're here, because..."

"Because I believe—in part—what you've just said," snaps Ripley. "Because I know we can never prove you've even swatted a fly...much less killed Christ knows how many men. And because I have a perverse sense of humor...I thought it might be a novelty to see Christmas in, in the company of two murdering bastards. *That's* why I'm here. That you invited me is only by-the-way."

Which is what I mean, when I insist that this guy, Ripley, is a very unusual cop...or, if you like, ex-cop. He is curious, and not just nosey. He has guts, and not just brass-necked nerve. He has self-assurance, and not just the blind arrogance of the average, top-line bull.

This man is a cop-in-a-million.

Gawne's face cracks into a grin, and the grin moves into a throaty chuckle.

He says, "Charlie, I love you—you, too, Fleischer ... you're both so bloody *innocent*."

Ripley pouts his lips into a sardonic moue, and moves his head in a cynical nod.

I growl, "Anybody with a gun pointing at his last meal gets very 'innocent' ... if he has any sense."

The chuckle dies and Gawne gets serious.

He says, "We were about to discuss a certain low-life character."

"Darley?"

"Darley is not a fit subject for a serious discussion."

"Then, who the hell ..."

"Carlo Gambino. The man who paid you to chop Gallo."

"Your mouth," I say, warningly. "It needs a little more control."

"Charlie doesn't mind. Charlie ..."

"Charlie," I rasp, "can go straight to hell. That he is here—whether, or not he is here—does not interest me. That your mouth flaps even more than it used to ... that is what interests me, Gawne."

"Now why the blazes," he asks, musingly, "does the name of one man make you sweat? Why? You're top dog, Fleischer. That's what you claim. The king hatchet man in the whole wide world. The big hitter to end all big hitters."

"Big enough," I growl.

"Puny," he sneers. "And how puny? We-ell ... you daren't even use your own name. 'Fletcher.' That's what you call yourself, and that's how big you are—how insignificant you are ... as insignificant as any run-of-the-mill clown who carries the name 'Fletcher.' It suits you, boy. It sums you up. It's one reason why you're here. One reason why I asked you to come. It's why..."

He stops talking.

The interruption is both sudden and absolute.

Lewis arrives. The Winchester, twelve-gauge pump-gun is levelled and steady and his finger is hooked around the trigger.

He stands about three yards to the left of Gawne's chair, sweeps the Winchester in a slow, threatening arc, then opens his mouth to speak.

He is good...but, at the same time, he is lousy. He is doing the right things, and the wrong things, both at the same time.

Ripley...

Okay—Ripley is an uninvited factor. He is something neither of us expected. But he is *there*...and nothing we can do will make him vanish into a genie-bottle. So-o, accept him and ignore him. That he is a cop—that you *know* he is a cop—is a minor nuisance. But nothing more. He is not immortal. He can scare—he can die...he is like every other man. That he knows *you*—that he can put an identity disc around your neck—is of no consequence. It is only as important as you make it. Okay—he knows you...but he is only one trigger-squeeze from *not* knowing you.

Gawne...

Forget the wheelchair, kid. Concentrate upon the guy *in* the wheelchair. He is not shackled...he only *looks* shackled. He is a freelance trigger-man—was, is and always will be—which means he is years better than you yet are...which, in turn, means *he* is the direction from which things are going to hit you. Watch the bastard. Watch him!

All the right things.

All the wrong things.

All at the same time,

And (again) all at the same time, there is noise and there is action.

There is a click, as the hammer on the Winchester snaps home onto a dead cartridge.

There is a crisp explosion—faintly muffled—and the blanket around Gawne's legs flicks outwards as it grows a tiny puncture and, between and above the eyes God gave him, Lewis suddenly has a third eye...an eye which is black, and perfectly round and which, even as it appears, begins to weep blood.

Lewis's head is punched back on its neck. For a split second he looks as if he will fall backwards, then his knees buckle, his center of gravity alters and he pitches forward onto, and across, the Winchester which has slipped from his grasp.

I make my move. I roll sideways in the chair...to snatch the S and W, before diving for what cover the armchair can offer.

Gawne bawls, *"LEAVE IT!"*

And I freeze—with my fingers not quite touching the taped grip...and I freeze because, if I do not freeze I, too, am due the cyclopic eye treatment via the Harrington and Richardson double derringer which is no longer under the blanket and which stares at me, as if anxious to demonstrate that what has happened to Lewis was no fluke.

I freeze then, very gradually, I relax and ease myself back into a sitting position in the chair.

Gawne watches me and, if you want to call the expression on his face a smile, go right ahead...but, for me, it has no humor.

"You're a lucky bastard, Fleischer," he murmurs and, for a moment I do not get the gist of the remark.

Then, it jells.

That which started the sequence of events—the click of
the Winchester's hammer... *and the Winchester was
beaded plumb onto my chest!*

The cop speaks.

He says, "It's a damn good job it was a misfire."

"No misfire," I growl.

"Eh?"

"Not unless sand has explosive qualities. I doctored the
cartridges, last night—took out the powder and shot—
emptied the caps... refilled them with sand." I sigh,
heavily, then end, "For a damn-fool reason."

"Pride?" Gawne asks the question in a low, soft
voice... asking the question, understanding the reason
and knowing the answer.

I nod and mutter, "Yeah... something a little like
that."

"What the hell..." begins Ripley.

"Pride, Charlie," says Gawne. "To be paid to do a job.
To have a reputation, and to be jealous of that reputation.
To make bloody sure nobody else can steal your thunder.
That young punk..." Gawne jerks his head towards the
sprawling, bleeding thing which was once Lewis. "He was
a diversion. A side-show. He wasn't going to chop
anybody... Fleischer made sure of that. Nobody was
going to be allowed to even touch the reputation of the
man who stiffed Joe Gallo." He looks at me, and says,
"Right?"

"Right," I check, gruffly.

Gawne watches my face. I send a silent message, and he
knows the derringer has become superfluous iron-
mongery. He places it on his knee, on top of the
blanket... ready, but no longer deadly.

The cop eyes the body of Lewis with distaste. He is a
cop—an ex-cop—therefore he has to perform certain

specified tricks... and (who knows?) maybe he means them.

"You people!" he snarls. "Judas Christ... you commit murder, according to your own cockeyed rules. You 'chop.' You 'hit.' You 'stiff.' The hell with all the fancy names... you *murder*. And you think you can get away with it."

"Charlie." Gawne uses a coaxing, mocking tone. "You were here. You saw what happened. Some young hooligan—some young tearaway... you know him, do you?"

"You know damn well I know him."

"Really? I don't. Fleischer doesn't... ask him." Gawne glances at the body, then at me, and says, "Do *you* know him, Fleischer?"

"I have never," I say, "seen the creep before in my life."

"See?" Gawne grins at the cop who looks like he has had boiling oil injected into his blood stream. "So-o... what happened, Charlie, is this. This tearaway—this *unknown* tearaway—rushes in here, waving a shotgun. He is liable to kill somebody. He is liable to kill *you*... and why not? There are a lot of mad young bastards who hate the fuzz. And, to them, you're still fuzz. Charlie. An opinion—for what it's worth—you're the one he was here to shoot. And in *my* house. And you're *my* guest. He even pulled the trigger... but, unfortunately, it was a misfire."

"It was no bloody misfire," hoots the cop. "Sand! The flaming cartridges are..."

"Ah—but I wasn't to know that, Charlie... now, was I? What I saw—what *you* saw—was a homicidal maniac, ready and eager to blow somebody's skull off. Luckily— very luckily—I had this little thing handy." Gawne touches the derringer with a forefinger. "I did the natural thing. I shot back. I'm—er—not too good a shot."

"You," snarls the cop, "could take the pips out of a raspberry at a hundred yards. You could..."

"I'm not too good a shot, Charlie," insists Gawne, cheerfully. "I meant to wound him. To cripple the poor, misguided berk. To stop him from killing somebody. Unfortunately, I hit him in the forehead."

There is a hush. A muteness. A silence which is far more than an ordinary silence; a stillness which lasts all of two minutes...so quiet—so complete—that we can hear the whisper of the flakes as the wind brushes them against the outside of the window-glass.

The cop is nailed to the floor. Gawne knows it. I know it. But it takes two minutes of silence for the cop, himself, to learn to live with it. It takes all that time for the steam-pressure to lower—for the blaze to leave the eyes and the jut to pull itself in from the jaw...and for all this to be replaced by a rueful grin of defeat.

As I have already mentioned, this one is a cop-in-a-million. He can take defeat gracefully. He even knows how to laugh, when the joke is on him.

Without rancor—without residual anger—he says, "Gawne...you're a liar."

"Of course," agrees Gawne. "Between these four walls. You know it—I know it—Fleischer knows it...but try convincing the coroner."

"I wouldn't waste my time." Ripley flicks a finger in the general direction of the derringer, and says, "It's probably a daft question. But do you happen to have..."

"A Firearm Certificate? A Gun License?" Gawne puts on a look of mockingly injured pride. He shakes his head and clicks his tongue, then says, "Charlie...would you be here, if I *hadn't*? Would I have conned you into being a witness, and left a loophole that size? I have everything, Charlie. Obviously. I'm a cripple. I live here, alone with my wife. We're isolated. I need *something*...your ex-colleagues all agree. I need something with which to protect myself when naughty men come knocking at my door."

"You are," says Ripley, with real feeling, "the most cunning—the most outrageous—bastard I've ever met ...and I've met more than a few."

"Well, thank you, Charlie. Coming from a man like yourself, I take that as a compliment."

And they grin at each other.

Ripley glances at the stiff, and begins, "I think we'd better..."

"Leave him," says Gawne.

"Look—for Christ's sake—there's a limit. I can't..."

"The telephone isn't working, Charlie."

"Oh!"

"You can't walk far. In this weather, you can't walk more than a few yards."

Ripley looks a little less amused.

Gawne says, "I can't leave here. Not without assistance."

"All right. Fleischer can..."

"Fleischer," says Gawne, "can notify the police, when he leaves." He pauses, gives me a very odd-ball look, then adds, "When he leaves...and, meanwhile, apart from staining the carpet a little, Lewis isn't doing anything particularly urgent. We, on the other hand, have some *very* urgent business to conduct."

And I know that the "we" does not include Ripley, except as an interested spectator. Ripley has fulfilled his function...what remains is a strictly Gawne-Fleischer shindig.

We start slow and easy. Using the weather outside as a simile, we push the conversational bobsleigh down a few gentle slopes before we hit the swoops and bends of the Cresta Run.

The cop listens...interestedly.

Maybe young Lewis takes time off, *en route* to Hell, to also listen . . . if so he, too, must be very interested.

But first, slow and easy.

I do a repeat of my unpaid-waiter routine. A hop-mix for the cop. Water, touched with whisky, for myself. Meanwhile, Gawne stokes up his ego with good brandy.

Then Ripley and I settle back in armchairs and draw smoke into our lungs from pipe-bowls. Gawne strips, pierces and lights a cigar . . . a very large, very expensive-looking cigar. He looks like an old-time movie mogul. Or maybe he looks like a rich and benign uncle, watching us and timing the point when he should spring the latest will-change surprise. Whatever . . . *he* decides when we are ready to start.

Then, we start.

Gawne says, "To be honest with you, Fleischer, you're getting old."

"From you," I murmur, "that is like Castro calling Tito a dictator."

"Ah, yes—but some people *get* old—other people *grow* old . . . but stay young. You 'get.' I 'grow.' That's the difference." He waves the cigar around, and says, "Age has damn-all to do with the body. It's a mental thing. Some men stay childish all their lives. Some men are oldsters, before they reach the fifty mark. Others—the fortunate ones—reach a peak . . . and stay there."

"You?" I suggest . . . not without a hint of sarcasm.

"Me," he agrees. "Apart from this bloody chair, I'm as good as I ever was. Better. And I've learned to out-smart the chair—learned to out-think it . . . I can't go to them, so I make damn sure they come to me. *You* came to me. You're proof that what I'm saying is true."

"Like Ripley, here," I say. "I was given an invitation. I accepted. That doesn't mean . . ."

"You were sent."

"Eh?"

"*Sent.*" He jerks his head. "Brought, if you like . . . by

young Lewis. You have been staying at *The Plough*. You arrived there yesterday. Before that, a motel in the Epping Forest area. Before that, London... Darley's place and a dropping-spot run by a bint called Valda. Need I go on?"

"You have," I growl, "a good idea of the itinerary."

"I should have. I planned it."

"Like hell! That motel. I know it from the past. It was my idea. *I* decided..."

"And *I* was notified. Before you'd had time to unpack your bags." He smiles, expansively; as if, all this time, he has been doing me a big favor. He says, "Why not, at least, let you pick your own beds? Why not, Fleischer?... just as long as you end up here."

I take a swallow of whisky and water. It is necessary, if only to kill some of the bitter taste which is invading my mouth.

I wait, and I do not have to wait long.

He pulls at the cigar a couple of times, then murmurs, "They want you out, Fleischer. That's what it boils down to."

"Darley..." I begin.

"Darley!" He somehow spits the name, without loosening his hold on the cigar with his teeth and lips.

"Okay," I say. "Tell me."

"Darley deals in tits and fanny."

"That, I already know."

"He isn't even a good pimp."

"That, I am prepared to believe."

"Darley's allowed, because he's useful. Because, if he was shifted, he'd have to be replaced by some equally insignificant mouse-dropping."

"That, too, I am prepared to accept," I growl. "Now... give me some news."

He enjoys some more cigar smoke, then narrows his eyes a little, watches my face, then asks, "How many hits, Fleischer? All told... how many?"

"Six," I mutter.

"Six?"

"Seven," I correct myself in a low, choking voice. "Seven . . . counting the Russian bastard I'd just smashed when we . . ."

"Seven? Including those you contracted under me?"

"Yeah." I nod and swallow. "Seven. Seven hits."

A voice says, "I take it we're talking about murder? Right?"

Without taking his eyes from my face, Gawne growls, "We're talking about 'hits,' Charlie. You call 'em whatever you like. You aren't included in this conversation. You're a listener . . . and only that, because you can't leave under your own steam." Then he throws the words at me, and says, "Seven hits? Seven times—seven contracts . . . and, on *that,* you've built a bloody reputation?"

"Ask around," I growl.

"I have . . . and what I have been told makes me want to spew, little man. A 'reputation.' What the hell! And they believe you . . . Sweet Jesus, they *believe* you."

I get a little cross.

I toss what is left of the watered-down whisky into my mouth, and make as if to stand upright.

I snap, "Look—I don't have to . . ."

"*Sit down!* . . . midget."

The derringer is still on his knees. He moves his right hand, and the fingers touch the grip.

I take a breath. Then I sit down.

"Seven," he says, as if he is talking to himself; as if he is having to repeat the number a few times in order to check that "six" is not, after all, the natural lead-in to "eight." "Seven . . . not even double-figures."

He shakes his head in wonderment, grabs the cigar from his mouth, then downs some brandy.

He says, "Let me tell you something, Fleischer. Let me name some of the trigger-men from your own country . . . men who made criminal history. Jack Mc-

Gurn . . . 'Machine Gun Jack.' Charlie Fischetti. Punchy Illiano. Those three, for a start. Heard of 'em?"

"I've heard."

"If not, I can name another three—another thirty-three . . . another three hundred and three."

"I've heard of them," I repeat, grimly.

"D'you know how many *they* chopped? How many *they're* known to have chopped? . . . not counting the stiffs nobody could dump on their doorsteps."

"I can guess."

"Don't guess Fleischer. I'll tell you. Fifteen score, plus . . . each! One thousand graves, shared between the three of them. And they aren't the top three . . . just three of the top hatchetmen. Three of a whole bloody army."

Somebody breathes, "Christ!" and that somebody is a cop who is stunned by what Gawne is saying, and what I know to be no less than the truth.

"Gorillas," I sneer.

"And what the hell are you?" raps Gawne. "What the hell do you provide that they didn't—don't still— provide? A body. A corpse. Work for some blasted undertaker. What the hell else?"

"Okay." I shrug. "Let us take the point. Where comes the beef?"

"Seven." He is back to that damn number, again. Mouthing it, like it has some mystery . . . like he wants to make sure he can pronounce it right. He gulps brandy, then snarls, "What sort of snot-nosed, lower-than-dirt, dog-puddled dwarf can lay claim to a 'reputation?' On *seven*!"

And, at this point in the cross-talk, I get the shakes.

Gently, at first—a tiny fluttering of nerve ends under my skin—which I can feel, but which are not yet visible to anybody watching. But I know they are there, and I have had them before a couple of times, and I know that they will eventually show themselves.

Gawne will know. The cop will know. And I will be
ashamed...and my shame will refuse me even the slight
solace of open honesty.

I decide not to fight Gawne; not to answer his taunts
but, instead, to concentrate all my will-power upon one
thing. To stop the tremblings. To hold them in
check...to keep them a secret from this tormenting
bastard, and the forensic fink who is a silent witness.

Gawne changes the key a little. The rasping snarl leaves
his voice, and is replaced by a tone of soft contempt. His
line of talk also switches. It becomes logic—sneering
logic—to which there is no adequate answer.

He says, "Seven hits. A 'reputation.' Nothing, little
man...less than nothing. A trick. A con. A P.R. job.
Believed by some, because you've worked like the
clappers of hell to put on a front. To sound big. Therefore
believed by some...but disbelieved by anybody with his
ear to the ground.

"Since the war, Fleischer. I've followed your progress.
My protégé—wouldn't you say?...therefore, I've followed your progress. And I *know.* Nothing! A couple—
three—killings...plus a handful of 'frightening' opera-
tions. That's what you've done. The sum total. And that's
how you've lived. How a pint-sized goon who's only done
that *has* to live. Lush—while he's actually on a job, with
expenses paid...but, for the rest of the time, in dirt.
Cheap lodging houses. Two-bit hotels...and, some of
those you left without paying the bill.

"And, some of the jobs. Some of the stop-gap jobs.
Hamburg...the St. Pauli clip-joint area...doorman, at
a dump where tarts wrestle in mud as a climax to the
evening's entertainment. You lasted a year, there. Just
over a year...until the *polizei* closed the place. Then you
bummed your way across Europe, and ended up in
France.

"Le Mans...remember Le Mans? The chemical

works?... the dump where they made sulphuric acid? The 'frightening' job you did for the management? The commie—the one who threatened to disrupt the whole shooting-match if working conditions didn't improve? You did a great job there, Fleischer. They wanted you to throw a scare into the poor bastard... and you did all that! You used the product of the firm. Acid. And, from then on, no more disruption of the factory... it isn't easy to be militant when you're handling a white stick.

"That was when the cops started chasing you... right? The Le Mans fuzz... so you high-tailed it for Paris. Then the Paris cops. The Sûreté. You were on their books, boy. You were a very much wanted man—and that's when it started... the image-building..."

Those goddam shakes!

They are getting worse. They are twitching stupid little muscles at my mouth corners and under my eyes and (damn and blast them!) they have a life of their own. They will not behave—they will not relax—and if I rub them, or even touch them, Gawne will notice them. He will know that he is getting through to me... and he will gloat even more.

Because that is what is happening. He is hitting me. He is hitting me with words and with memories, and every one is a goad. And every one hurts, and every hurt adds to a previous hurt, and my whole stinking being is building up into one great hunk of trembling pain.

And I have this crazy feeling.

That, all my life—since that day in May 1948—I have been running away from this big bastard. Dodging him. Trying to outpace him—trying to shake him off my trail... and never quite making it.

And now, he has caught up with me.

"... and the continent got too damn hot for you. You tried the U.K. You tried the Billy Hill and the Jack Spot outfits.

Let it be known who you were—what you were . . . what you *claimed* to be. And that you were 'available' for any job their own boys couldn't handle.

"You lived dangerously, little man. Spot and Hill. Both claiming to be 'boss' of London . . . and both 'retaining' a miserable little punk called Dave Fleischer for extra-special jobs. A punk who knew how to sell himself. A cockroach who claimed to be a tiger. Y'know, Fleischer—I could almost admire you for what you pulled in those days . . . the tales you circulated about yourself. The hot-line garbage you quietly put around.

"Clever . . . but stupid. Because neither Hill nor Spot wanted a villain like you around. A villain you *claimed* to be. You were a potential menace . . . to both of them. A 'big man' like you! You could get ideas. You could be the next king.

"So-o, they used you a couple of times. One killing. A nothing—a nobody—a stupid little tart who boasted she could blow London's gangland wide open. She had to be buried and, in case she'd already dropped hints—named names—by somebody 'unofficial.' The only woman you've ever chopped, Fleischer. Not important . . . nobody even missed her. Nobody ever knew she was dead. She's buried on the moors, here . . . not a million miles from where we're sitting. Right?"

Ripley begins, "Look—if that's a fact, I want . . ."

"Shurrup, Charlie." Gawne does not move his eyes from my face, as he silences the cop. "There's no proof . . . not what you'd call proof. And, suppose you find her—which I doubt—she'll be beyond recognition, by this time. She's one of many. Leave it at that. But the first one Fleischer killed. The first woman—the *only* woman . . . and he was blind bloody drunk for more than a week, afterwards. Tough—a hard man, with a 'reputation' . . . and that's *how* hard . . ."

You (you who are reading this) have you ever been hit by a

searchlight beam?

Let me paint the picture. Night-flying. Ten- maybe twenty-thousand feet. A clear night, but with no moon, and not too many stars. Way up top, over enemy territory, but surrounded by blackness on all sides, and blackness above and blackness below. Coming home, after a mission. Safe and comfortable in a good ship. Easy in the knowledge that, because you can't see them, they can't see you. Doing what you've been trained to do. Doing it automatically, while your mind goes on ahead and thinks about a hot meal and a warm bed.

Then, suddenly...

WHAM!

They have you...just like that. Pinned. Crucified in light. Blinded by the beams, and knowing that you still can't see a damn thing, but they can now see *everything*.

It has never happened to me before—I was strictly ground-based—but I have known flyers who have tried to explain it...who have lived through the experience and tried to describe the taste.

Rest easy, boys.

I now know what you mean...exactly what you mean!

"...but you hid it. You foxed 'em...Billy Hill and Jack Spot. They still had you tabbed as real opposition. A tough nut. So-o, they used you a couple more times. Not killings...nobody *needed* killing, at the moment. Fortunately. Fortunately for you...for your 'reputation.' Just a couple of muscle exercises. A little leaning. A little smacking of loud-mouthed squirts who wouldn't fall into line fast enough. That's all...and even *you* could do that.

"Then, somebody tipped you. Hill and Spot had this one thing in common. They wanted rid of you. They were both worried about this Yankee tearaway—this Dave Fleischer character—who just *might* topple one, or even both, of them.

"Which is why you were on the run again. Back home

to America. Sense, would you call it?—wisdom?...or cowardice? Or maybe just making bloody sure this 'reputation' wasn't tarnished.

"America?...we-ell, America." Gawne makes an interval in this potted biography, in order to take in some brandy. He enjoys it. He enjoys a long and thoughtful pull on the cigar, then continues, "America is a pretty big place...and you're such a *little* man. I lost track. There are gaps in your travels. Gaps I can't fill. But I know enough. I don't know all the places you visited...but some. You moved around. Philadelphia, Cleveland, Wisconsin. Then there's a gap, before you turn up in Salt Lake City. Then you go south, via Denver to Dallas. Then there's another gap until I pick you up again, in Nashville. You hung around there for a while. In that district— Nashville, Louisville, Memphis...you seemed to like that area.

"The jobs? They all had different names, but they all meant one thing. Bouncer. Frightener. Muscle-man. Gambling joints, dance-halls, clip-joints. A couple of brothels—now, doesn't *that* make you big?...official chucker-out to a couple of cat-houses.

"That's when you killed the pimp. Remember? Memphis? The less-than-nothing who tried to tempt one of the tarts from the vice set-up? I don't even know his name. His name isn't important...even less important than he was. But, he was a nuisance, and you were given the job...and you did it. A doped drink, a belt across the skull with a blackjack and a few yards of heavy chain...and, as far as I know, he's still at the bottom of the Mississippi.

"Then, back to the bawdy-houses. Back to the knocking-shops, and dealing with obstreperous customers. Until '66...remember '66, Fleischer. Autumn, 1966...when you were offered a contract? A real contract?...your first *real* contract?"

I say, "Yeah," and it comes out like it is choking on

phlegm. I clear my throat, and mutter, "Sure, I remember 1966. Why the hell shouldn't I ..."

"The Kray Brothers. The 'Firm,' as they liked to call themselves." He continues talking. Softly—dreamily—as if my interruption had not happened ... as if the questions he is asking are not questions which need any sort of an answer.

He says, "The Kray boys ... and a stupid, whisker-faced wide-boy called Angus Sibbet."

The cop murmurs, "Denis Stafford and Michael Luvaglio."

"Keep dreaming, Charlie." Gawne whips a quick grin in the direction of Ripley, then returns his attention to life-story telling. "Up north, here. The Krays controlled the fruit machines. The One-Armed Bandits. They were fixed ... with the Krays, everything was fixed. They had them by the thousand. I mean that, Charlie—as if you didn't know ... literally, by the thousand. Clubs, night-spots, boozers, hotels, Bingo halls ... everywhere. And their 'collector' was Sibbet. A big man, with a beard, and no brains. No brains at all. He was greedy. He lived high on what the Krays paid him ... but not as high as he wanted to live. The Krays fiddled the machines. So-o ... Sibbet fiddled them even more. A fiddle, on top of a fiddle. He ended up by twisting the Kray Firm out of a cool thousand a week. One thousand pounds, every week ... nicked from London's top terror gang."

Gawne chuckles at his thoughts, then says, "The big, stupid bastard. He had no sense. He was living on borrowed time ... and he hadn't the gumption to know."

The cop is looking worried.

He says, "Stafford and Luvaglio."

"Ah, yes. Stafford and Luvaglio."

"Are you saying ..."

"They were flash people, Charlie. They were slightly bent, and they talked big."

"That's not what I want ..."

"I know what you want to know, Charlie. And I'll tell you." The dreaminess has left Gawne's voice. The tone carries a take-it-or-leave-it ultimatum. "Sibbet was chopped. He was gunned to death on a cold and frosty night, in January '67. Stafford and Luvaglio were charged, convicted and sentenced. Nobody bent the coppers. They had a case . . . and the case held up in court. That's all. That's all a copper asks for. When he gets that, he's satisfied."

"There were doubts," insists Ripley. "There are *still* doubts. What are you saying, Gawne? That Stafford and Luvaglio were framed?"

"We-ell, now . . ." Gawne resumes his dreamy voice, forgets the cop and talks to me, again. "Let's go back to the autumn of '66. The contract the Kray boys held out to you. It was big money, Fleischer. A man with your 'reputation.' Nothing to it. A quick trip north—bang, bang, bang . . . then a fast journey back to the Big City. And an alibi. Fixed. Unbreakable. A seat booked on a plane back to the States. And you . . ."

"Is that how it was done?" asks the cop, grimly.

"Leave it, Charlie."

"Look—Gawne—I want to know. I want to . . ."

"Nothing!" The word is an explosion. It is roared across the few feet separating Gawne from the cop, and it travels like it was solid and supersonic. Gawne pulls the plug, and bawls, "Forget it, Charlie. Everything you hear in this bloody room . . . forget it. You aren't here. You don't damn-well exist. You were asked for a purpose, you've served that purpose. As of now, you're a blasted spectator. You're not included in this particular game. Not as a copper, not as an ex-copper . . . not as *anything*! Now—as a favor, and for your own good—knock it off. Sit there—listen . . . then forget."

I wipe the back of my hand across my mouth, and even my

goddam hand is starting to tremble. The fingers—the hand ... the whole stinking arm.

Because I am scared. And I am scared because this big, wheelchair-bound bastard knows too many things. He knows more about me than any man should know about another man. It is like he has been locked away, inside my skull, all these years. Watching—tuned in to my thoughts ... and remembering every damn detail.

I look at the back of my hand—my still-trembling hand—and I see the smear of sweat from my face, and the slide of spittle which I have wiped from the corner of my mouth.

I see these things, and I know I am licked.

I am licked stupid ... unless I fight back.

And I go crazy. I become a complete fool.

I decide to fight back.

Gawne downs what is left of the brandy, turns in his chair to re-fill his glass and, as he does so, takes up his verbal vivisection of myself and my life once more.

He says, "The Kray Firm sent for you. They..."

"They sent for me," I agree in what I hope is a hard, flat voice.

He glances sideways at me, as he pours booze ... surprised that I am kicking back.

He says, "They were never renowned for common gumption."

"They were the top mob in the U.K."

"They sent for a punk like you."

"Some punk. There was nobody in their own territory..."

"That's what they *thought*. That's what your own P.R. talk had done for you. I'll grant you that."

"They sent for me," I say grimly.

"They did, indeed." He corks the bottle, turns to face me, tosses a measure of brandy into his face, then says,

"And that was a wasted bloody journey, if ever there was one."

"The set-up was all wrong."

"For you—I agree . . . it was a little dangerous."

"Gawne," I snarl, "don't push it. Not *too* far."

"Or?" He grins, and the grin is loaded to spilling-over point with mockery.

"You will," I say, very deliberately, "be able to compare notes with Gallo."

"Gallo! *Gallo!*" Gawne almost chokes on the words, then starts laughing. Not soft laughter. Loud—raucous—rake-hell laughter . . . the brand of laughter I last heard him use, pre-1948, on the continent. Laughter he used in the face of goons—stupid bastards—who thought they could out-smart him.

"Joey Gallo," I say, quietly, and try to keep the tremble clear of my voice.

He makes like the full name is the punch-line to a very funny joke. The laughter comes stronger. It shakes him—makes the wheelchair squeak at its axles—slops some of the brandy onto the blanket covering his knees.

Then he stops. Suddenly. Like dropping a blind—closing a soundproof door—and all that is left is a big fat grin into which he tosses another measure of booze.

He says, "Tell me about Gallo, little man. Tell me . . . I'm interested."

"In front of a police witness?" I glance at the cop. "You figure my marbles have gone?"

"You killed him," he says . . . still with the grin as big and as fat as ever.

"Cool it, Gawne," I warn.

"Of course you bloody-well killed him."

"Knock it off, big man. What you are saying is . . ."

"You hit one of the biggest cats on earth—and stayed alive . . . and *that* was the miracle."

"Gawne. I'm telling you . . ."

"Not that you killed the bastard. But that Diapoulas

didn't kill you. *That's* the part that went wrong. Fleischer. This big, big 'reputation' you throw around, little man. You didn't earn it. It was given to you—by mistake...because a stupid Greek gunsel thought he could hold his liquor, and still shoot straight."

I stare at him, then whisper, "You don't know what you're saying, Gawne. You have the facts all wrong. Somebody..."

"All right." He nods—smiling—as if to an unconvinced child. He says, "Gambino—Carlo Gambino...he fixed the contract. Right?"

"I am not answering a stupid question like that, Gawne. With a bull in the same room, and you want me to..."

"All right. All right." The patience is still there, in his voice. Smiling and long-suffering. "Tommy Ernst and Frank Ferriano made the approach. Set up the contract...on behalf of Gambino. To knock Joe Gallo. Right?"

I do not answer...for reasons already given.

"Tommy Ernst and Frank Ferriano," he repeats, softly and with meaning. *"Two of Gallo's own mobsters."*

"So?"

"Setting up a corpse-job, on their own boss?"

"It happens," I growl.

"For Gambino?...Gallo's rival for the top seat?"

"They cross each other...all the time." I put conviction into the words. More conviction than they deserve. I steady my voice, watch his face, and say, "Gawne, these are my people. I know them. They would cross their own grandmother...just for the exercise."

"Inside their own mob?" He nods his head in solemn agreement. "They jostle around for power, within their own outfit. But they don't go outside...because that would be bloody dangerous. *Bloody* dangerous! Unless, of course..." He pauses, and the rest of the sentence comes out like the purr of a cream-filled cat. "Unless, of course, you're big enough—important enough—to make it safe...to put you beyond suspicion."

The big man is hypnotizing me with hints and riddles. His voice—the way he pushes truths and possibilities in my direction—is gradually driving me nuts. In the whole world, there is only two people. Gawne and myself. In this room—in the whole world...just Gawne and myself. Nobody else. No cops...I have forgotten all about cops. Just the two of us—no bodies...I have forgotten all about what was once Lewis, and what is now stiffening on the carpet.

And I have to know.

What the hell it is, I *have* to know!

In a whisper which carries to the wheelchair, and not much farther, I say, "Quit playing with me, Gawne. Give. You claim to know certain things. Okay...make the claim stick. That, or shove your goddam snide up your ass and sit on it."

"Are you man enough?" he asks, mockingly.

"Try me," I snarl.

And, by Christ, he does!

He says, "Four of you. Ernst, Ferriano and Bruno Carnevale. And, yourself, of course. Ernst and Ferriano—two of Gallo's men—to set it up...in the name of Gambino. Carnevale—one of Gambino's own soldiers—to drive the getaway car...supposing the million-to-one shot came off. You get the set-up, I hope. A combined. Gallo-Gambino operation...to eliminate Joey Gallo.

"And, if you remember, little man, there wasn't a street war after the killing. There should have been—past history insists that, when one top man gets knocked down, suspicion falls upon the rival mob and there's a whole round of killings and counter-killings...but, this time, there wasn't. Nothing unusual...despite Joey's sister. She screamed what she honestly believed to be no less than the truth...'The streets are going to run red with blood, Joey.' Her exact words, Fleischer. Heard by a score of newshounds, and quoted verbatim.

"But she was wrong... they *didn't*.

"Think about it, Fleischer. Think about what that means. What else, but that the whole thing was a fix? What else, but that top men had arranged the hit?... and with something in mind?

"A combination... what else. Gambino, and..." He pauses, lifts an eyebrow, then says, "Not Joey. That's a ridiculous idea. Not Joey's family... that's just about equally ridiculous. But *somebody*. Somebody big enough in the Gallo mob to hold the lid down. Big enough to step into Joey's shoes... once Joey was out of the way. Somebody above suspicion... because that 'somebody' was going to kill the killer."

He stops and waits for it.

I give it to him on a single breath.

I say, "Diapoulas."

"Who else? Pete the Greek... Gallo's right-hand man." Gawne chuckles at the thought of it. "The man most likely to succeed. The next chief. And, in next to no time, joint boss of a Gambino-Gallo super-mob. The biggest 'family' in New York."

And he is so right... he is so rotten *right*!

I know these people—these hoodlums... they are from my country. They have a history and, if you care for that history, it is a very interesting insight into man, and his capabilities, at the lower end of the scale.

Gangsters—the popular name for them—can be divided, straight down the middle, into the "organizers" and the "roughnecks."

The "organizers"...

Those with the necessary gray stuff under their skulls. Those who go in for Capone's original thesis of "strength through combination." "Scarface Al" was an animal, born without a soul, but he *always* gave the opposition a peaceful way out. He always said, "Share it, or we take all." And those with sense cut their losses, shrugged their shoulders and lived.

The "roughnecks"...

"Big Jim" Colosimo. The O'Banion gang. They were gun-happy and bomb-happy. They did not believe in talk—they had no time for "propositions"... what was not given to them, and without even asking, they buried. When Capone started to "organize," they oiled their pistols and looked around for some punk to shoot at.

For "Capone" read "Gambino."

For "Colosimo (or "O'Banion") read "Gallo."

It ever was, and ever will be... and it certainly was in '72.

Gambino wanted to expand. He wanted co-operation between the outfits. But, unfortunately, the Gallo mob defended their territory like dogs fighting for their own back yards. So-o, there had to be either a war, or a cross. And the cross needed a man inside the Gallo army—a big man... a man capable of taking over, and going into partnership with Gambino.

Diapoulas... who else?

From then on it was easy. Find the patsies. Give Joe Gallo a nice funeral... and make damn sure nobody is left around to talk.

I should have died in the early hours of Friday, April 7th, 1972. I was allowed into Umberto's Clam House—I was allowed to chop Joey Gallo... but then, I should have died.

Brother!

Old Man Luck had his arm around my waist on that day... nor has he been too far away, ever since.

Consider...

Bruno Carnevale—the driver of the Chev which timed things so perfectly, after the killing—the boy behind the wheel of the getaway car. The *late* Bruno Carnevale! He was found, beaten to broken-boned pulp, then shot dead, in Queens village ... and for no known reason.

Frank Ferriano—one of the duo who propositioned me a few days before the killing—the Gallo man who claimed to be talking for Gambino. Another entry in the obituary columns! The last thing he saw was a Manhattan parking lot—just before a shotgun blast tore his head apart ... and, again, without good, or obvious, cause.

Tommy Ernst—the second of the propositioning duo—the smooth guy, who did all the talking. He, too, made some mortician very happy! He died on home ground—Staten Island—and he died of lead-poisoning ... the quick way.

Me?

I figure I must have a gypsy forefather somewhere down the line, and the gypsy blood has, so far, kept me above ground ... that, plus more luck than I deserve. Canada ... Winnipeg, Prince Albert, Edmonton, and all points west. Across to Italy, and up the leg ... Naples, Rome, Florence and Milan. Then around the continent of Europe ... ending up in Amsterdam. A few score jobs all the same, but all different ... selling muscle, where muscle was needed. Back-alley work. Acting like a man running away from sudden death, even though I did not know it.

Luck!

And now, my luck has run out.

I say, "Diapoulas?" and I feel my breathing coming quicker and shallower.

"Naturally." Gawne nods.

He is holding the derringer again and its two eyes, one above the other, are staring me in the face.

There is a sound. Quick and soft. An indrawing of breath, as the cop prepares to speak.

Gawne says, "Save it, Charlie," before the first word has time to pass the cop's lips.

The cop stays silent.

And I can feel moisture, running down the nape of my

neck. Sweat. And some of the sweat has gathered in a single pearl, and hangs above my eye, in the hairs of my right brow. It demands my attention. It dominates my whole vision. One goddam globulet of sweat which hangs there and mesmerizes me.

"You had to come," explains Gawne, quietly.

"Yeah." I almost nod. I stop myself from moving my head, just in time...in case I disturb that damn sweat-drop.

"You had to come to me. Obviously...I couldn't come to you."

"Yeah...obviously."

"Darley was a ploy...obviously."

"Again...obviously."

"I'm glad you understand, Fleischer. It's right that you should."

"And Lewis?" I ask.

"That—er..." He allows a quick smile to float across his face. "That was your idea."

"It is nice to know that *some* of it was my idea."

"It could have been a very deadly idea," he reminds me. "He could have done Diapoulas's job for him...instead of me."

"Yeah." I almost nod, again. "Except for the sand."

"Except for the 'reputation.'"

"In which case, he would have earned himself a reputation."

"Possible," he agrees, thoughtfully. "The man who shot the man who shot Joe Gallo...it's possible."

"Why rob him?" I ask.

"*You* robbed him...with the sand in the cartridges. I only killed him."

"Okay. Why kill him?"

"I didn't know. How could I? He was a man with a twelve-bore. He broke into my house. He was obviously going to shoot *somebody*...that 'somebody' could have been me."

"Gawne," I say, heavily.

He lifts an eyebrow a thickness of a cigarette paper.

"We are well past the kidding stage."

He moves his lips, as much as he has moved his eyebrow, and something which might be the wraith of a smile pays his mouth a quick visit.

He murmurs, "I didn't like his old man. Use that as an excuse, if it satisfies."

It is an excuse. It does not satisfy me... but it is the only excuse I am going to get.

The sweat-drop grown too heavy. It falls onto my lashes and explodes into a curtain of semi-transparency. I brush it clear with the back of my hand.

"Christmas," muses Gawne.

"Yeah... Merry Christmas."

"You came here to chop me, Fleischer."

"That's what I *thought*."

"And Lewis came here to shoot *you*."

"It would seem."

"Unseasonal. Not the true spirit... wouldn't you say?"

I glance at the derringer, and crack, "That is no bon-bon you are holding, friend."

"Ah... but I haven't used it."

"True."

"I could have done," he admits. "I could have waited for you to make your play."

"Dangerous."

"No." He shakes his head. "I, too, have a reputation. Unlike you, I earned it. I almost beat Lewis... and I was watching you, when he started blasting."

"Nobody is arguing," I concede. "You are fast. You are accurate."

"And you," he says, softly, "have been within a trigger-squeeze of a shroud since you opened the door."

"I believe you."

The cop makes himself heard once more.

In a very loud, very harsh and very indignant voice, he

snarls, "That's enough! A man's been shot. Murdered..."

"Self-defense, Charlie. I've already..."

"I'm calling it what it *was*. Not what some putty-brained bloody jury's going to call it. What we all three know it was. But, by Christ, if you think I'm going to sit here, like a kid on its potty, and watch you two lunatics shoot it out with each other—if you think I'm going to do *that*—you must be out of your bloody..."

"Nobody else is going to get killed, Charlie." Gawne interrupts the fuzz-flow in a gentle, but very deliberate voice. "Fleischer knows when he's licked. He is going to take his mac, carry it over his arm, and walk out of our lives. Meanwhile, we're going to enjoy one more drink—you and I...one for the road. Then—who knows?—the telephone might be working again."

"Why?" I ask...and it comes out little more than a whisper.

"You live." Gawne gives me a slow, lop-sided smile and, maybe I am kidding myself, but I have the impression that it is touched with sadness. He says, "You live, because I say you're going to live...let's say for old times sake. You're not much, Fleischer—you're a fraud...but, even as a fraud, you're a shade better than Diapoulas. And, at least, you *did* kill Gallo."

It is a reprieve. I have been sitting on the hot-seat and, as the screw threw the switch, there was a power cut...and that is exactly what it feels like.

Maybe being born feels like this. Terrifying...but a relief.

I stand up from the chair, drape the mac across my shoulder and step off towards the door. I walk around what was once Lewis; the blood has soaked into the carpet, and the gloved hands are still wrapped around the pump-gun.

I walk out of the room, and close the door.

I should be dead...but, instead, I am alive.

● ● ●

The drive south is uneventful.

Uneventful, that is, if you do not count the confetti-sized flakes which give the headlight beams a consistency of watered-down milk. The snow is acting like it has come to stay. Not flashy; not blasting all its energy in a single, short-lived blizzard. Instead, like a good fighter, it is pacing itself; a steady, relentless wearing down of what opposition there is left and a gradual, but implacable taking over. It is taking over; the ling is already covered and only the taller spikes of the half-dead couch-grass stand higher than the snow-blanket.

It is Christmas Eve—Christmas Morning—and, as the Volvo descends from the wilderness of the tops and reaches for wider roads, it threads its way through villages where, for this hour, there is an unusual activity.

People are around. Groups of villagers walk, over-coated, scarfed and bent against the snow. Greetings and "Goodnights" pass, from group to group and, although they cannot be unaware, they are disdainful, of the weather. It is Christmas, and the watch-night services, held in tiny churches, have ended—the Christmas Communions have been taken—and there is a unique "Englishness" abroad.

No other country can conjure up this magic . . . nor, come to that, can the "townies" of even this country.

As I drive the Volvo from the tops, it is all around me; as real—as identifiable—as the snow itself.

But, if you do not count this, the drive south is uneventful.

Uneventful, that is, if you do not count thoughts.

But such thoughts! . . . such conclusions! . . . such real-izations!

I have been *made* . . . let that be clearly understood. I have been manufactured—created—as surely and as completely as any coin-operated robot at any fairground. I perform certain tricks. If the appropriate stimulus is injected I travel along pre-ordained paths.

I am "reliable"... as "reliable" as a good car. I handle well; I start without trouble, I steer easily, I travel at any required speed and I am cheap to run.

I do things. I terrorize, and I kill. I am purely functional, and I function beautifully... and my function is to be inhuman.

And yet I started *as* a human. As a babe. As a child. But, somewhere on the way, I was de-humanized; I was stripped of honor—drained of feeling—and turned into what I now am.

I was *made*... therefore, I am a machine.

Next question—big question... who made me? Whose label do I carry? From which particular carton did I originate?

There are a lot of easy answers, and every easy answer is also a glib answer... and glib answers do not bake too many beans. But it is a long drive, and I have plenty of time; I have time to identify the glib answers and time to toss them into the ashcan. I have time to take myself apart; to examine each cog, to check each pawl; to take a long, hard look at every coiled spring and every balance-wheel... and then decide.

Who made me?

My folks?

We-ell—biologically... who the hell am I to argue with nature? But that is not the tune I am strumming. They made a baby, and I was that baby... okay. But what else? They gave me a home, but it was not a good home... but, to be honest, nor was it a bad home. It was a home... period. It was a not-too-clean, not-too-dirty house in which was stored not-too-good, not-too-bad furniture, and the furniture was used by two adults (one male, one female) and six kids (two male, four female). These adults, and these kids, lived with a dog (of mixed breed), a brace of cats, a hamster, a couple of goldfish and (hidden away, someplace) an unspecified number of mice and maybe a rat or two.

So-o—what have we got?

A home and (if you want to go sentimental) a family.

The old man got drunk, sometimes. The old lady screamed at him. When we were well-behaved (and, if they were available) we kids were given dimes as a reward. When we misbehaved ourselves we were slapped down.... and, in that house, "sex-equality" was always practiced.

Now, I know, the various "oligists" could build a six-inch-thick dossier around the Fleischer family. They could winkle-pick what they would call "proof" of what they would also call "tendencies;" with superlative hindsight—which is their main tool-of-trade—they could foresee the past with dazzling accuracy.

Okay—but I happen to have lived it... and I know damn well that the Fleischer family was no worse, no better, than ten-million other families. We kids were mid-stream, first generation Americans. And that is how we behaved. And that is how we thought. And, if one of us turned out a screwball... do not blame the family.

So, who?... who made me?

It would be nice—it would be very cozy—if I could slap the parcel squarely in the lap of a fat-gutted freight-yard guard, with a woman's voice and a perfervidity for shooting dogs. To argue the point would not be too difficult... but the argument would be built upon a false premise. The dog was the innocent party... not the dog's owner.

The owner of the dog was a bum. A teenage bum... but a bum, nevertheless. He had run away from home (and this, for no good reason) and, for some considerable time, he had lived by thieving. He was in the freight-yard to thieve. What else?

A thief and a freight-yard guard, with a dog caught between. Blame one, and you have to blame the other. Blame both, and you are maybe touching a little of the truth... maybe.

The freight-yard guard was a bastard. Agreed. But no

bastard leaves a trail of machines behind him.

So, who?... who made me?

We are hitting the big roads, now. The tarmac arteries of a nation which is also an island. The A-class roads and the motorways; the trunks and the dual-carriageways.

And now, Christmas Day—Christmas Morning—is not so much like Christmas. It is like any other night... but with snow. It lacks the magic—but, maybe not quite... maybe it just lacks *all* the magic. Because— and maybe I am kidding myself—some of it seems to be still around. An echo, maybe, from the real Christmas which, at this moment, fills the rural places of this land with solemn and silent sound. Could be that some of that special magic leaks off, from where it is born, and touches places which cannot give it birth, and people who have never known the breath-taking magnificence of the real thing are given a springier step because of something they have never experienced.

So (and whatever) it is Christmas Morning, and a time for cars to be driven fast by happy goons with an above-average booze-count in their blood; to be driven along brown and slushy roads which run between banks of plough-piled whiteness... no matter, it is still Christmas Morning.

And the Volvo is pointing south, and it is an uneventful journey.

Except...

Except for the big question which refuses to stop bouncing around inside my skull.

Who—what—made me what I am?

The war, maybe?

Who the hell am I kidding? What sort of crappy excuse is a war? A war is a war, and people fight and people die, and a lot of guys learn how to point guns at other guys and, because they are ordered to do so, they pull triggers.

But what the hell does that prove?... that every guy in the combat area is a killer?

A soldier is not a killer... not a *killer*! He is not a professional hit man. He is a bank clerk—a plumber—a schoolteacher—a truck-driver—an insurance agent... he is all these, and many other things, dolled up in fancy dress. Christ, it is arguable that he is not even a *soldier*!

He is just a guy who has been fed the necessary bull. He has been told, and he is dumb enough to believe, that the future of mankind—the continuation of the world—is dependent upon him leaving his home, being shouted at by some other dumb bastard, carrying junk from point A to point B, living on hard-tack, being shot at, shooting back, killing and maybe even dying. He is a poor mug who has been conned, by the professionals, into believing all this.

He is there by the thousand—by the tens of thousand—by the million... and, when it is all over, he goes right back to being a plumber, a schoolteacher, a truck-driver, an insurance agent, or whatever else he was before the P.R. goons told him he could also be a hero.

So, what the hell excuse is a war for anything?

For me?... what the hell excuse is a war, for me being what I am?

And that includes a certain Rusky who, on a September evening, in a booze-joint which was part of a crippled city, felt like pulping a U.S. Army sergeant. The poor jerk was an animal, behaving like any other animal, and he was an animal because creeps a few thousand miles to the east had indoctrinated him and taught him to be just that... an animal. Okay—I killed the poor slob... but I killed him because he had been placed there to be killed. He had been set up. The patsy to end all patsies. And, if it had not been me, it would have been somebody else... and it is a million-to-one shot that that other person, whoever he might have been, would have ended up like me.

So-o, this is one Red who is not under my particular bed. He provided a certain highlight of my life, but he did not change that life.

And we are back at the start-line.

What the hell made me what I am? What? . . . or who?

The trees of the forest wear the snow like it is white-fox fur, and their branches are arms along which are draped the stoles. It is, I know, a very hackneyed description, but it fits . . . perfectly. And I am a little too tired to aim at improving perfection.

The night-clerk at the motel is sleepy and irritable; maybe he has downed too many free drinks . . . maybe he does not remember that this is Christmas Day.

A note to the value of five English pounds works wonders; it awakens him, and cheers him up, at one and the same time.

I ask him my questions. About a dame, who stayed here, alone. A description, and the date she booked out . . . and what is her name, and what is her address, and what is her telephone number?

He opens a filing cabinet, tools around with a card index, mutters some possibilities to himself, eliminates those possibilities, then comes up with a name—and the info that goes with the name clinches it . . . it *has* to be her!

I jot down the details, thank him and move out of his life.

I point the bonnet of the Volvo south, again, and aim the car for a certain dump which is in Reve Street, Soho.

Gawne? . . . David Gawne?

I would dearly love to say that the responsibility is his; that he took a blue-eyed, innocent, all-American boy and turned him into a slaughtering machine. It would be so easy, and it is very tempting.

But it would be so much crow-shit.

Gawne polished me—okay . . . maybe that. But the

potential was there, in the first place. He did not create me. He is no Svengali. All he did was take what was already there, and use it.

What he also did was carve me, straight down the middle. If he created anything, he created a schizo...and not even that! Because each half knows about the other. In a cockeyed way, each half almost admires the other.

What Gawne did—if he did anything—was take the prototype of the original mixed-up kid, and unmix him...and now (a couple or three hours back) he cut the final link.

He held a mirror to each half, and let each half see itself for the first time.

So-o...

Who the hell else—what the hell else...not Gawne!

Reve Street has that morning-after look. The whole of Soho is suffering a monumental hangover and, if it were possible for bricks and mortar to have red-rimmed eyes, they would be there. There is puke on the pavements, and smashed bottles in the gutters. There are cheap perfume boxes in corners, and used condoms in shop-doorways. And there is the stench...the once-in-a-year stench which follows, and is payment for, the wildest night of the year in a place where wild nights are for sale every twenty-four hours.

Christmas Day...Soho-style!

The pale blue Merc is parked outside *The Striponium Club,* and my journey has not been unnecessary.

I park the Volvo and push my shoes through the mush and muck which carpets the pavement. It is still snowing, but the impression is that the flakes have lost their whiteness—have surrendered their virginity—long before they touch the stones. Dawn is yawning its way over the rooftops; a slate-gray dawn...a dawn clothed in half-mourning for all that lost innocence of the previous night.

I wear my mac unfastened and the hard weight of the Smith and Wesson bumps against my hip as I descend the stairs to the upholstered cellar. I like the feel of those bumps. They are very reassuring.

The main room—the glorified telephone booth, with a stage at one end and a bar at the other—looks like two earth-moving machines have had a fight to the finish within its confines. Some of the tables—some of the chairs—are still upright... but not too many. I feel the crunch of broken glass under the soles of my shoes. The drapes of the stage have been torn. The beautiful bottles which line the wall behind the bar look like they have been used as a makeshift coconut-shy... and maybe they have, at that!

The room is not empty. Two guys are asleep (that, or dead!) with their backs to each other, squatting on the floor by the stage. There are also two other sleepers; a dame who has her skirts hitched high above her waist, and a guy with a stomach, who has his pants around his ankles and who was obviously concentrating upon wild-oat sowing when the curtain dropped upon himself and the meadow he was aiming to broadcast—they look hilarious... if you have a taste for very sick jokes!

Then a door opens, and I am no longer the only person in the room who is not asleep.

The goon sees me, remembers me, and suddenly looks very satisfied. This time he is not going to allow me ducking-space. This time, he is going to be ready for the crippling footwork. And, this time, *he* is going to be the one who uses a bottle.

He grabs one from the nearest table, smashes it into a saw-toothed hand-weapon against the edge of the bar-counter and moves forward with a not-very-nice grin of anticipation smeared across his face.

I take my hand from the mac pocket, line the S and W automatic on his navel... and he stops moving and stops grinning, both at the same time.

"Breathe," I say softly. "That is the only excuse I need."

He hates me with his eyes, wills me to drop dead and loosens his grip on the neck of the bottle. The broken bottle hits the carpet, and rolls under one of the tables.

I make a circulary movement with the forefinger of my left hand.

He knows the rules of the game. He turns his back to me, clasps his fingers together and places his hands on top of his head.

I step over to him, ram the muzzle of the S and W into his spine and say, "No talking, fink. Just nod. Where is he?"

He moves his head in a single, tiny jerk towards a closed door to one side of the apology for a stage.

I murmur, "I hope you are right . . . for your sake."

With the last word I move, and make the movement too fast for him to duck or even know it is coming. The steel of the automatic hits him hard, at the base of the skull and he loses consciousness and bends in the middle. I step to one side and use a knee to steer his falling body clear of a table, and he does not make too much noise as he joins the broken bottle on the carpet.

I make a quick check that I am, once again, the only person in the room who is not asleep, then I move to the door alongside the stage, turn the knob and walk into what is Darley's office . . . or something.

It is a nice room. Not too large, not too small; nicely decorated, nicely furnished; it has a small, but impressive desk and a small, but impressive divan . . . and the divan is in full production!

Darley is wearing four articles of clothing. Two of them are shoes, two of them are socks and (even at a moment like this) I waste a split-second of eternity wondering what sort of dumb creep removes his pants and shorts, without first removing his shoes. The dame is wearing an expression of ecstasy and (unless you count the gemmed ring which encircles one of the fingers which are clawing into Darley's back) that is all. The hair on her head says she is a titian redhead. The rest of her hair calls the hair on her head a liar.

They have reached what crude bastards like myself would call "the short strokes."

I notify them of my presence, by saying, "Tie a knot in it, Darley. You would make a stinking father."

The dame squeals, opens her eyes, becomes bashful, twists so that her ass is pointing in my direction... and damn near emasculates lover-boy. Darley yells as the pain hits him, drops his feet to the carpet and sits on the edge of the divan... like the lead nudist carrying the flagpole in some crummy procession.

I murmur, "Surprise—surprise... I have brought my Christmas box, personally."

For a moment, everybody freezes. And who can blame them? The S and W is the most important article present; it commands absolute and complete attention.

The dame widens her eyes, as a prelude to opening her mouth.

I snap, "Keep it corked, sister. No noise is very good advice."

She keeps her eyes wide, but keeps her mouth closed.

Darley nurses himself, and says, "What the hell are *you*..."

"Doing alive?" I finish the question for him. I say, "That, buster, is what Diapoulas would have asked you... but it is a question which need no longer worry you."

As he is working it out, I gaze at him.

Edward Darley—Ed Darley—"Safron" Darley ...Christ on a flagpole!

And this is a man? This is a specimen of the human race? This thing with a skin the color of mild nicotine stain; with a smooth, hairless chest and sweat-shined black tangle squirting from each armpit; with a paunch which slopes out north of the navel, then swoops back in to form a dewlap with a beard of pubic hair from which sprouts an already shrinking erection; with skinny, flabby-muscled legs which end in splay-toed, boney-ankled feet.

And this—*this*—is a man!

"You ain't gonna use that thing, Fleischer." He nods at the automatic, but the nod does not carry conviction, and the voice is uncertain. He says, "You ain't that dumb. I got Diapoulas behind me, Fleischer. Diapoulas and Gambino. You ain't gonna..."

"At this moment," I say, harshly, "all you have behind you is a cheap stripper who is not even wearing her G-string. What you have in front of you is *Me*...A guy you crossed. A guy you bundled off to be chopped. *Me*...the guy who is now going to kill you."

I squeeze the trigger of the S and W three times. The first gets him in the throat, smashes his voice-box and stops any yelling he might have in mind; it knocks him back, across the dame's calves and she jerks her legs up tight and clear of his body. The second gets him at chest-level and the third gets him in the gut.

He is dead—he is bleeding...but I know my trade well enough to know that he is already stiffening.

There is some gore around. Some of it has hosed onto the dame's thighs and is running, like an open wound, down towards the back of her knees. She watches it. Voiceless. Conscious...but only just.

In a very hard voice, I say, "Where you are, lady. And as long as you like. Shove your tits out of this door too soon, and you can go with him...finish what it was I interrupted, in hell."

I think she would nod...if only she could find the strength for even that small movement.

I do not give a damn.

I move out of this office-come-knocking-shop and close the door behind me. I cross the main room of *The Striponium Club* and hurry up the stairs, to the street.

I turn the key in the Volvo and, as I do, my eye catches the dial showing the amount of gas in the tank. Not too much... which is understandable, after the drive south from "Diasc Farm." As the engine kicks into life I make a decision. I kill the engine of the Volvo, climb out and walk to the pale blue Merc.

The doors are open and the keys are in the ignition.

I climb into the Merc, start the engine and watch the dials. This one is well-filled with gas. I decide to borrow it—and why not?... Darley no longer has a use for it.

I know... it is a damn-fool idea.

My excuse?

Just that—that I am a damn fool... and, at the moment, I am not thinking too clearly.

Bristol... good old, snow-covered, memory-jerking Bristol!

It is the same place. Exactly the same. Last time, I arrived in a Triumph Vitesse, this time, I have arrived in a pale blue Mercedes-Benz... but Bristol does not change. Last time, I was not alone, this time, I am not merely alone I am also very lonely... but Bristol does not understand what the word "lonely" means. Last time, I was within sighting distance of what might be called "happiness," this time, I am too scared to figure out just how scared I should be... but what the hell does Bristol care? Come to that, why the hell *should* Bristol care?

Why Bristol?

Why come here?

There is no sensible answer to some questions. Just questions... followed by question-marks. When we hurt, we yell... but not because yelling eases the hurt. When we sleep, we dream... but not because dreams refresh either our minds or our bodies.

There are some things people do, because... period.

It is why I have come to Bristol.

Because.

And, if that is not a good enough reason, there is no reason.

I find a nice restaurant, where they serve me with a nice breakfast, and after the breakfast I smoke a slow pipe of tobacco.

Then I find a telephone booth, check the number I bought from the night-clerk at the motel, then consult the S.T.D. list. I dial a number, and wait.

A man's voice answers, and I start feeding the coins into the slot.

I ask him his name, and he tells me. His Christian name is James.

I say, "You are back early, friend."

"Early?" There is puzzlement in the question.

"From buying oranges and lemons."

"What?"

"Italy," I explain.

He says, "I've never been to Italy in my life," pauses, then says, "Look—who is this, anyway?"

I chose my words with care.

I say, "I—er—I know your wife . . . vaguely."

"Are you a friend of her sister's?" he asks, and there is worry in his voice, this time.

"Her sister's?"

"She has an invalid sister. She visits her, occasionally. She's just got back . . . a couple of days ago. Are you . . ."

"No," I hear myself say, in a flat voice. "Not her sister. I do not know her sister."

And the hell of it is, I like the guy; from the sound of his voice I get the impression that he is a very kind—very patient—man.

There is music in the background. Faint music, which I recognize.

I ask him, and he says, "Yes—if you must know—we're listening to the stereo . . . my Christmas present, from my wife."

"Handel?"

"Yes. The *Christmas Music* from *Messiah*. But what the devil..."

In a very tired voice, I say, "As a favor, friend—as a favor to a guy you do not know, and will never know—when they reach *Worthy Is The Lamb*, turn it onto full volume. Then break the goddam record."

Before he has time to ask why, I drop the receiver onto its cradle.

There are some great bridges around. Brooklyn Bridge, for example; a beautiful piece of engineering art. The Victoria Falls Bridge, too; that, also is a sweet bridge, with a single arch which spans five-hundred feet of chasm. The Golden Gate—the Blue Nile—Boothferry...all sweet, sweet bridges.

But none of them quite up to the Clifton Suspension. That guy—Isambard Kingdom Brunel—had magic. He was not just an engineer...not just an *engineer*. He was a visionary. None like him...before, or since.

This bridge—this Clifton Suspension Bridge—is as near perfect as makes no matter. It links the cliffs on each side of the gorge, like a silk thread held firm by twin paperweights. That is what it looks like—that is the measure of its gossamer beauty—and yet it is steel-strong...it shrugs off one hell of a weight of traffic.

But not the blue Merc.

That car has been white-hot property since before I climbed into it. Maybe I knew. Maybe I did not give a damn...maybe I have not given a damn, since Gawne allowed me to live.

The Merc is parked near the toll to the bridge, and the cops have found it. It has taken them longer than it should—but, okay...it is Christmas Day, even for cops.

Without looking, I have watched them talk to the toll-keeper. I have seen the car—and unmarked Austin—cross the bridge to the west toll. I have stood, with my forearms on the ironwork of the parapet, and I have waited.

And now there are only the cops and myself. We have the bridge to ourselves... and that is how I planned it. I stare out, for a moment, at the Avon, below... at the snow-clothed cliffs, on each side... at the parks, and the hotels, and the houses which all go to make a fine city.

I turn, and rest my back against the parapet.

They are coming in for the arrest, east and west. Two groups—uniformed and plain-clothes—walking cautiously to where I am standing.

I put my hand into the pocket of my mac, and bring out the Smith and Wesson automatic. And they hesitate. They do not halt, but they slow a little. They advance more cautiously.

Gallo?... he would have crouched there, and shot it out. But Gallo was "Crazy Joe" Gallo, and an animal who gloried in blood-letting.

Diapoulas?... he, too, might have shot it out but, with him, it would have been on the run. He would have picked the weaker of the two advancing groups, and he would have tried to blast his way through to freedom. Because he was Diapoulas, and a reputed trigger-man.

Gambino?... he might have used his tongue and, after his tongue, his bank balance. Gambino would not even have had a gun. Gambino paid other mugs to carry guns. Therefore, Gambino would have been inconvenienced for a short while, but nothing more than that.

Gawne?... he would have...

God knows what Gawne would have done? Gawne would have been Gawne, and Gawne would not have allowed emotion to take over, therefore Gawne would not even have chopped Darley... therefore, what Gawne would have done is only of academic interest.

Me?...

The nearest cop is now within talking distance.

He edges forward, holds out a hand, and says, "The

gun, Fleischer. Don't do anything stupid. You're in enough trouble."

I move the hand holding the S and W and he freezes.

I smile, and continue the movement, and the automatic arcs over the parapet and joins the falling flakes in their journey towards the surface of the Avon.

They come in at a rush and pin my arms.

The cop who led the arrest—the cop who wanted me to give him the gun—says, "Fleischer? David Fleischer?"

"You already know the name, friend," I murmur.

"I'm arresting you for the murder of Edward Darley. I have to warn you. You're not obliged..."

He goes through the patter, but I do not listen.

Why the hell should I? What difference will it make—what I say, or what I do not say—now that I have worked everything out? Now that I know?...what the hell difference does anything make?

The answer has taken some time to soak through, but it has arrived.

Who made me what I am?

Myself... *who the hell else?*

I am what I am... because I am what I am... because I am what I am... because I am what I am...

And the answer goes on, forever; into eternity—like a mirror facing another mirror, with a never-ending series of reflections.

And each reflection makes me stink that little bit more!